Wheel of Fate

Wheel of Fate

Book 1

Yvonne Pastolove

Table of Contents

Chapter 1

Paris, 1836

Slowly, two young women walk across the '*Pont au Double*' and turn towards Hôtel-Dieu, one of the oldest hospitals in France. Rozenn, the older and taller one, is not patient and has lost what little patience she ever had. It has taken her forever to convince Jannet that Hôtel-Dieu's 'Tour d'Abandonment', most often simply called 'The Tower' is her only choice. She kept resisting, repeating, "I'll be better soon," until Rozenn shouted at her that she was off her head, that even a half-wit would see that she is getting worse, not better! How many times did she have to tell her that if they didn't leave now, they'd lose the cover of darkness? Or did she really want to do this in broad daylight, under the eyes of the curious?

To make matters worse, the arranged ride on Gilbert's farm cart had taken them only part-way. Rozenn had heaped every curse she could think of on the young man's sullen head, dangled the promised coins before his eyes, then quickly pushed them back into her shirt, saying he'd be paid on the return trip or not at all. After that they had to skirt around vagrants and drunks who weaved in and out and across the maze of alleys, especially near the all-night pawnshops and taverns - she'd had to support Jannet the entire way because, by then, she could scarcely set one foot before the other.

And now the poor thing staggers, intent only on holding the small bundle safely to her. At the slightest sound from her little girl who is just two days old, she bends more closely over her and whispers soothingly, "Don't worry, my littleMadeleine, I won't leave you. I could never do that."

Rozenn steadies her friend around the next street corner and recoils, the heat of Jannet's fever is burning from her shirt into her own.

"We're almost there - for the love of God 'n' all His Saints, do ye have to keep sayin' this? Why don't you understand that this is the only thing ye can do?" She doesn't wait for an answer because, thank God, they have arrived.

"Look, Jannet, we're here!" She pushes her friend towards the tower. "All ye need to do slide the door to the left to open it, like this', but for the love of God quit talkin' 'bout not leavin' her!" she hisses at her. "Don't ye know it's the only thing ye *can* do?"

She wishes she could walk away from Jannet - but she cannot. She has sworn by all the Breton Saints to see her friend through this. If she doesn't, it might not go well afterwards, when she *will* need the Saints' help; that was the bargain she struck, but soon impatience and frustration burst out of her again.

"Ye have to leave her, there's no other way. I know it, ye know it, everyone would tell ye that. I'm gettin' hoarse explainin' it a thousand times. For the last time: yer labor was long, ye lost a lot of blood, 'n' then the bad fever got ahold of ye. Ye're sick with it, Jannet, very sick. There's no one to help ye 'cept me. Ye can't take care of yerself, how on God's green earth do ye expect to take care of her? The Sisters will, that's what they do here. Now do it!"

When Jannet doesn't move immediately, she reaches past her and briskly shoves the door sideways. The turntable creaks before it revolves slowly and stops in front of them. There is a folded blanket inside the basket.

"Look how lucky ye are, they don't always have blankets ready. She'll get clothes inside, remember I told ye? A bonnet, shirts 'n' a necklace with her name 'n' date stamped on it, 'n' she'll be baptized tonight. Doesn't that make you feel better? Hey, Jannet, are ye listenin' to me?"

The infant chooses this moment to stir. She opens her blue-green eyes. How can they already be so much like her father's? The soft fuzz of her hair is curly and sticks out in a cowlick, much lighter than his, but so much the way his did. Jannet swallows a sob. Infants do not see clearly during their first few days, she knows that. It is also what that old nun, leaving church and assuming Jannet to be one of "them easy street girls", had said. Age-spotted hands clasped piously together under her chin she had proclaimed in a voice so holier-than-thou that it made Jannet cringe, "Forgiveness is *not* for the likes of *you*!"

"Yeah? And there is more starch in yer heart than in yer wimple!" Rozenn shouted back, loudly enough to be heard above Jannet's low, "Don't, oh please, don't."

Jannet is convinced her daughter saw her, really saw her - but she will not remember. She will not know her. Rozenn is right; she is ill, so weak she can scarcely stand. She is too ill to take care of Madeleine. The money Pierre gave her has dwindled down to a few small coins … the Sisters are her only hope … but leaving her Madeleine … it is leaving her heart.

"Quit dreamin', just do it!" Rozenn commands harshly.

Jannet chokes down another sob and wills back her tears because tears would blur the only image of her child she'll ever have. She kisses her daughter, again and again, and gently places her in the basket. The blanket is nice and soft - who will see to it that Madeleine is cozy and warm? Safe and loved? May the good Lord watch over her always, watch over her … suddenly the other worry pushes back into her mind.

"Rozenn - please tell me, where is … ?"

"Good grief, not that again!" Rozenn interrupts her in an angry shout. "How many times do I have to tell ye: the boy didn't breathe! A thousand times I told ye that: he did not breathe, he never did. He didn't live! Nothin' anybody could do for him. Sure it's sad, but I can't stand around here all night watchin' ye do nothin'! Do it quick-like, it goes easier that way. Give the table a good push!"

Jannet doesn't hear. Her arms are empty, she is empty, but as long as her hands remain on the basket, her child is still with her.

"Tonnerre de Dieu, why do I always have to do everythin'?" Rozenn reaches around her, pries her hands off the basket, sends the turntable out of sight and gives the bell-pull a few angry tugs.

The sound startles Jannet. Such a pretty sound, and yet it cuts deep, so deep …

"Well, that's done. Now the Sisters know they have a guest. Come, it's late. Time to get goin'."

Rozenn is in no mood to wait for Jannet to return from wherever her thoughts have taken her. Roughly, she pulls her away. One quick look at her friend's face

- she is worse, much worse. Won't be easy, getting her all the way back to where she lives.

Jannet is convinced her daughter saw her, but she will not remember. She will not know her. Rozenn must be right. She is feeling so hot and so weak and the pain is so bad she can barely stand. She knows that she is too ill to care for her child. She knows. There are women, wet nurses, who take infants into their homes for money, but she has heard ugly stories that some pocket the money and don't feed the children - how could they not? The money Pierre gave her has dwindled down to a few coins. She has nothing and only a little time left, the sisters are her only hope. She knows that, she knows, but leaving Madeleine …

"I said it's time to go." How is she going to get her back to her place? The lady of the house, Jannet's distant relative, has let her work for room and board, on the condition that the arrangement comes to its end before the arrival of a screaming infant. She has been lucky at that; other employers would have put her out as soon as she started to show. Well, delivering her back is the last thing she has to do. Rozenn is in a rush to get back to her own place where she is paying cook's helper half a month's wages to watch over the boy, *her* boy, to keep her mouth shut and him quiet, just for a few hours. What a handsome little fellow he is, bigger than his sister, of course. No wonder it was such a difficult birth.

Jannet lets herself be steered across the bridge and

into the labyrinth of rutted, cobbled streets where drunks still totter around aimlessly and where mongrel dogs, interrupted in their search for food among rotting piles of garbage, snarl at them. She knows how ill she is, but she needs to tell Rozenn something important. She touches her elbow.

"What?"

Jannet doesn't answer, the pain is getting worse. Rozenn sees that her face has gone pale and blank. Rozenn thinks how she knows how to read and write, was used to a different life although she never talked much about it. And what good did all of that do her? She is surprised at a fleeting sense of pity, thinks about what she has been told of that fever after childbirth, that it almost always ends badly. The women were right - Jannet is not long for this world. Well, nothing she can do about that. She has kept her promise.

After what seems like an eternity, they reach the crumbling stone steps which lead down to the cellar kitchen of Jannet's great-aunt or whoever the woman is. Jannet's bed there is a thin mattress filled with straw ticking, set into a kitchen alcove.

"I have to hurry back," Rozenn says. "I told ye, me mistress is a witch, gets up *before* the crack o' dawn even on Sundays to make sure we're all at work. Ye'll be all right now. Sleep if the old biddy lets ye. Madeleine is in good hands with the Sisters."

Not sure whether the fever is catching or not, she gives Jannet's shoulder an awkward little pat before she disappears into the night. She hopes the child is in good hands; one can never be sure. Lately people have been saying that Hôtel-Dieu is so crowded that they have to put two babies into one crib, and sometimes they run out of milk and food. Of course she didn't tell her that. Perhaps it isn't even true. They also say that half the children there don't live to see their first birthday. She had not believed that either, not until her own son was not in the lucky half ... She sighs. All that is water under the bridge, like they say. Time for her to go back to Brittany. With her boy!

Jannet stands there for a long time before she realizes that Rozenn has left. I never thanked her. Sluggishly the thought works itself into her consciousness. She tries to see the uneven steps which lead down into darkness, but her eyes keep closing. She leans against the wall, it feels cool against her back, she lets herself slide down to sit, only for a moment. She knows it wasn't the fever talking then, and it isn't the fever talking now. She had pleaded with Rozenn to let her hold her boy for just a little while, but she wouldn't. 'He's dead', Rozenn kept repeating, 'he is dead!' Even if he didn't live, let me hold him for a little while, please? I know he cried. Why did she take him away? Why? I am not imagining this, I heard him, I heard him.

Please . . .

I am so tired I cannot think ...

Because now nothing matters ...

Nothing matters ... now ...

Nothing.

Chapter 11

Five years have passed since the most trying days of her life, but Rozen has never forgotten the nightmare of leaving Paris in Gilbert's cart. Nicolas screamed the entire way, his face scrunched up in fury, mottling into an angry, purplish red. She could never tell why - hunger, wet, gas, too cold, too warm, rash, needing to be changed again? What else was there? More than once, Gilbert threatened to put her and her screaming brat down by the side of the road.

How could such a small person be so ornery, so contrary, turn her life into such misery? It felt as if his aim in life was to wear her out. And what a silly notion that was, almost as silly as believing that the joy of being a mother again would instantly become hers. It couldn't be punishment for telling Jannet that he was dead, could it? Nae! Divine retribution, if that's the right word, never happens that quick; it comes on ye later, when ye least expect it. Most likely something is wrong with the boy - why does bad luck always single her out?

When they stopped at a cheap inn, the elderly woman who was waiting on tables limped over to their corner and commented, "Got yerself a tough little one there, ain't ye? Raised six of me own, four still livin' with their children. Want I should have a go at 'im?"

"Sure. Here - take him!"

Rozenn would have handed him to whoever asked, including the Devil! To make matters worse, all the woman did was jiggle Nicolas up and down, exactly as she had done and he stopped crying. Hiccupped a few times before he caught his breath, gulped down all of the watered-down milk, burped wetly, yawned and settled down to sleep. At first, Rozenn was merely annoyed and embarrassed, then enraged at how this boy made her look like such a failure - but there was always more than one way to look at things. Could be this was a sign she wasn't meant to take care of an infant. All she could see stretching out before her were endless years of drudgery and sacrifice. Why did Nicolas let the woman change him without one peep of protest? With her everything was a battle.

A little while later, gossiping over several glasses of cider, the strong kind, and while Nicolas was sleeping like the little angel he was not, the woman mentioned Berthe Leroux, a wet nurse who lived outside a village only two hours away. And another sign surely: she was looking to take in another infant although she'd just had one of her own and was raising several older children.

"Of course she's respectable," the woman answered Rozenn's question, "Would I mention her if she weren't? If yer wonderin' why she be doin' this: she needs to earn somethin' on the side, her man bein' a sailor. Comes home only once a year, but never fails to leave her with one in the oven! Men!"

They snickered knowingly until Rozenn asked, "How much, ye think?" When she learned that Berthe's charge for her services was reasonable, her mind was made up. Of course this Berthe was either an idiot or a saint, or a combination of both, saddling herself with someone else's children.

Either way, she would do fine for Nicolas for the time being. Things were bound to change, might work out as he got older. He'd be easier to manage then; he might even grow into the son a mother could rely on, could be proud of. She had nothing to reproach herself for; she had saved his life, hadn't she?

As expected, Nicolas was back to being his miserable crying self when they continued on their way, so much so that she frightened herself by coming dangerously close to shaking the badness out of him.

She held the screaming boy for what seemed like endless hours, not letting Gilbert stop until they found Berthe's home.

Well, hovel more than a home, she thought, but at least Nicolas had stopped wailing.

Within a short time the two women came to an understanding which included visiting on Sundays. Berthe's newest child looked rather puny, but the four older ones, all with rheumy noses and stringy black hair, seemed healthy if rather dirty - well, it was the end of the day, wasn't it? They apparently shared two straw-filled mattresses in a corner of the kitchen which doubled as an 'everything else room'. Well, she had slept on worse and had survived. So could he!

Although it was with tremendous relief that she left him with her, Rozenn thought it would not be amiss to make sure Berthe saw and heard her sniffling at having to part from her dear son. She pulled a handkerchief out to dry her eyes which, needless to say, did not require drying.

She visited for the first time three months later; what difference could it make to one so young how often she came? Monthly, or better still, every other month while he was so young suited her just fine. She didn't mind paying in advance.

When Berthe asked about his birth certificate, she tearfully told her that she'd had him on the first of September, but that the paper was lost during their travel. She quickly added that work might keep her from coming regular-like, she'd do the best she could and would make sure to be there for his birthday.

She did arrive on that day and was in for quite a

surprise. Nicolas had grown into a handsome little boy who stubbornly tried to walk and picked himself up no matter how often he toppled over or found himself sitting down abruptly. And, will wonders never cease, he did not cry!

Rozenn handed him the carved wooden horse she had pinched from a stall at the previous year's autumn fair, but it immediately disappeared into the hands of Berthe's five-year-old son and remained there. Nicolas didn't seem to mind, so she didn't either. Anyway, he did not deserve a present, not the way he had struggled against sitting on her lap. It was good that Berthe had not seen that she had slapped him. Only once and not hard, but it did make him lose his balance. He didn't cry then either, just sat there, staring at her in mute dislike.

The next few years she started to pay for several months in advance and came less and less often, once with a knitted cap she had found which Nicolas immediately tore off his head and threw on the ground.

"Yer expectin' too much, give 'im time," Berthe tried to tell her. "The boy doesn't know ye. How can he get used to ye when ye miss so many Sundays?"

"I have to work," Rozenn countered hotly, "I work hard. Most Sundays I'm so tuckered out I can hardly move." She thought but did not say that she saw no point in walking all this distance only to find what she already knew but could not understand: Nicolas wanted nothing to do with her.

During a short visit after his fifth birthday (which she had missed), Berthe tried to tell her what a good worker he was. "He is not afeared o' horses, can ye imagine? Not of the cows either, he takes them to pasture for one of the farmers. Knows to watch out for the ornery ones, knows to move 'em away from places that be overgrazed without bein' told. Rozenn, have ye noticed the scratches on his arms 'n' legs? Ye haven't? He got those goin' at a boy who was twirling a cat 'round by its tail! He sure does love his animals. 'N' he is smart, real smart. Sits with the children when the young priest comes to teach 'em their prayers. He remembers every word after only *one* time! Much better than my Marrec who's older 'n' named for me husband - 'n' the questions he asks, there's so much goin' on in his head! The other day he's makin' lines in the dirt, tells me he is writin' - did ye ever?"

"No!" Rozenn was getting tired of saying, "Really? You don't say! Is that so?" and finally said, "Enough, enough!" Berthe must have a bloomin' imagination or be talkin' 'bout some other boy: Nicolas did none of this when he was with her. He'd simply stand there, mute, sullen and poised to run. He shook his head at every word she said, stubbornly refused to call her 'Mother', never kissed her, only stared at her with those disconcertingly unblinking, blue-green eyes before he'd suddenly bolt - well, nobody could say she hadn't given it a good try. Very little in life works out as one expects, but when enough is enough the smart ones walk away.

She took another large sip of apple brandy, a deep breath and confided in Berthe that … well, that Nicolas was not hers, that he weren't her son at all.

"What yer sayin', what kind o'story yer tellin' me now?"

"No story. It's true."

Rozenn told her how she had taken him out of the goodness of her heart, to help his poor mother, her dear, dear friend who had died giving birth to him, God rest her soul. Died from that terrible childbed fever, ye know 'bout that, don't ye? She did, just two days later. But as he had never taken to her, for no reason that she could see - what was the point of visiting?

"What ye mean? He is a good boy, 'n' so smart. In time he might … "

"He's never good with me. Ye like him so much - ye keep 'im!" She threw a fistful of coins on the table. "I can pay for this year 'n' one more if ye insist, but not more. If he is half as good a worker as ye say, this'll work out to yer advantage; am I right, huh?"

Berthe had heard enough. "It's a bad, bad mistake yer makin'. Take back yer money: ye know where ye can put it!"

"Hey! No reason to talk dirty to me. Suit yerself." Rozenn gathered up the coins and dropped them back into her pocket. "Who're ye to tell me I be makin' a mistake, huh?"

"*I* know Nicolas. Ye sure don't!"

"Oh, have it yer own way!"

This was turning out better than she had expected. Rozenn left immediately. Although she had never been one to look back, a small, niggling voice kept questioning her decision, but only for a day or two. She looked forward to being unencumbered and was eager to get back, not to work so much as being with a new man she'd set her sights on. Later, who knows, perhaps . . .

Berthe was happy and Nicolas was relieved. He did not like the woman who always insisted he call her 'Mother' when she came. When he wouldn't, she'd get real quiet, with a bad kind of quiet that came before she'd look at him with eyes gone real hard, and suddenly she'd be screaming angry. He wasn't sure how a mother should be and didn't much care because he had Berthe. Rozenn not coming back, that was good. Very good. He had run away from the angry conversation between the two women and returned with some firewood for Berthe when it was almost dark, when he could be sure 'she' was gone.

That same evening, Berthe sat him down and in her usual no-nonsense way announced that he could stay

with her as long as he was willing to earn his keep. He
didn't let his relief show. After a short ponder, he merely
asked, "What is keep?"

"Beggin' 'n' cow-herdin' for pay," she answered.
"Hey, no need to make a face. Beggin' is 'onorable work.
It says so in the Bible. Me children do it, too."

She looked him over and frowned. "Too bad you're
tall for yer age, but we can't shrink ye, can we? Yer sorry-
lookin' enough 'n' thin as a spoon's shank. That's good
- who'd believe a fat beggar-boy that he be starvin', eh?
Ye start tomorrow mornin', bright 'n' early. Go to the big
farms 'n' beg grains for yer supper. Bring food home if
ye want to eat that night - that be our rule. And no need
to wash in the mornin'."

Nicolas didn't understand why but never considered
not doing as Berthe said and went to sleep.

"Grains, like I told ye," she repeated before he set out
the next morning. "Now listen good: look *miserable sad*,
stick out yer hand like so, ask for a liard, barley or oats,
please madame, or a crust of black bread, for the love of
God, please - hey, ye might even get a crêpe! Wouldn't
hurt to cough a little, squeeze out a tear or two. Why
barley 'n' oats, ye think?"

Nicolas pushed that around in his head for a while.
"Cause that be what grows hereabouts?"

"Clever boy," she beamed, "but never answer a

question with 'nother question. Folks believe ye when ye sound like ye know what yer talkin' about. Remember that."

Nicolas nodded; that made sense. "But what's a liard?"

"Why, a penny's worth; comes to about a handful." She adjusted the double-pouch begging bag she had sewn for him around his neck and tucked the bags down, one in front, one in back, inside his old and much-mended shirt.

"Now, this is important: don't pay attention if people wants to tell ye scary goblin stories, or that the Devil hisself was born in a cave not far from here - or even that yer devil-fisted." She chuckled. "Don't know what I'm talkin' 'bout, boy, do ye? Devil-fisted, that's what folk hereabouts call them as always use the *left* hand. Don't pay 'em no mind. Born with two hands, aren't we, so why should one hand be better 'n' the other? Some folk say things just to annoy or scare ye. They just stories, 'n' we sure got more here than other places! But that's all they be, stories. They're not real."

Nicolas nodded again. This was going to be all right. Not as good as school would have been, but all right. He had no clear idea what school was anyway, had only heard it was the place where rich boys learned to read and write. Maybe other things, too. There were no such places for boys like him, but he was glad to be off to see new places, new people. That was learning, too.

The first weeks were hard. Most farmers had nothing or only very little to give away. Some were curious, wanted to know where he was from, who his folks were. When he answered, "Don't have none," the younger women especially must have felt bad; often they'd put a ladle of groats into his bag. Quick, as if they didn't want to be seen doing it.

Old women always asked whether he had come through the forest. He found out that if he said yes, they'd launch into scary tales about night prowlers or gnomes or bad fairies, and if he didn't look scared enough they'd whisper, "Just wait, ye'll see soon enough, the night-screamers or Bugul Noz will get ye! Are nobody's legs fast enough to get away from them."

That night, Berthe explained that night-screamers were children who had died without being baptized; that's why they wandered, crying, through the woods of the world at night until Judgment Day.

"Am I bapt ... a baptize? What does that do?"

"Course ye are. It's done for babies so their souls can go to heaven. Father Alphonse can explain it better when he comes next year. It's like I told ye, there are more scary stories here than any other place in the world! Don't worry yer head over them; they're only stories. Why ye still bothered?"

"The night-screamers - why didn't *they* get a baptize?"

"Lord, aren't ye full o' questions! Either they be sick 'n' the priest didn't get to 'em in time, could be a hundred other reasons! Now go wash, 'specially those dirty feet. Save yer other questions for Father Alphonse."

Nicolas did as he was asked, even though he'd had no chance to ask about Judgment Day and Bugul Noz; he didn't like the sound of either, whoever, whatever they were. One thing was sure: from now on he would avoid caves and forests. If he couldn't, he'd make sure to be in and out double-quick, and in the daytime only. Berthe said that telling a lie was a sin, but he figured there were times when lying was smarter than telling the truth. From then on, if asked whether he had come through the woods, he simply said, "Oh, no, I never!" Too bad if the old women were disappointed.

On summer evenings, when it didn't get dark until very late, Berthe let him look at her most prized possession which, she said, were from her 'better days': the heavy 'Lives of the Saints' and the even heavier Bible. "Ye earned it," she'd say, carefully taking the volumes down from their high shelf.

By the end of the summer, a few letter arrangements had begun to make sense to him because some words reminded him of the prayer book words, or, at least, parts of them did. He looked for words that looked the same or almost the same, tried to sound them out and realized that he could figure some out. Only short ones. The more often he looked, the more he understood, but it was hard, too, because "The Saints" were in French and not Breton, which, Berthe explained, was what he and she and all good Bretons spoke.

He marked his place by putting a dried leaf in the book and replacing it before it turned too brittle; he would never hurt a book by turning down a page corner. If he ever had money, he decided, lots of money, he would buy a book; no, a dozen books, a hundred books, 'n' read 'n' read 'n' learn from them. He felt surrounded by questions and secrets that no one had answers to.

Questions, for instance, about the moon 'n' the stars, why the moon changed its shape regular-like, and why it didn't fall out of the sky. The stars, too. Why could birds fly, but other animals could not? Was it because of what was inside their feathers? Other animals could swim; he had seen fish 'n' frogs 'n' water snakes. Why did the leaves change color when summer was over, and then they fell from the trees? And how did summer 'n' winter come 'n' go? Where did snow come from - he liked to picture an enormous barn inside the sky, and when God pushed the barn door open and tipped it downwards, it snowed. That set him wondering about heaven 'n' hell again, heaven bein' high above 'n' hell down below, the priest had said. There had to be a net nobody could see to keep the good souls from falling back down to earth, but the others - where was fiery hell? Way down in the earth and far, far away from where he lived, he hoped. And if souls could not be seen, like the priest said, how could one be sure there was such a thing as souls? How could they have a voice, like the night-screamers? How could they get out of a body and a nailed-down coffin that was buried under big mounds of dirt?

He had his first inkling that the entire world was not like where he lived when Berthe's husband Marrec came home. He overheard him telling her about something called 'ocean', where they could not see land for months, only water 'n' more water, but each evening they could see the sun slowly drowning in it. When they went ashore, that's what he called it, ashore - they all staggered around like drunks after being on the ship for so long. They saw men with yellow skins 'n' straight black hair braided down their backs 'n' slitty eyes. They jabbered in a language no one understood and ate their meals with sticks. Nicolas tried to picture eating soup with sticks - no, that couldn't be right. He must have heard wrong.

Marrec tended to ignore the children except when he hollered for someone to fetch something. He could be in a right temper if no one came running.

"Brandy 'n' baccy," he shouted to no one in particular one evening after supper.

Nicolas, being the closest, ran and handed over the bottle and the tobacco pouch. Succumbing to curiosity he asked, "Monsieur Marrec, how do the yellow-skin people eat soup?"

"Huh - what was that?" Marrec's eyebrows shot up almost to his hairline in astonishment. "Ah, it's you, the boy with a thousand questions." He took several slugs of the home brew. "With spoons, small spoons."

Nicolas nodded. "What other places have ye been?"

"Still here? Why are ye askin'?"

"I like to find out 'bout things."

"Hmm - Well, sailed 'round Africa twice where folks have real dark skin 'n' don't wear much, it bein' so hot; there's lions there, giraffes, elephants, monkeys, parakeet birds in all the colors of a rainbow. 'Nother time we sailed the other way. Sailed north a long time, saw wolves, later seals, bears white like snow, not brown like our bears here; got ourselves stuck in ice for days 'n' nearly froze to death. Toes haven't been right since then, but never mind, boy, ye don't know what I'm talkin' 'bout, do ye?"

"No, Monsieur Marrec, but I like hearin' it all the same. That time when it was so hot, when you sailed month 'n' months 'n' could only see water 'n' every evenin' the sun fell into it? Now, the sun didn't really drown, did it - but how could it get back up into the sky in time, I mean for the next morning?"

Marrec scratched his head. "How ye know 'bout that, Big Ears?"

"I ... I heard ye talkin' to Madame Berthe, monsieur."

"Listenin' at the door, were ye? Off with ye now, Big Ears. Tell ye more next year - hey, might make a sailor of ye when yer older, what ye think o' that?"

"Oh, yes, Monsieur Marrec, yes." Marrec was already snoring and didn't hear him.

Africa, that was a name he wanted to remember. Snow-white bears and rainbow-colored birds - he knew about rainbows. They sometimes happened when the sun came back after the rain. But what were seals, what did they look like? Well, he had an entire year to think about sun questions, different people and strange animals ...

There was no next year. Marrec did not return around the usual time. At first Berthe did not seem very concerned; this had happened before. Once he had not made it back for almost two years and could not let her know because he had never learned to write. But somehow this felt different. She began to worry. Nicolas saw her brush tears away after she prayed, but only when no one was watching. She prayed more often now. He didn't know whether he ought to say something to her or not, so he tried to help more.

It was many months later that an oilskin package for Berthe arrived, intact but very much the worse for wear for having traveled so far. Inside were Marrec's seaman's cap and his old much-mended sweater, his knife, a coin-filled purse, a ceramic soup spoon and a note penned by one of his mates and signed by the captain. Berthe asked Nicolas to read it, but he had trouble with the handwriting and most of the words. She had to wait for Father Alphonse.

He arrived several days later and condescended to read the letter out loud. Seaman Marrec had died instantly when their ship was caught in a violent three-day storm and the main mast broke off and fell on him. He was buried at sea.

What happened to him then? Where did all that water take him? Nicolas didn't like to think of Marrec's body being tossed about by big waves; that had also to be awful hard for Berthe to think about. He didn't ask whether she minded that he was getting the spoon when there was nothing for his own children. Perhaps that was why she took it and put it away someplace. He thought of all the things he would never be able to ask Marrec; when he saw her sadness he was sad, too, and said nothing.

Meanwhile, he continued to try to learn written French and had no idea how to say what he was looking at. Much was confusing, but he didn't mind. He liked thinking about complicated things.

Thinking of confusing things put him in mind of the other night when something very strange happened in his sleep.

He didn't know what to make of it; all he remembered was that, just before he woke up, there had been two of him. Two faces. He knew for sure because he had once sneaked into Berthe's corner, looked through her things and had found a small, cracked mirror. That's how he knew what *he* looked like: not at all like Berthe's children who all had dark eyes and dark hair. His hair was light-brown and wavy; his eyes were between blue and green. There had really been another one of him - although the other one could perhaps have been a girl; she had longer hair, but why didn't she wear one of those white lacy caps all the girls wore? He just didn't know. When he reached for that other one, she disappeared, was gone. He had wanted to ask, "Who are you? What do they call ye," but he woke up and she was gone. He couldn't make sense of this, and the strangeness of it bothered him so much that he told Berthe.

She laughed, but not in a making-fun-of-him way; she never did that. "You had a dream, me boy, just a dream. Dreamin' is nothin' to worry 'bout, it's not real. Everybody dreams. Folks go to sleep and dream. Sometimes it's good, some-times scary, sometimes ye don't understand what ye dream. 'N'sometimes," she laughed again, "sometimes ye remember nothin' in the mornin'!"

That might be so, but did others dream about someone who looked like them? He was curiously unsettled about this and wished he could do something to make the dream happen again.

There were other things that worried him even more, but he was learning to keep some of them to himself.

For instance, there was the merciful God he had learned about from the young priest. How could that God be on the thieves' side? He had to be on the lookout for them every day when he went out to beg. He had overheard them call the most terrible curses down on farmers who didn't hand over what they demanded - like sickness or death for their families, failed harvests and swarms of locusts for their crops. They lay in wait for beggar boys like him towards the end of the day and tried to steal everything that they had collected. The farmers were so afraid of them that they handed over whatever the thieves demanded.

That same God also looked away from poor and sick folk and was not merciful. Berthe's two youngest boys died on the same day, one an hour after the other, after one week of being shaking-sick with a bad fever, a bad cough and wheezing chests that hurt so bad they couldn't breathe right. They could only suck on small rolled-up pieces of cloth that had been dipped into Berthe's special herb tea; it had soothed sore throats before, but not this time. After a few days they didn't cough much, just lay there, pale and quiet. Berthe, who never used candles during daytime, lit a candle stub for each boy. A bad feeling crept over Nicolas as he watched the flickering shadows they cast over the small faces.

"These be holy candles, to guide me boys into the next world," Berthe explained, her face closed up tight, her voice choked with tears.

Nicolas understood that Rémy and André would not live and worried. Didn't stubs burn down very quick? What happens to being guided if they didn't burn long enough? Why should it be up to holy candles whether a child makes it into the next world or not, and anyway, what was that next world? It seemed all right to him when old folks died, but why did children have to die? He couldn't get Berthe out of his mind, the way she suddenly crumpled down on the floor one night when she thought he was asleep.

Was he going to die, too, even though he hadn't been sick in a long time? What if no one lit a candle for him?

He asked Father Alphonse who came to pray and talk about funeral costs with Berthe how a merciful God could allow this and got his ears boxed real hard for being an ignorant-impertinent-insolent heathen who had the effrontery to question God's will. Nicolas could have repeated the names the priest called him without knowing what they meant; his red-angry face was proof enough that they weren't good words.

Later, when the priest rushed through the prayers at the boys' funeral, sounding as if his mind was far away on something more important, he was so angry for Berthe that he felt he needed to say that it wasn't right. Several times he opened his mouth and closed it again. It seemed wiser to keep certain thoughts and questions to himself.

It was now up to him to do even better with food-begging and avoiding the men-thieves became harder. Younger boys didn't have much of a chance against them. He was glad he had those strong, long legs and on early mornings often ran just for the joy of it, while his pouches were still empty. The thieves never bothered him now, probably also because of his dog Chien who had appeared out of nowhere one day, dragging his bloody leg behind him, limping and snarling. After Nicolas shared what little food he had, the dog let himself be carried home. Berthe took care of the leg, and now Chien followed Nicolas wherever he went and turned ferocious if someone as much as raised his voice at him. Chien obeyed commands even before Nicolas was done talking.

Every day and at night before he went to sleep he tried to think of ways to learn things. Things that Berthe didn't know, things that could only be found be found in books. Or in school. School was not for him, he knew that, but he had heard that in school you could get answers.

School must be wonderful . . .

Chapter III

His luck changed when he was eleven.

Nicolas had grown. 'Like a weed, yer all legs 'n' arms,' Berthe used to say, shaking her head. The handed-down and much-mended pants which had hung from him only a few months earlier suddenly threatened to come apart at the seams. From working hard he was getting muscles and developing strength and was not afraid anymore. He roamed farther afield, looking for new and better places to fill his larger pouches. He understood the necessity of begging and did well at something he hated doing.

One afternoon, coming out of the cool woods, he walked along a meadow humming with bees in the summer heat when he happened on three big boys who had knocked down a fourth; at least that's what it looked like. Two were still hitting and kicking him although he was down, lying in the dirt, trying to protect his face and his foot at the same time. The third one was going through a bag, tossing out books, papers and pencils.

Looking for money, of course. Nicolas remembered having been caught like this once, years earlier. He had come home, bloodied and sore, both pouches torn and empty. Berthe had handed him a wet rag to clean his skinned knees and scratched legs and took care of the cut on his chin which left a white scar. There had been no supper that night, but she managed to fix him something for breakfast before she handed him the mended pouches. Three against one? That was wrong! So was throwing away books and good paper and pencils!

Nicolas whistled for Chien, commanded sternly, "At 'em!" and set about pulling the attackers off the boy. The dog's bared teeth and ferocious growls were enough to scatter them.

Nicolas walked over to where the boy lay curled up into himself, still protecting his head under both arms.

"They're gone. Can ye get up 'n' stand?"

"Don't think so." The boy groaned, sat up slowly and wiped his eyes. "They threw a rock at me, that big one over there. It hit me in the back and made me trip. My leg twisted and I fell on my ankle, hard. Ow, it hurts."

He tried but could not stand.

"Must be real bad then - where ye live?"

"Fougères."

"Whew! Why are ye all the ways out here?"

Nicolas waited patiently until the boy answered.

"What's it to you? I tried to run away from them into the woods and got lost . . ."

"Well, try again, see if ye can stand." Nicolas, who had finished collecting the boy's belongings and had carefully placed everything back into the bag, extended a hand towards him. The boy struggled to his feet but groaned and shook his head as soon as he put weight on the injured foot. He sat down again and looked like he was about to cry.

"Well, guess I'll have to carry ye. What's yer name?" Nicolas helped the boy hop over to a tree log and to sit while he hung the school bag around his own neck, facing forward.

"Alain Caradec. What're you talking about? You can't carry me!"

"I'm Nicolas Favreau. Bet I can. Now when I bend down, grab me 'round the neck. When I say 'now' hold on real tight till I stand up. *But don't choke me!*"

They had to stop often. Carrying Alain, who moaned and complained all the way, was a struggle that lasted more than an hour, the longest and hottest hour of Nicolas' life. He stumbled a few times and every time he did, Alain's arms tightened into a stranglehold and he yelled, "Hey, be more careful!" Thank God he lived at the near edge of the town, just ahead.

Nicolas had never been this way before, could not look around properly but still caught glimpses of large, important-looking houses with too many windows to count, and big gardens. There was also an old, odd-looking stone building that went on and on with many high round towers and slits in the thick walls.

"Who lives in that big place over there?"

"Now? Nobody, silly, that's the old Fougères Castle. Everybody knows that. It is one of the biggest castles in all of Europe," Alain explained proudly. "We're almost there."

Europe? What was that? Nicolas stopped to catch his breath and with the back of one hand wiped away the sweat that kept dripping down his face. A little later he pointed upwards with his chin.

"And that, up there?" He had never seen such a large round nest atop a roof either.

"You don't know much, do you? That's a stork nest; we get one every year, it means good luck. That other part of my house, over there on the left, that's where my father works. He is a very good veterinarian."

Nicolas didn't get a chance to ask what that meant.

A woman, anxiously running up and down the street, turned around at the sound of Alain's voice and screamed, "Alain Oh Alain thanks be to God you're safe I was so worried about you what happened Alain your poor face you're bleeding and why can't you walk oh I see it's your foot let me see oh no your ankle looks bad it's swollen badly I hope it's not broken oh my poor, poor boy." She tried to grab him.

At least that's what Nicolas figured Alain's mother had been saying. He couldn't be sure, he only understood a word here and there. She wasn't speaking Breton. Her son, visibly embarrassed at being fussed over, shouted at her not to let go or she'd make him fall.

Nicolas wiped his face again and dried his hands on his pants as three servants rushed outside. Two immediately linked arms and carried Alain inside. The third grabbed the school- bag off Nicolas' neck and checked it over. "Hey boy, what ye steal out of this here bag?"

"Nothin'." Insulted, Nicolas stood there, stretching and rubbing his sore neck and shoulders. He was about to turn away when Alain's mother called out from the open door. "Don't go away, boy, Cook is setting out a plate for you in the kitchen. Go right in." Waving him inside, she disappeared back into the house.

Food? Nicolas hoped that was what was being offered, he wasn't sure, but his mouth had filled with saliva at the mere thought of it. He ordered Chien to stay and followed a young man into the kitchen where tempting aromas made him feel light-headed. He sat down at the end of a long table and immediately drank down the entire mug of cold cider before he ate the best meal he had ever eaten in his life. He couldn't have said what it was: the only things he recognized in the creamy sauce were pieces of potato and some vegetable, what else would be green like that? He ate everything, savoring the tender meat and the slices of crusty, buttered bread set before him and drained a second mug of cider. He had finished eating and was wondering what to do - he didn't want to leave without thanking somebody - when an important-looking man walked into the kitchen.

"So, you're the boy who rescued my son and helped him get home? I just heard the entire story. I am Docteur Caradec." He sat down opposite Nicolas.

"Alain says you're quite a fighter. Took on three older boys; is that true?"

"We'll, me 'n' me dog did."

"Why?"

" Three against one, that isn't right, 'specially with the one down already. Wasn't much of a fight after I told Chien to go at 'em: they ran like the Devil was after 'em." He grinned at the memory.

"I can imagine. How did you know that three against one is not right?"

"Berthe told me. Now I jest knows it."

"Berthe? Is she your grandmother?"

"No, I just live with her."

"I see. Tell me, what do they call you?"

"Nicolas."

"Nicolas and - ?"

"Favreau, Nicolas Favreau."

"What about your parents?"

"I don't have parents. I live with Madame Berthe, way over on the other side of the big woods."

"How old are you?"

"Almost twelve."

The man wasn't saying anything else, so Nicolas sneaked a look through the open door into a corridor. Several large colored pictures of horses in shiny yellow frames hung on the walls. People who could buy so many pretty but useless things to hang on their walls - they had to be rich.

"I see you have discovered my horse paintings," the man said after a while. "They are by Stubbs, a great horse painter. He is British. He gave them to Alain's grandfather who was a veterinarian, as I am."

Assuming that the word meant nothing to the boy he explained the term.

"I see, thank you." Nicolas would have liked to ask what 'British' was but didn't have time.

"Now, where were we? Right - my son says you gathered up his books and papers and that you carried him and his bag all the way home. You really did that?"

He scrutinized the boy - cleaned up he might be presentable enough, and Alain had begged and begged and begged him until he had said all right, I'll think about it, I'll see, perhaps. Alain was not the only boy who feared these older boys who tormented the younger ones on their way to school, and he flatly refused to go accompanied by a servant. That would only make everything worse, he insisted; he was probably right. The boy was two years older than Alain and looked strong.

"Yes, I did."

The next question came after a long pause. "Ever been in trouble with the law?"

"The law?" Nicolas repeated slowly, not sure what Docteur Caradec was talking about.

"A gendarme ever come to where you live? To take you to jail? For stealing or for destroying public property, or for doing something worse?"

Nicolas' "No!" was a vehement near-shout. "I don't steal, never. No gendarme came. Never!"

Docteur Caradec suppressed a smile, said, "Good,," and thought for a while.

"Well, Nicolas," he finally asked, "what would you

say to living here for a few weeks and making sure Alain gets to school without trouble? Just until his ankle is healed?"

Live here?

Nicolas was sure he hadn't heard right. Living here, in this big stone house with the many windows? Eating *without* begging? He wanted to whoop with joy, but suddenly the suggestion lost its appeal.

"I cannot do it," he said sadly.

"Why is that?"

Nicolas explained his two reasons: Berthe, who relied on him, and Chien.

Docteur Caradec, who prided himself on being a good judge of character and of seeing through most people, found himself taking to this dirty youngster who had helped his son, felt loyalty towards the woman he lived with, didn't forget his dog. Didn't take the easy way out. It showed character.

He thought how Alain dreaded the way to school, how the big boys scared and made life miserable for him, and how nobody could do anything about them; how lately Alain had gone as far as threatening not to go to school, and that was simply unthinkable. Having Nicolas go with him might solve the problem which had mother and son close to tears many mornings . . . of course getting Alain to and from school remained a problem.

"And if I had a servant ride over to Madame Berthe, right now? Who would explain everything to her, bring back some of your belongings? It wouldn't be for very long, only until Alain's ankle is healed. Your dog can stay, too, of course, but in the shed."

Well, this was different! Beaming, Nicolas agreed immediately. "I don't need nothin' but the boots, please. But I have to go soon 'n' explain everythin' to Berthe meself, too."

"Naturally." Docteur Caradec understood that. He looked down at the boy's callused, dirt-encrusted feet.

"Very well. Now there are some things I have to make clear to you that we do differently in our home: We wear shoes at all times. Inside *and* outside. Madame Caradec will see to a pair for you and some clothes. We say prayers every day, morning and evening, with family and servants attending; that includes you while you live here. Cursing is forbidden, strictly forbidden. And there is no card playing, singing, fiddling, dancing or knitting on Sundays. You understand?"

Nicolas nodded. Prayers and *new* boots - how difficult was that? And as far as the other rules were concerned - according to Berthe he couldn't carry a tune to save his soul, so he didn't have to worry about singing; he didn't know how to play a fiddle or how to dance and had never even seen playing cards, and as far as knitting went - that was for *girls*! As to cursing

- he could always do that in his head, without making a sound.

But there was something he needed to ask urgently. "Sir, how do I get Alain to school with his bad ankle?"

"That is the question, isn't it? How can we?"

Docteur Caradec rolled a pencil back and forth while he deliberated.

"Our doctor is still here; the ankle is being taped as we speak, and Alain is not allowed to put weight on that foot for three weeks. I wish you knew how to ride a bicycle, then Alain could sit on the handlebars - no, what am I saying! His mother would never allow that! Too dangerous et cetera, et cetera - and anyway, you don't know how to ride a bicycle."

"No, 'cause I never tried - but I just thought of a way! Do ye have somethin' cart-like that Alain could sit in? I could push or pull him. Then when we get to the school, all I have to do is piggy-back him inside."

"You would do that?"

"Yes!"

"Let me think about this. Wait here."

School was important, and no better solution came to mind. Finally his wife Sylvie gave him a dubious 'yes', provided he agree to have one of the servants follow at a distance so the boys would not be aware of him - but did he really think it was prudent to have such a dirty boy come live with them? Most likely he had atrocious table manners or none and oh, no - what if he had lice?

"He'll learn our ways, and if he has lice, we'll get rid of them. He'll get cleaned up and it's only for a few weeks," he reassured her. "Let's give him a try."

"If you say so. He'll eat with the servants, of course."

"No, dear, with us. I'll tell Cook on my way out to give the dog something."

"But outside only, please. I'm sure he has fleas," she said unhappily.

Chapter IV

A nd so Nicolas became a member of the Caradec
household. He did not mind the prayers; they were
short, and he got used to wearing the new boots which
really fit, not like his old ones with the flapping soles
which were too big, even with rags stuffed into the toe
parts.

There were other changes in his life.

His first bath was quite different from dunking into
the cold creek on a summer day or splashing water over
himself at Berthe's kitchen sink. He wore store-bought
clothes now, not hand-me-downs. No holes, no tears,
no patches; they were neither too big nor too tight, had
no old spots, weren't worn through at the knees, and
had never belonged to nobody before! Actually, they
were so stiff they weren't comfortable the first few days.
The only time he protested was when they wanted to
throw away his old boots: they belonged to Marrec and
were not his to get rid of.

Chien, having befriended Cook, lived well, too, and still followed Nicolas everywhere. Every day he waited outside the schoolhouse until the boys were dismissed. He bared his teeth at whoever yelled, "Here comes donkey with his load!" and grabbed boys who kept up the chant by their pant legs. They soon gave up.

But none of this was as important to Nicolas as going to school which Docteur Caradec had arranged, even though it turned out to be much different from what he had imagined. The boys didn't bother him after he won fights against the two tallest and strongest ones. They contented themselves with calling him 'a rude, nasty little peasant'. Nicolas shrugged that off. Getting only one out of four words right was nothing to brag about!

The teacher, Monsieur Mathieu, didn't like him. He made no secret of the fact that he considered Nicolas an unsuitable addition to his class. "You may be a decent enough pushcart pusher" - at this the boys laughed uproariously, as if on cue - "but I am told that you don't speak our beautiful language. Neither speak nor read it. T-t-t-t-t, in this day and age, how is that possible? I assume you also lack even a nodding acquaintance with our multiplication tables. How about addition? Can you add two and two, or is that too difficult for your brain, assuming one is hiding under all that hair?"

Nicolas wasn't sure what the teacher had said, but it made the boys laugh again.

"Let me help you. Two and two." Quickly the teacher held up two and two fingers, then three, four, five, nine in rapid succession. "So - which is it?"

When Nicolas answered, "Four, monsieur," but ignored other equally insulting questions, the teacher ended with, "Well, what should I do with such an uncouth imbecile in my class? I know, let's begin with simplest lesson." With his bamboo stick he pointed to the illustrated official-looking sign above the blackboard and, tapping on each word and enouncing slowly, recited:

" Il est interdit de parler Breton et de cracher sur la terre."[*]

"The authorities must have had him in mind when they created this sign, don't you agree, class? We certainly shouldn't expect to hear much from him."

Again, the boys erupted in shrieks and guffaws which bothered Nicolas. He understood what the sign said but not why it should hang in school and why the teacher made fun of him. He had no intention of spitting on the floor or anywhere else. Berthe had not allowed spitting. Confused and saddened by the daily humiliations, he tried to ignore them. He was where he wanted to be, in school.

During the following weeks, Monsieur Mathieu grew visibly perturbed. Learning came easier to this peasant than any boy he'd ever had in his classes: the

---

[*]   It is forbidden to speak Breton and to spit on the floor.

yokel followed the lessons without trouble. Hearing something once seemed to be all he needed to remember it, word for word. Having to take a lowly peasant into his class was bad enough, but a quick learner, that was adding insult to injury! He'd show him: he would never call on him!

Nicolas learned to recognize the signs: Monsieur Mathieu struggled to retain his composure only when *his* hand was raised! It always began with his left eye twitching, and then he'd tug at his stiff shirt collar and look anywhere but at him. Nicolas stopped raising his hand. Being ignored suited him because comparing his answer to the correct answer was all he cared about.

After a week of watching this, Alain grew annoyed.

"What's wrong with you? Why aren't you angry?" he shouted at his new friend on the way home. "You know all that stuff! Why do you just give up? Why don't you raise your hand?"

Nicolas shrugged.

"No, I want to know. You'll never get points that way."

"I don't care about points, whatever they're good for, but all right, I'll tell you. Reason number 1: He would not see me anyways, so why raise my hand? You know he won't call on me. Or if he did, he'd laugh about how I pronounce whatever the answer is. Reason number 2:

I'm not goin' to give wrong answers to make Monsieur Mathieu feel good."

"Oh!" Intrigued by his friend's logic, Alain loaned Nicolas his Breton-French dictionary and read to him from a French book or newspaper every day, putting a finger under every new word as he pronounced it repeatedly. He didn't like Mr. Mathieu either, but he envied the ease with which Nicolas learned.

Nicolas found several things about his new life challenging: cutting meat as effortlessly and cleanly as the Caradecs; sleeping in a bed smothered by soft pillows and a duvet after years of curling up on a straw-filled sack on Berthe's kitchen floor; the stiff Sunday collar that still chafed his neck and gargling' those French *r*'s the way everybody else did so effortlessly. Most of all he disliked having to go to bed so early; Madame Caradec believed that growing boys needed a great deal of sleep. "Sleep is one half of your health" was one of her favorite sayings. Another one was, "Wait for the night before saying that the day was beautiful."

He woke at dawn every day and didn't know what to do with himself. After a few days he tip-toed downstairs and looked for Docteur Caradec's newspapers which he had seen in his study. Sitting on the floor by the window where the light was good - no one was allowed to touch the new lamp - he tried to read and got stuck. There were too many new words. But there were advertisements in "La Presse", accompanied by pictures which helped. The other paper, "Le Moniteur Universel", was much too difficult.

He began to memorize words every morning and tried to copy them down for Alain, who explained and pronounced them. Very slowly, the Fougères, Rennes and Paris news began to make sense - fires, accidents, robberies, births and weddings, and those black-framed notices about people who had died. For sale offers for farming equipment and other advertisements. Foreclosure notices he did not understand at all. Politics - he read paragraphs over and over and still there were too many big words. Of course he took the greatest care to put both newspapers back, folded exactly the way he had found them.

Nothing much happened for three weeks, and one week later Alain's ankle was pronounced sufficiently improved. His doctor allowed him to walk to school, slowly and carefully, of course. No rough-housing. Every day, Nicolas expected to be told that he wasn't needed any longer, that he would have to leave. That school was over for him.

The evening he was called into Docteur Caradec's office after supper he was convinced that the dreaded day had arrived.

"So - hmm, Nicolas, I've been meaning to ask you for some time - someone sneaks into my office very early in the morning and reads my papers, and I think, no, I *know* it is you," he finished in an unusually stern voice. "I don't remember giving you permission to do that." Docteur C.'s brow was creased and he sounded displeased - this was worse than what Nicolas had expected.

"Yes, Sir, I go into your study. Very early. And no, sir, ye can't remember sayin' I could 'cause ye didn't - I mean, I know ye didn't say I could."

"And why would you be doing this?"

"I want to learn how to read regular French while I live here. Berthe has no newspapers. I think reading newspapers helps me 'n' at the same time I can find out 'bout so many things, but there is much I still don't understand. I always put both papers back, folded exactly the way you do. Sir."

"Yes, that is true."

The boy was a quick learner. Even his speech had undergone a change for the better. There was a long silence while Docteur Caradec packed his pipe.

"Well, let's put this newspaper business aside for the moment. I have another question for you, Nicolas, one that may be difficult for you to answer: do you *have* to, or do you *want* to go back to Madame Berthe? What I am asking is this: Would you consider remaining here, living here for a while longer? Take a couple of days to think this over before you give me your answer and the reasons for your decision, whatever it is."

Living here? Still going to school? The one thing he had never expected. Never! That was wonderful, amazing, incredible! Why would he need a couple of days to think over the easiest decision in the world?

"Alain 'n' me, we're friends now," he started, speaking so fast that the words tumbled over one another. "I never had a friend before. Yes, I want to stay here with him, with ye 'n' with Madame; I can learn here, things I can't learn from Berthe. I learned things from her, too, but now I needs to learn from books, many different books. I don't need time to think it over. No, sir, I don't. Thank ye, sir, yes, yes," he said again, nearly out of breath. "Yes, sir, I would like to stay."

Docteur Caradec suppressed a smile and nodded. "That's it then, very good. I'll take care of the paperwork to make you my ward, temporarily - meaning that I shall be responsible for you while you live here. You are sure, quite sure?"

"Oh yes, very sure! But …"

"Speak up, boy. There is a 'but'?"

"I must tell Berthe myself. It's not right if I don't."

"Of course."

Docteur C. had not expected anything different; still he wondered how Nicolas knew this. Well, perhaps the boy had it in him; perhaps that was who he was. He'd had a good feeling about him from the very beginning. Discrete inquiries about his background had resulted in nothing except the bare facts of his arrival at Madame Berthe's.

More importantly, watching the growing friendship between the two boys, he realized that he had fewer worries when Alain was with Nicolas. Even his mother was less nervous about her son, and Alain had stopped complaining about school so much. Perhaps if there had been other children … .

"All right then," he repeated, "but think about it some more. It is always a good idea to sleep on important decisions. One more thing: from now on, the old newspapers will be in the *salon*. Use the lamp there *if* needed, carefully, of course, but my study is off limits. Do you understand off limits?"

"It means - don't go in there?"

"Yes, that is precisely what it means."

"Yes, sir, thank you, sir." Nicolas felt that he had been given a huge present and couldn't stop smiling, but he remained standing.

"Why don't you call me Docteur C. from now on? Is there anything else?"

"I was wondering if . . . if I could watch you some time, when you take care of sick animals?"

"What makes you ask?"

"Well, when I found Chien, or he found me, he was in a bad way. His leg was bloody 'n' stuck out at a strange angle, he was whimperin' somethin'awful; he wouldn't let me get near him at first, but I talked to him quiet-like, then he let me carry him home. Berthe cleaned the leg 'n' put ointment on it, then she put a piece of wood against it 'n' wrapped a cloth around it. Chien is good as new, only limps a little if he runs around too much or is tired. I'd like to learn about helping sick or hurt animals, perhaps after school when Alain starts with fencing lessons again?"

How ironic, Docteur C. thought. This boy is interested in what I do while my son's stomach turns at the sight of blood. He won't go near an injured animal. He'd had great hopes to see Alain become the third generation Caradec veterinarian.

"Why not?" he said. "Let me think about it."

When Nicolas tiptoed into the salon the next morning, the newspapers were there on one of the small tables as promised, neatly folded under a book. Nicolas picked it up. "Aesop's Fables"?

Who was this Aesop who owned something called fables, and what might they be? What a strange name,

Aesop! He opened the book and saw that there was a story on each page, with pictures next to it which was a good thing because some of the stories seemed to be about animals he had never seen. Immediately, he thought of the time Marrec had told him about Africa animals.

He began reading - about a cricket and an ant (that was easy, those he could picture); a tortoise and a hare (why was it necessary to have another name for rabbit?); a lion and a mouse (now he knew what a lion looked like); a fox and a stork; a fisherman and a little fish; a dog and a wolf. He didn't know who was who about the monkey and the dolphin and wondered about elephants. They must be the biggest animals in the world!

As he tried to read and understand what was called 'the moral' at the end of each story, some things came together in his mind. Not only made these fables sense because the animals behaved like people, or maybe it was the other way round - either way, they were like a door opening onto something he had no name for. A few mornings he nearly missed breakfast and getting ready for school.

Alain liked riding but was not permitted to go out alone yet. He went to his father with a proposition: didn't Father agree that riding with Nicolas would make more sense, apart from being more fun, than going out with a servant who now would be free to do whatever work he was supposed to be doing?

"Cogently argued, son," Docteur C. said, pleased by Alain's unusual initiative. "You might make a fine lawyer someday, son; what do you think of that idea?"

Alain, so relieved his father had not mentioned veterinary school, answered, "If you really think so, Sir, why not?"

Docteur C. turned to Nicolas and explained 'cogently argued' before he gave his permission, provided Nicolas was not afraid of horses and took to riding. Within a month, the two friends went out together. It was on such an outing, weeks later, that Nicolas mentioned to Alain that he had asked his father whether he could watch him take care of the animals. "He said he'll let me know. We'll go together, of course."

"Oh no, we won't! What's wrong with you? Don't you remember that I'd hate it, that I never want to watch? Anyway, what made you ask? Oh, it just dawned on me, now I know: you're trying to get on Father's good side."

"What are ye talkin' about!? That's a stupid thing to say!"

"Who you're calling stupid? Of course you're trying to get on his good side! What did you think, that I would not put two and two together? Hah!"

"Hah, yourself. I'm doin' nothin' of the sort. What've you got in your head - wool? Fightin' over this is too stupid for words!"

"Stupid, is it? You know damn well how he hates it that I cannot stand the sight of blood; he used to call me 'sissy' all the time. Had it all figured out how I was going to follow in my grandfather's and his footsteps. I bet he didn't mean a word of it, about me becoming a lawyer."

"Listen, I did not say *you* were stupid, I said *fighting* over this was. I don't know a thing about the footsteps you're talking about. But don't you think you'd better get over fearing the sight of blood if you're goin' to fight for your country some day?"

"Don't you dare call me stupid again, and don't tell me what to do either!"

"Didn't you hear what I just said? I didn't call *you* stupid, I said *fighting* about the word was stupid. I'm not telling you what to do either, don't you know that? And for the last time: *I am not* tryin' to get on your father's good side! Don't you know me better 'n' that?"

"Hell no, I don't! What's more, I don't believe you!" With that Alain yanked his horse around and raced off.

After a few seconds' hesitation, Nicolas followed. He already regretted using that word. How often had Berthe told him that was a sure way of making things worse? Angry and hurt by Alain's accusation he would have liked nothing better than to turn around and ride away in the opposite direction. But he had promised Madame Caradec never to let Alain go off on his own.

He recited all the curses he could think of to himself, Breton and French and out loud, until he caught up with him.

They didn't talk on the ride home.

They'd had fights before, misunderstandings and disagreements, all dismissed as 'boy stuff' by Docteur C., one boy trying to outdo the other and with Madame C. always siding with Alain. Nicolas could win most times if he wanted to, at anything, but he didn't need to. This was different. There had been real resentment in Alain's voice, and that made him think. Why? Did Alain resent not sharing something with his father while *he* might be able to?

Or was it because his help was no longer needed? Nicolas easily kept ahead of most of the other boys in just about every subject. Perhaps - was there some hurt underneath Alain's anger? That was something else that Berthe had talked about, how folks who are nasty or angry all the time may not want to let on that they are sad or disappointed, that they hurt on the inside. At the time, he had thought that she was talking about Rozenn and was not willing to accept anything that explained her, but what Berthe had said might make sense for others. Now Alain spoke to him only if his parents were in the room. He knew it was up to him to do something about that.

He mulled this over for some time, and it took several attempts to make Alain understand how important their friendship was to him. He explained what living with the Caradec family meant, that they were the only people who didn't think of him the way the teachers and most boys in school did: a school-smart but otherwise worthless, ignorant nobody who didn't know who his parents were, whose 'father' could have been a bum or a thief or, God forbid, a murderer'; whose mother - well, nothing was known about *her* and what that might mean was anyone's guess, wasn't it? The boys in school didn't talk about him anymore, true, but they didn't have to. He knew what they thought about him.

He tried to tell Alain that he was his friend, forever, he hoped; his friend, not his brother. And that as far as seeing blood was concerned, didn't that go back to when he was much younger? Most likely he had gotten over this a long time ago, perhaps even without realizing it, so how about watching his father at work together sometime? He would ask for something simple and not very bloody because he didn't think *he*'d be ready for something very gory.

Alain grunted something before he punched him on the shoulder.

Everything was all right again.

A few weeks later they were invited to watch Docteur C. at work. First, he showed them the ink-drawing portrait of the lawyer and veterinarian Claude Bourgelat who had pride of place on a wall in his office.

"He was born in 1712 and lived until 1779 which means he was born during the reign of *Louis XIV*, lived through the reign of *Louis XV* and saw the beginning of *Louis XVI's* reign. Three kings. Isn't that amazing? Of course Alain has heard all this before."

"Has he ever!" Alain nudged Nicolas and whispered, "Only hundreds of times, and *he is bored stiff.* Father talks about the kings every chance he gets; as if I cared about how long any Louis lived or ruled or when he died!"

"All right, all right, Alain, we shall leave royalty for now, but I want Nicolas to know that Claude Bourgelat was an exceptional horseman who was connected to the Royal Court and had studied the ailments horses are prone to, specifically Rinderpest, also known as Glanders. You have to think about how important horses always were for armies and their cavalry regiments. Anyway, in 1761 and by order of King Louis XV's Council of State, a 'Royal Veterinary School' was established in Lyon and headed by Claude Bourgelat: for the very first time, principles and methods of curing livestock diseases were taught in a learning institution. Two years later another school was founded near Paris, in Maison-Alfort. Now let's go on to the next gentleman, Alain's grandfather. He and Dr. Bourgelat met at a riding competition, came in first and second and became friends. Alain's grandfather was one of the first students to enroll in Lyon; two years later he received his diploma and opened a veterinary practice right here, in this house. Here I might as well tell you that in your grandfather's time people looked down on veterinary doctors - they were even called 'cow doctors'. Only doctors who treated *people* were true doctors; only they deserved respect. Grandmère Jeanne's family felt that way, but after a while her father changed his mind. I always suspected because of the royal connection. Your grandfather obtained permission to call on her, they obtained permission to marry, and in due time, I was born, grew up, and followed in my father's footsteps."

Nicolas who happened to be looking towards Alain at that moment knew exactly what he was thinking - 'Here we go again with those damn footsteps!'

"But that's enough of an introduction. Time to go to work. Stay back and don't touch anything."

He preceded them into a treatment room where a very nervous elderly woman was trying, without much success, to calm her cat which had been on the losing side of a cat fight.

First, Docteur C. washed his hands saying, "I used to be the butt of much ridicule for doing that. Why wash hands for animals when doctors don't bother doing it for people? Well, I happen to believe in proper hygiene for both, but especially for myself." He dried his hands, put two drops of liquid on a small cloth and draped it briefly over the cat's nose.

The cat went limp and the woman wailed, "Mon Dieu, mon Dieu, Chou-Chou is dead. You have killed my Chou-Chou!"

The boys grinned at each other.

Docteur C. cut off her wails by saying calmly, "No, Madame, he just sleeps for a few moments!" He proceeded to set the cat's leg, splinted and bandaged it. Then he took needle and thread and very delicately and quickly stitched both badly lacerated ears. After that, he cleaned the bite wounds on the cat's back before he handed him back to Madame, saying, "He'll be awake in a few minutes. May I suggest you keep him away from that other cat!"

The next patients were two Brittany dogs - a hunting breed Nicolas knew more closely than he cared to, having been chased by several during his food-begging days. Both limping dogs had stepped on glass shards; their badly cut paws were seen to with the same effortless dispatch. Cleansing and a few stitches followed by another cleansing and taped bandages. Alain looked on with grudging admiration but carefully guarded his look of non-involvement. He left with a curt 'thanks' to his father while Docteur C. checked the contents of his bag and announced that he was off to one of the largest farms in the area.

"Sick cows," was all he said, looking concerned.

Nicolas was fascinated and in awe of Docteur C.'s

dexterity. The cat and the dog would wake up and be fine, he was sure of it - and come to think of it, *he* had better wake up, too! This was all extremely interesting, but it would come to an end, at the latest when they would both graduate from the Lycée. Alain would be leaving for Paris and his law studies. He'd be on his own then. Perhaps not immediately, but soon. He had better give some serious thought to what he wanted to do, but meanwhile, there was still much to learn.

Life was good, but Nicolas did not forget Berthe and continued visiting her at least twice a month. She was not old, he thought, but she looked more tired these days, although she never said so. He could tell that her back bothered her by the way she got up and held herself. Must be from heavy lifting all her life. He made sure to bring firewood every time he went to see her and filled her water pots.

He still had that disconcerting dream when he saw his other self, sometimes twice in a row, sometimes not for months. The face was not exactly like his; after all, she was a girl - still, it was like looking at himself. She always disappeared as suddenly as she appeared, and each time he was left with a strange sense of loss, and then he'd wake up. He needed to talk about this with Berthe again, only her; she knew him better than anyone, and she knew things one didn't find in books. "That was only a dream," she had kept telling him, but what about having the same dream again and again?

Didn't that mean something? And how could he dream about someone he had never met, did not know?

When he told Docteur C. that he intended to visit Berthe some afternoon soon, he said, "Of course." Then he looked at him for a long time and suddenly added, with a big smile, "but from now on you don't walk. You take Duc. He might as well be *your* horse the way he has taken to you and you to him."

Nicolas was speechless.

"Go on, he is yours. Yes, I mean it. Of course I expect you to take care of him."

Duc was his horse now? Docteur C. really meant it? All Nicolas could say when he got his voice back was, "I promise to take the very best care of him. Always. And thank you, thank you, Docteur C., thank you!" He ran to the stables.

While Chien raced ahead and sniffed every tree, bush and blade of grass to his heart's content, he collected enough firewood to fill the large flour sack he had borrowed from Cook, and sang happily and loudly off-key the entire way.

Berthe was asleep on the bench by the open door, one hand on a square wrapped package held together with string. The Chinese spoon was under the string, and so was the wooden horse, missing a leg now. She seemed smaller, sitting like this. He thought of her as always in motion, rushing, doing ten things at once. The same strand of hair, grayer than he remembered, had escaped from the tight bun at her neck. The image of her tucking it back in was lodged in his mind.

He shushed Chien and tied his horse to the only piece of fence that had not collapsed. Berthe was snoring softly; her spectacles were beginning their slide down her nose. Nicolas caught them and set them down on the bench beside her. Everything looked ready to fall apart; the old swing had lost its last slat, the empty rope swung in the breeze.

He realized he saw things with different eyes now and went inside to stack the wood. Noticing that the roof still leaked, he emptied the bucket into the vegetable patch and returned it to its spot. She had lived here by herself for how long now? Her last boy had left, must be going on more than a year. Was he wrong, remaining in town?

When she woke up and saw him, she greeted him with her wide smile. "Look at ye, all growed up, come on a horse in ridin' boots 'n' fine clothes; it's a true city boy ye become!" She looked for her spectacles and settled them back on.

"No, no!" Nicolas shook his head. "I'm no city boy, I'll never be that, but I did learn to speak 'n' read proper French. School is good 'n' I read newspapers every day. Books, too, but I still like that first one best, the stories called fables, remember? The ones 'bout animals, but they're really about folks 'n' what they do" - and I shouldn't go on so much about this, he thought and quickly added, "But I learnt good things from ye, too. Important things!" He didn't tell her that Duc was his horse now.

"Did ye now, me boy?" She patted the bench. "Come sit by me."

"Sure I did," he nodded and sat. "Like tellin' the truth. I used to think I was so clever hidin' somethin' from ye, but ye could always tell when I *didn't* tell true. Then ye'd explain how one lie leads to another 'n' another till yer so tangled up in 'em ye can't tell what be true 'n' what isn't! I'm old enough now to ask ye: why didn't ye paddle me backside like ye did yer own children? 'N' another thing: I don't like thinkin' 'bout ye bein' all by yer lonesome out here." 'Funny, he thought, how I slide right back into her way of speaking.'

"Bless yer heart, that's me boy, always thinkin', always full of questions. That's what my Marrec, may he rest in peace, called ye, 'the boy with a thousand questions.' But 'bout that other: ye didn't need paddlin', ye learnt quick without it! 'N' that other thing: yer not to worry, Marie's fetchin' me in a few days."

"She is?"

Berthe looked towards her kitchen and shrugged. "She says this place not fit to live in for years, but now ready to fall down any day now. So I goin' to live with her, help with her little ones. I'll like that - but ye know, I been wonderin' how to get ye out here so's we can have ourselves a chat 'bout something very important. I was that glad when ye sent word ye were comin'."

"Well, here I am. What is it?"

She took a deep breath and grabbed his hand. "Nicolas, ye remember yer mother at all?"

"Rozenn? Course I remember her. Don't know why, but I never believed she was my mother."

"I knows, but did ye have to shout, 'No, yer not me mother!' into her face? Every time she come see ye? Knowin' how spittin' angry it made her?"

Nicolas shrugged. "Every time? Wasn't that many times, now was it? Anyways, I don't think she really liked me, not the way she had of lookin' me over, wantin' I should call her 'Mother' when I hadn't seen her in a long time. Always wantin'. Wantin' I should sit on her lap, wantin' I should kiss her. I used to watch for the meanness in her face to grow, when she'd get angrier 'n' angrier afore she'd start hollerin' - that's when I'd run 'n' hide till she was gone. I hardly think about her."

Berthe grabbed his hand more tightly. "Yer not thinkin' 'bout her, that be good. It makes it easier, tellin' what I got to tell ye."

She paused for a moment, thoughtful. "All them

years I been practicin' tellin' ye, quiet-like by meself, so I don't forget. See, gettin' old has a way o' sneakin' up on ye, ye forgets things 'n' don't even know it's happenin'. Names, places, 'specially. Come, sit closer." She patted the bench again and pushed her spectacles back on her nose. Nicolas thought how she must be doing that a hundred times a day . . .

"Now, Rozenn, she talked 'bout this only the one time," she started, "only once. T'were many years ago, ye were livin' here, but ye were only five."

She paused for a long time before she sat up with a determined look on her face. "It's hard for me to tell ye; must be harder fer ye to hear it, so I'll come right out with it 'n' tell it plain: *Rozenn said you weren't her son!* She said her friend was yer mother. 'Why did ye do that?' I shouted at her but she didn't answer, just went on talkin'. Said that very sick the friend was after you was born, on account she got the bad fever. She - she died of it. Now Rozenn had promised to take care o' ye if somethin' bad happened. She said she did, or tried to, 'cept she didn't know how to be mother to a fussy little boy n'heavens, were ye fussy with her! Awful fussy. That's why she brung ye here, to me. I asked 'bout her friend, your mother. Rozenn said she was pretty 'n' nice; very smart, too. Knew readin' 'n' writin', was used to a better life. Her name was Jannet. Her husband" - she frowned in concentration, "I needs to get this right: her husband was Pierre Favreau, that's how come ye be Nicolas Favreau. He built houses 'n' died in an accident, don't know what kind or where. He was not from 'round here but place way down south, or did she say south-east? The name of his village, that's what I can't remember, been tearin' me hair out tryin' to think of it ... Now Rozenn never said how they knows each other, she 'n' yer mother, but very different the two were, I'm sure. Couldn't tell ye sooner; ye were too little. But now that yer all growed up 'n' soon done with school, it's yer right to know - even if there be hurt in the hearin' 'n' in the knowin'."

"Hurt?" Nicolas put his arm around Berthe's shoulder and said, "Don't you worry about hurt. And no more tearing your hair out. There is no hurt, only surprise."

He had never thought of Rozenn as his mother and was relieved that she wasn't. It was good to think of his mother as someone smart and nice and pretty - everything Rozenn wasn't - and it was sad that his parents had died so young, but he didn't know how to feel about people whose names he had not known until a few moments ago, people he couldn't picture in his mind. Especially having become part of another family, 'with all the normal ups and downs, just like brothers', Docteur C. had said again only a few days ago, laughing and shaking his head when Alain and he went at each other over something silly, but as far as knowing who his parents were - he didn't quite know what to do with that. But he was glad Berthe had told him and he liked his mother's name, a good old Breton name.

Before he had to leave he asked Berthe where Marie lived and tucked the information away into his memory, along with his parents' names.

Today was not a good time to ask about the dream he'd had again about a month ago. As always, it had left him with the strange sensation that he knew the dream visitor. Anyway, Berthe probably still thought that it was only a dream.

"I bless the day ye come to me," Berthe said and crushed him to her while she called down the blessings of every Breton Saint on his head.

Then she handed him the package and said, "The horse was yours anyways, 'n' the spoon be yours now. Go, go now, me boy, go." She pushed at him and quickly turned away.

Nicolas rode back slowly. Berthe had been right about keeping all of this from him until he was older. He understood why she had kept the spoon until now, but he had always thought the horse belonged to one of her sons. Now he also understood what always pulled him back to her. He wished he had told her that if he thought of 'Mother', it was *her* face he saw. He never had, thinking it would make her weep, and he was not at all sure that he wouldn't have either, although he never did. He hoped she knew without hearing the words, but suddenly there was an unfamiliar tightness in his chest, a kind of pain, thinking about her and his mother.

Roughly, he wiped at his eyes; something must have gotten into them.

He wiped them again, later, when he opened her package and saw her 'Lives of the Saints'. Of course she had to take her Bible to her daughter's home: the entire life of her family was written inside: births and marriages and deaths. But to give him the other book that meant so much to her … he could never receive a greater gift.

Berthe's eyes followed him until they blurred and he disappeared around a bend in the road. She thought back to Nicolas the infant who survived and her own little boys who didn't; to Rozenn who always looked like she had swallowed milk that had gone off. She thought back to the little boy who clung to her and how he used to nod in that serious and wise-beyond-his-years way when she told him something important; how he was fevering so bad with a chest cold and cough when he was four and she picked an apron full of herbs and yellow daisies to add to her special fever-lowering tea, and her immense relief when it worked. How he once sneaked into her vegetable patch to check on the wild raspberries she protected from birds under a large piece of see-through cloth and the amazed look on his face when all she said was, "So, Nicolas, they sweeter 'n last year's?"

How he helped take care of her two youngest boys when they took sick with sore throats, fever and coughing and cried so pitifully because swallowing hurt so bad and sleep wouldn't come - how he sneaked out early mornings and shook the dew off the tree leaves into a mug because she had once said that dew was more soothing than any other water - how he stayed up through the nights with her and never minded washing and changing them, doing whatever had to be done, and then his sadness when the end came - and his anger and clenched fists when the priest rushed through the funeral prayers with such haste. Such a thinking boy he always was -

She thought of the summer when his voice suddenly plunged from high to low and squeaked back up to high again; how he never forgot about her after he had moved away, always brought her something besides firewood, potatoes, apples, a jar of preserves, a bunch of wild flowers - how he always made time for her.

She had missed him somethin' awful after he left, but it warmed her heart that he'd have the chance to learn. She had never doubted that he would do well: ye have this thirst inside, ye learn, it is what ye need to do. But how many have goodness to go with it? Me boy, he always had both, will always have that . . .If only I could live to see what he makes o' hisself when he is all growed up ... "Oh, quit dreamin', ye silly old bat!" she scolded herself and marched inside. He could be anywhere in this world by then, and she long gone from it.

When she saw the neatly stacked firewood, she

brushed the last tears away. She was going to take that with her, no matter what her daughter might have to say about it.

All of it!

Chapter V

Docteur C. still put out a book for Nicolas as soon as he had read and returned the previous one, larger and harder books now: history not only of France but of other countries, art and architecture, biographies of famous men, and poetry some of which Nicolas liked even if he didn't understand it. The more he read, the more he wanted to know, and the greater his urge was to see something of this world, to go places that were unfamiliar to him, to see people who were different.

Some years earlier, in 1848, there had been a great deal of talk about the Second French Revolution which, he had learned from the newspapers, ended something called the Orléans monarchy and led to the creation of the Second French Republic. Nicolas was familiar with the word but unsure what exactly turned a republic into a Republic with capital "R." It had to be more than the mere absence of a king.

Alain and he had noticed how many young men were talking about this and going to Rennes in order to enlist in the army. Rennes was not far, only about twenty-five miles from Fougères. Of course Alain was too young now, but only by a little over a year - wouldn't that be something?

Then they made the mistake of bringing up the subject at the dinner table. Alain's mother immediately burst into tears and rushed from the room. Docteur C. started to go after his wife but sat down again, threw down his fork and banged his fist on the table so hard that it set his glass dancing and the wine sloshing over the rim. He righted the glass, threw his napkin on the spreading stain and made it clear that Alain could forget about this insane idea. Now and forever.

First: He was seventeen. In other words: under-age, which meant he would not be accepted into the French Army. Period.

Second: A young man who enlisted owed the army many years of his life, possibly twelve, unless the law was changed which was not likely. Had he given any thought to what it would mean, being stuck in the army for many years? At miserably low pay, fighting, ready to die for causes which sometimes made sense only to generals?

Third and most important: He was not raising his only son to become cannon fodder! No need to look so surprised, that's what he said and that's what he meant. Since Alain was doing well at the Lycée, studying law in Paris would be an excellent alternative for him, one that guaranteed him not only a better and safer future but a longer life! Meanwhile, he expected him to put the idiotic notion of enlisting out of his head. Forever. He turned to Nicolas and added, "That goes for you, too; you're older and ought to have known better."

Fourth and last: He did not want to hear another word about this ever again. Was that understood?

"Yes, Father."

"Yes, Docteur C."

It was not lost on Nicolas that Docteur C. had talked about his *only* son. He had not expected anything different, but it did make him think. There would always be this difference between them; he was treated like family but was not *of* the family. Alain and he were still on fairly good terms, but there were times when he didn't like him very much. Lately, Alain only did what *he* wanted and could be stubbornly mean about it.

Apart from that, he couldn't see himself living here while Alain was studying in Paris. Surely Docteur and Madame C. would not expect or want that either, even though he had been helping Docteur C. with his animal patients, two to three afternoons a week, for the past few years. More than once Docteur C. had commented that he was a natural, but Nicolas felt that simply sliding into veterinarian school was not for him.

He was grateful for the education he had received. There had been some very good teachers along the way, good in every sense of the word. Even spiteful Monsieur Mathieu had changed his tune after the first year, modestly taking credit for his most outstanding pupil's advancement every year and, later, his excellent performance at the Lycée.

But - meanwhile his most fervent wish was still to see something of this world. That was one of the reasons why both Alain and he still hoped for the excitement of another war. In secret, of course! According to the history books, wars happened with astounding regularity and everywhere. Just recently there had been articles in the newspaper about the Russian Bear trying to expand his influence beyond the Black Sea, which was sure to ruffle French, British, and Turkish feathers - meaning, Nicolas assumed, that those powers would not be content to sit idly by and watch. He decided to look in the atlas to see where exactly all this was happening. Were the French and the British really on the same side now? Either way - surely there would be another war before they were too old to join up!

Chapter VI

Afternoon was the time of day Anne Desrosiers loved best because, over Nanny's objections, she spent it in the nursery with her daughter.

The servants went about their tasks, she had discussed meals with Cook, was done with her correspondence and other obligations and did not expect visitors this afternoon - these hours belonged to her and Madeleine. Sometimes she still could not quite believe that after so many years they were so blessed, and it had all come about because they had gone to see her sister. And, of course, because Louise was who she was.

A year earlier, her husband Henri had insisted on taking her away, away from the place of her miscarriages - the lost years as she thought of them.

"It cannot change what happened, what is, but it might do you some good," he'd said. "We haven't been to see your sister in a while. I'll clear my desk, and first we'll take a month, go to Rome and Florence to visit most if not all the works of your beloved painters. Then we'll travel back up to Paris and visit Louise on our way home. And if you are sure that you want to do this, a thousand percent sure - well, then we'll talk about it again."

Of course she was sure, more than ten thousand percent sure! She could think of nothing else, and wasn't it strange how they both shied away from the word 'adoption'. Traveling to new places together, no matter how beautiful, no matter how interesting, would be very nice, very pleasant and she so appreciated what he was trying to do, but not even seeing every single one of The Seven Wonders of the World could fill the emptiness that had grown larger with each child she had lost.

But now she had something to hold on to, to take hope from. Her Henri was a man of his word. They *would* talk about it again. She knew how fortunate she was and she didn't mean because they could afford to take long vacations. With opportunity and dedication his father had become a wealthy merchant and had left it all to his only son as soon he was old enough to take over. More important, Henri was a truly good person, had an innate gentleness that had set him apart from the other young men who had shown an interest in her, although he always knew best. Well, all the men in her world believed they knew best.

Many years ago and over strong parental objection, Louise, her older sister, had left home to train as a nurse in Germany before entering the convent of the Hôtel-Dieu in Paris. It had made no difference to her that most people looked down on nursing as a vocation unbecoming the daughter of a successful attorney. She was intent on doing what she had talked of doing ever since she was a small girl: taking care of the ill and infirm.

She'd been writing to Anne every few weeks and, very much aware of her sister's despair during the last several years, had begun to describe how every week she spent one or two nights at the 'foundling wheel', waiting for the bell to ring. How much it meant to her to take in the infants, and how she felt the anguish of the mothers who had to resort to this.

She didn't go as far as to make a suggestion, Anne knew she wouldn't, but she mentioned, every now and then, how easy it was to adopt one of their babies. In her last letter she had written that, once again, it was getting so crowded in the ward that sometimes two newborns had to share a crib.

When Anne had first mentioned adoption, Henri had resisted in his usual calm, reasonable, but forceful way.

"Anne, you wouldn't know anything about the child you're adopting," he kept saying. "There is no way of checking a child's background with the children who are left with the Sisters; regular adoption channels have at least *some* information that can be made available to prospective parents. What if the child turns out not to be healthy, or, God forbid, not normal? What if the father was an alcoholic? A thief? Worse? What if the mother was - well, you know what I mean."

"Yes, I know, but Henri, you can never be sure what children are going to be like, not even your own," Anne said.

"True, we know that only too well." They were both thinking of friends whose only child was born so severely malformed that he never came home. He had lived out his short life in a hospital.

"And there is something else that concerns me: I ask you, what mother gives up her child in the middle of the night?"

"A young woman who is alone - or one whose husband is ill or has lost his job - or one who isn't . . . . "

"Married, or one who's never had a husband!" he finished the sentence.

"I'm not naïve enough to believe that doesn't happen," Anne agreed, "but there *are* women who fall on hard times through no fault of their own, and a woman who brings her child to the sisters is doing what will be best for that child. Don't you think that is also likely, or at least possible?"

"Of course it's possible - it is also the easiest way to

get rid of a child, isn't it?" Shaking his head, Henri sat down and put an arm around her.

"Sorry to be so blunt. My dearest Anne, you are always so ready to think the best of people; it is who you are, and I love that about you, but you might feel differently if you were out in the business world the way I am."

He thought for a while.

"But I know what having a child means to you, you have gone through so much already, I'd have to be an ogre not to - "

"Oh, Henri, would you really consider it?" Anne didn't let him finish and hugged him. "I know it's a leap of faith, but - could you really do that?"

"My dear, I'm not making any promises. What I was going to say was that I'd have to be an ogre not to consider it. *Consider it*, that's all. Yes, we can look into it when we are back in Paris."

He kissed her and left for one of his meetings.

She kept hearing his "we can look into it"; that had to be enough for now. After seven years of marriage, Anne knew her husband and had expected that, like most men, he would resist the idea of adoption. They had so looked forward to having children - the day when Dr. Jeannerot finally told her it was unlikely she would carry a child to term, and that further attempts would put a severe strain on her health, was the worst day of her life. After that last miscarriage she was ill for months, ill in mind and body. She had tried to bury her grief and sorrow deep within herself, and it had taken her a long time to find the way back. She was better now and knew it would not have happened without Henri's love and patience.

Thinking how she always used to enjoy sketching and painting, he had the small room off the morning room painted a cheerful light yellow and outfitted as a studio; she had always said how perfect the light was in there. He had the room furnished with two easels, canvases, paints and brushes, sketchbooks and charcoals; he had a chaise lounge placed in one corner next to a small bookcase which held her favorite books. During alterations the room was kept locked. Anne never questioned why; she took no interest in what was happening around her.

Henri waited until her July birthday, and instead of sitting down to breakfast with her, led her to the locked door.

"Anne, I need you back," he said, handing her the key. "Take it, it is yours. I know you need to be by yourself, sometimes; lock the room when you feel that need if you want. But I hope that someday soon the door will remain open."

They went inside, into the cheerful room that was

filled with summer sunlight. Anne saw all that Henri had put into it, and for the first time in months, she felt that what had been weighing on her so heavily was becoming lighter. She looked at Henri, saw the uncertain, worried expression on his dear face, and knew she had to make more of an effort. She handed the key back to him because there were no words that could express what this gift meant to her. Returning to painting and sketching was what she had needed. She came to think that it had saved her, at least the part of her that could be saved.

When they talked about their upcoming vacation, she made notes of the Rome and Florence dates, and especially of the time they expected to spend in Paris. Henri had already arranged to meet with two photographer friends; he liked to keep up with the newest developments in the field, although he considered himself merely an amateur.

She had never done anything behind his back but convinced herself that there was nothing wrong in informing her sister of their travel dates without telling Henri. As she sealed the envelope she hoped that Louise could still read between the lines. Since childhood they had almost always known what the other was thinking.

Louise wrote back immediately that her request for additional tower time during July and August had been granted. Most of the sisters, especially the older ones, did not relish sitting night after night on a hard wooden bench waiting for a bell that might or might not ring, although they would never say so. Anne read the last paragraphs over and over again - yes, they still had it!

Anne and Henri left on their travels in August and visited more museums and galleries in both cities than Henri felt he needed to see, but looking at his wife, smiling and almost animated again, he thought it was worth standing in front of every Leonardo, Raphael and Michelangelo *and* all the other painters and sculptors whose names he didn't bother to commit to memory. He also caught her a few times looking longingly at little children and realized that he had better do some more soul-searching before seeing his sister-in-law.

Anne enjoyed the leisure time with her husband but secretly counted the days until they could leave Italy. There would still be a two-day stay in Lyon before traveling on to Paris, which they expected to reach during the first September days. She also tried not to read too much into Louise's last letter, tried even harder not to let her hopes grow too high, telling herself that it was only a beginning. What mattered was that Henri was willing to talk.

She could not help herself; her thoughts revolved around a child. Years later she would admit that yes, she knew that they had gone to Lyon but that she couldn't remember their hotel, had no recollection of whom they saw, or which restaurants Henri took her to! He would always confirm that this was quite true, that she had gone through those days in a trance, as if enveloped in an impenetrable fog!

When they arrived at the Hôtel Pavillon de la Reine, a message from Louise awaited them in their room, asking them to come to the Hôtel-Dieu the next morning.

Henri looked at his wife and said, "My dear - hmm - there must have been, shall we call it a bit of correspondence going back and forth between the sisters, seeing that Louise wants to see us tomorrow morning? Are you sure you don't want to sleep late, after all our travels?"

Blushing, Anne admitted that he was right and wanted to explain.

"No explanation necessary. It may save us some time. Just as long as you don't intend to adopt on your own!"

"Henri, I would never" - she started before she realized he was teasing.

In the evening they went for a stroll in the hotel gardens during which Henri gave up involving Anne in conversation. She may have been on his arm, but she was miles away.

The next morning they were taken to one of Hôtel-Dieu's small reception rooms in the foundling wing where Sister Louise joined them within minutes.

She knew that Anne had to be sitting on the proverbial pins and needles, so after hugs, greetings to Henri and very little small talk, she said, "I have been instruct-ed to ask whether both of you are in agreement before we get started."

Anne looked at Henri who, frowning, sniffed the hospital air but immediately answered, "In principle, yes, but I cannot say more without seeing the children."

Louise nodded.

"Of course. And by the way, Henri, that odor is chloride of lime, a disinfectant used in most hospitals. But what I wanted to tell you is that sometimes we have couples where one or both want to see as many children as possible. They insist on going from room to room, bed to bed. Looking for a particular child, one that will fit into their family, has the 'right' look, the desired hair color, the 'right' color eyes. This is very difficult for the older children, but even two- and three-year-olds seem to know what these visits mean. It is heart-breaking to hear them plead, 'Take me, I promise I'll be good; take me, please take me!'

Older children don't say much; they know that most couples are looking for infants. As far as I am concerned, too large a number of children 'viewed' - and I am talk-ing about dozens and dozens - tends to be more confus-ing than helpful."

Anne had an inkling of what Louise was leading up to when she walked them towards another small room, opened the door and went inside.

Anne and Henri waited.

"Are you - are you thinking what I'm thinking?"

Louise smiled yes at Anne and waved them inside. Henri looked on, bewildered: they were at it again. Although it should not have come as a surprise, he was still taken aback whenever he witnessed one of the sisters' wordless communications.

He turned to Anne. "What are you two conspiring about?" Louise nodded to her sister to go ahead.

"Henri, I think Louise may have found - ?" She turned back towards her sister who quickly supplied 'a daughter'. "She thinks she has found a little girl for us."

"She has? When could she have done that?" While he let the information sink in, something else must have passed between the sisters again because in one second, Anne was into the room and at the crib. The baby was asleep, one tiny fist tucked under her chin; she was the sweetest, most beautiful little girl she had ever seen.

Henri followed her and from a distance decided that she was not bad-looking for a new baby; she did not have that scrunched-up red face he had seen on friends' new babies, but getting answers to his questions was more important.

"Well, Louise, what do we know about her parents?"

"Very little, I'm afraid. You see that she wears our

necklace. All infants receive this piece of identification with the date of admission and a number on it. It helps us keep accurate records. She came to us with a note from her mother. It gives her birthday as September 1 and says that her husband and father of her child was Pierre Favreau, and that he died before their child was born. She wrote that only hours after she gave birth she came down with a high fever. From how quickly it climbed and how high it remained, she realized that it had to be puerperal fever which meant she was very ill. Her condition worsened overnight and she understood that she would not recover. The last sentence of her note reads, 'May God watch over Madeleine and keep her safe.'

'Very touching, there is nothing to find fault with in this note,' Henri thought, but now Anne interrupted his thinking again.

"Oh, Henri, come quickly. She just moved a little."

"In a moment, dear, I need to ask your sister some more questions. Sister Louise, puerperal fever, if I heard right: what is that? Is it contagious? Dangerous to the child? To others around her?"

"No, the danger is only to the mother. I'll explain in a moment."

"But that's all the note said? Nothing else?"

"Yes, it is all, but these few lines tell us more than

you think at first glance. And that little shirt the baby came in? It was hand-stitched and of the finest cotton. The mother wrote a flowing, legible hand and expressed herself clearly, easily - all of which, I believe, points to an educated young woman. It was *not* written by someone who struggled to put a few words on paper: there are no errors, no corrections, no awkward phrases. But what really convinced me is that she used the word 'puerperal.' I doubt that all the Sisters here are familiar with the term; we always speak of *childbed fever.* Even our doctors do. I looked for it in a medical handbook: it is caused by an infection of unknown origin which often develops during or following childbirth. Fever can rise to 40 degrees C.* or even higher; unfortunately we have nothing to fight this infection. Many mothers die of it, far too many."

"How do we know that the mother wrote the note?"

"You are right, there is no proof. But I have read mothers' notes for years; you develop a sense for what is heart-felt. Not a scientific approach, I grant you, but that's all we have. And the signature matches the text of the note."

Anne, standing bent over the crib, exclaimed again, very softly, "Quick, Henri, she is waking up! Oh, come look, she has the most beautiful blue-green eyes!"

He walked over and looked down at this little person

---

*   approximately 105 degrees Fahrenheit.

to whom his wife had already lost her heart. Anne was cooing to her, and one look at her was enough: how could he take away from her what in one moment had put so much joy into her life? She looked radiant. Still, he had a few more questions to ask. He went back to Louise.

"She has been examined by your doctors?"

"Yes. She was two days old when she came to us, which makes her two weeks old now. She had been well cared for. I know it is too soon to tell, but I do see many newborns, and she does seem very alert." Louise proceeded to give Henri details, height and weight, the latter being slightly below average.

"What does that mean?" he interrupted her.

"Could that be a problem in the future?"

"No, not at all. We are talking about less than three hundred grams. Besides, many babies tend to lose some weight during their first week, but not this little one. She is gaining!"

She looked over at Anne and said, "Of course you may." Henri looked at the sisters with a "what did I miss now?" look.

He had his answer when Anne, tears in her eyes, lifted the baby from her crib and nestled her in her arms, signaling him wordlessly to come closer.

"It's all right, you can touch her," she whispered.

He did, on the small fist which suddenly opened, seemed to search for something and curled around his finger. How could he feel like Anne when he hadn't finished asking Louise his questions?

He went back to her.

"There is no other information on her?"

Louise shook her head. "No. You are, of course, welcome to speak to our doctors, and you will be given the results of their examinations and the mother's note once all the formalities are completed. I have already spoken to our Mother Superior and hospital administrators; your generous annual donations, I am happy to report, will help the adoption process to move forward smoothly. And a box with baby necessities should be at your hotel as we speak - I hope none of this was presumptuous on my part and that everything meets with your approval."

"Thank you, of course; thank you," Henri said quickly. He wasn't at a loss for words very often, but he was now, and Louise understood his unease at everything happening so quickly and without him; she had witnessed that reaction in prospective fathers many times, and there was something else she had to tell him.

"Henri, it may help you to know that I was at the tower the night this little one was left. You cannot hear what is said outside unless someone speaks very loudly, and only if the door has already been opened. That night, I could tell that there were two women outside. One was getting very impatient and urged the mother on loudly, 'Go ahead, just do it!'

It must have been very painful for her because it took a long time until she moved the turntable again, but then the bell rang, several times. I picked up this perfect little girl - we always say prayers for the children, but that night my prayer was that this little one would go home with you - and there is one more thing I need to tell you. All children are baptized the next morning because so many come to us weak, even ill. I spoke to our Père Antoine and he agreed to wait. I thought in case you wanted to change her name."

She had thought of everything. He looked over at Anne who was in another world with the child in her arms. His immediate thought was, 'This is completely out of my hands. I don't have a say in this. It is as if I were invisible when those two join forces against me. How can something so important, so crucial, be decided so quickly, without me? I would fire any employee who would dare make such an important decision without exploring alternatives, and it's not that I don't trust Louise. I do. She has experience in this and I don't - and, he reminded himself, hadn't Anne once said to him, 'Henri, this is not a business decision? Hadn't she once called it a leap of faith? It seemed to him that he had no choice but to take that leap - except, he knew, he had already taken it.

Later, when they talked about their daughter's name, he admitted that he would have liked Claire for his mother. Anne thought about it for a while, but he could tell she was not taken with the idea.

She shook her head. "I don't think we should take that away from Madeleine's mother. It must have been important to her or she wouldn't have mentioned the name in her note; she may have taken solace from knowing that her little girl would always be Madeleine - if you don't mind too much, could you settle for Madeleine Claire? That does have a nice ring to it, doesn't it?"

Again - how could he say no?

On the train ride back to Rennes, a few days later, with Madeleine sound asleep with Nanny and their two servants in an adjoining compartment, Henri broached a subject that had been very much on his mind. It had taken quite a bit of time to persuade Anne to let Nanny be in charge of Madeleine on their way home.

"Anne," he began earnestly, "you are not going to spoil her, are you?"

"With love I most definitely intend to! But I know that's not what you meant. I think about how Louise and I were raised, with affection and patience *and* with a good amount of discipline. We were given more freedom than most of our friends whose parents' only goal, it seemed, was to prepare their daughters for marriage and motherhood."

"And what is so terribly wrong with that, my dear?"

"Nothing, as long as it isn't everything. We had lessons in many subjects, not all of which I enjoyed, but Louise did. We weren't only taught good manners, penmanship and needlework, but history and languages as well! We did have music lessons, of course, but not in order for one sister to play a little piano and the other to sing prettily for company. We had an art student for drawing and painting; you know I loved that. The first thing he did was throw away a shape-tracing tablet that some well-meaning friend of the family had given us, saying, 'Girls, rule No.1: not only do my students invent and draw their own shapes, I want it understood that coloring within the lines has nothing to do with art!'

More important than good lessons, looking back, was that we loved our parents, but we had to respect them and the boundaries they had set for us, and we did, not without some clashes!"

All of this sounded good to Henri, at least in theory.

"I don't know whether I ever told you how Louise always brought injured birds into the safety of our house (several of our neighbors kept cats) and tried to nurse them back to health," Anne continued. "I also don't remember her dolls ever being without bandages. Once she really frightened our mother by wrapping both my legs in bandages, all the way above my knees, smeared red paint over one leg and ordered me to hoist up my dress and limp! Apparently I limped very convincingly but could not moan without laughing. Poor Mother!"

She smiled at the memory but quickly turned serious again.

"Naturally our parents were angry and disappointed when Louise announced that she wanted to train as a nurse before joining the Sisters in a Paris hospital. Not only did they already have an eminently eligible suitor for her waiting in the wings, nursing was considered totally unsuitable, beneath daughters of 'good families'. It was not acceptable, it just wasn't done. Even today most people have a poor opinion of nurses. My parents said 'no' and asked Louise to think it over for a year. They relented before the year was up because they realized that Louise would never change her mind. They let her go.

"And as for me, I always had all the art supplies I needed and wanted, and Mother took me to museums and galleries - you aren't really worried that I'll spoil Madeleine, are you?"

"Well, I'll have to see, but now I suddenly wonder whether *I* was considered eminently suitable or eligible, too - and by the way, Anne, that was quite a discourse!"

"I can't help myself. I am so happy, beyond happy,

that I can't stop talking. And of course you were, eminently suitable, I mean, and you'll be a wonderful father to Madeleine."

Glad that they were in a private compartment, she leaned against him and sighed contentedly. "Don't I have the most remarkable sister in the world?"

Henri made a face. "And here I thought you were going to say 'the most remarkable husband'! Anyway, you're wrong: remarkable doesn't begin to describe Louise!"

"I agree. And looking ahead, could we go see her with Madeleine, once or twice a year? Visiting the Sisters is restricted, I know, but she is her aunt and godmother, and seeing her would mean so much to Louise."

"For once I am ahead of you! I have thought that we should definitely do that, and that it will also give me the chance to catch up with my photographer friends. Perhaps I'll even get to meet Roger Fenton; he is an amazing English photographer. I read somewhere that he is planning to do some work in Paris soon."

And so the Desrosiers settled into a happy family life.

Madeleine was an easy child until she turned inquisitive. She mastered walking before her first birthday and perfected the art of disappearing within seconds at about the same time.

Keeping an eye on this fearless little person navigating under tables, trying to climb on anything available was fatiguing. Anne was more than relieved that Nanny had come out of retirement to look after her beloved Henri's daughter.

Nanny immediately decreed that children that young belonged in the nursery. Behind closed or, preferably, locked doors. Even there Madeleine could sit on the floor, absorbed in trying to fit little boxes into each other, but take your eyes off her for a second and she'd be precariously perched on her rocking chair. Needless to say she was furious and frustrated when she was rescued from any dangerous situation and wailed loudly. Needless to say, her father reveled in what he called her 'sense of adventure'. He enjoyed the fact that she seemed to know what she wanted at such an early age and liked to say, "Thank God she is not one of those timid little girls who are only interested in the color of new hair ribbons or dresses but are afraid of anything with four legs that is larger than a kitten."

She certainly was anything but fearful and would have petted every dog, no matter how large, if Anne and Nanny had let her. When they tried to explain that some dogs might not want to be petted, might even try to bite, she'd shake her head and insist, "No! Nice dog."

If she wasn't sure what to do, she'd frown and bite her lower lip while thinking, sometimes for a long time. If something didn't go her way, she'd cross her arms and announce, "I not speaking" as soon as she could say the words. Then she'd stalk out of the room, her pretty face screwed into a fierce scowl, while at the same time making sure that her displeasure was noticed.

Both parents were concerned when it became evident that she favored her left hand. Henri was of the opinion that this bad habit should be trained out of her as soon as possible.

"Put everything into her *right* hand," he ordered, "and I mean everything: spoons, toys, pencils, books, whatever you give her." Anne tried for weeks and secretly admired how consistently Madeleine switched everything over to her left hand, always with an annoyed, 'Why don't you understand that I don't like it this way?' expression on her face.

When Anne overheard Nanny muttering darkly that Madeleine's 'Devil's fist' was so powerful and so dangerous that it ought be totally immobilized until she learned to use her right hand for everything, she made it clear that she didn't want to hear such talk ever again.

Every now and then, Anne thought of the young woman who didn't live to have the joy of watching her child grow into this little girl who could be so full of tempestuous mischief one moment and so sweet and affectionate the next. She was almost six years old now and had recently announced to her parents that she was ready to go to school, just like the boys she had seen on their way there, through the window, and wasn't it a good thing that the school is so near?

Told that there were no schools for girls, she shouted, "Why not? I *want* to go to school! Now!" Then she started to cry.

Her mother tried her best to explain the situation, but didn't come close to satisfying Madeleine.

"I'll ask Papa when he comes home," she announced confidently. "He'll fix it. Papa fixes everything." She did ask, and it was the first time that a sad and pensive Madeleine understood that fathers cannot fix everything.

Later that same evening, Henri said to his wife, "I gather the school question is far from settled where our daughter is concerned. I know you don't read all the newspaper articles that have to do with government issues and politics, so let me give you some 'ammunition' if she ambushes you with questions again." He explained how it all went back to 'the good old days' when women weren't allowed to learn how to read and write and had no say in anything except running their household; how there was a movement under way, named the Falloux Law after the Minister of Education, which would require all communities with a population of over 800 to open a separate school for girls; but how even if the law were to pass quickly, which was not all that likely, there would be the inevitable delays of searching for suitable sites, obtaining building permits, the building passing an inspection, and finally finding and hiring qualified teachers, etc. etc. etc. In other words: change was not likely to happen in time for Madeleine.

"Too bad," he added, "a good teacher could have made her switch hands. Why is she so stubborn about using her left?"

"I suppose because it feels natural to her; she does very well with it. Perhaps we ought to let her be, but we'd better find a tutor for her soon, don't you agree? And by the way, that was quite a discourse, too!"

When Anne went into her daughter's room as she always did, a few weeks later, Madeleine was just waking up. She sat up, rubbed the sleep from her eyes, looked around and asked, "Where did boy go?"

"Where did *who* go?" Anne asked, bending down for her good-morning kiss.

"Boy. The boy. He was just here."

"In your room?"

Aware of Madeleine's vivid imagination, Anne thought she had better go along with her until she understood who or what her child was talking about.

"N-no, not 'xactly. But I saw him. I really did!"

Anne sat down on the bed. "Sweetheart, you must have been dreaming!"

"No, no! It isn't like that."

"It must have been a dream. Was he someone we know, or a boy from one of your story books? What's his name?"

Madeleine shrugged. "I don't know, but he looks like me, 'xactly like me. Really. Our eyes are the same between-two-colors, and the hair is the same, too."

Anne felt Madeleine's forehead. It was sleep-warm, not fever-hot.

"You *must* have been dreaming, sweetheart. Some dreams can feel very real, especially if they happen just before you wake up. So much that you feel they weren't dreams at all. Don't you worry about this - ready to get up and have a nice breakfast? How about a croissant with raspberry jam?"

Madeleine was not convinced but hungry and jumped out of bed. While Nanny dressed her, Anne kept wondering about 'the boy'. She had read somewhere that some children invent imaginary friends, talk to them, play with them. She didn't remember whether the article dealt with 'only children' or not. Madeleine had never mentioned the boy before - did this mean that she missed being with other children? Thinking about this reminded her how she had broached the subject of adopting another child to Henri some years earlier.

"Absolutely not," he had answered in a tone he

rarely took with her. "We were, I mean we are so very lucky with our Madeleine, I am not about to tempt fate again!"

And that was the end of one of their rare non-discussions.

Chapter VII

The following summer, a new family moved into the house next-door that had been vacant for years - with Cecily, a girl two years older than Madeleine. The parents met, liked each other and lost no time introducing the girls to each other. They started to spend every other afternoon together. It was decided that they would be taught together by their mothers at home three mornings a week, alternating houses, until a suitable tutor could be found.

Henri had made it clear that he wouldn't settle for a retired nanny or schoolteacher but hoped to find a young person who had recently completed courses in languages, literature, history, perhaps also in geography, science and mathematics.

"And art and music," Anne added.

"And art and music. Someone who loves what he or she is doing and makes the lessons interesting. There is nothing more mind-numbing than the monotone drone of a teacher who only goes through the motions. I know. I've had to sit through hours of that. I'll put out the word that we are looking; we'll see what happens."

"You expect all that in *one* person?" Anne sounded dubious.

"Absolutely. Why not? By the way, Armand leaves 'all things domestic' - his words, not mine - to Pamela, who, being British, has her own ideas on the subject. We'll have to get together with them to discuss the details."

For the time being, the girls got along well during their play afternoons, although Cecily was still very much interested in creating lavish tea parties for her large array of fashion dolls while Madeleine preferred board games or looking at her new friend's books. That led to some minor spats which the girls were able to re-solve quite amicably amongst themselves.

It was probably inevitable that one of these spats would escalate. Like many spats, it started with some-thing trivial, in this case with an argument about hair color.

Much preoccupied with her upcoming twelfth birthday, Cecily, in the middle of play, started twirling a strand of her hair around her finger and asked, "Do you like my hair, Madeleine? It is blonde and my mother says that I can have it curled for my birthday. With hot irons! Let's do one more tea party with the new Sunday dishes."

"Of course I like it. My hair is light-brown and doesn't need hot irons because it curls by itself" - she dangled a curled hair strand for emphasis - "but Cecily, we've played tea party *three* times already. Four silly tea parties in a row, that is too much!"

"My tea parties aren't silly, and four is not too many … and just so you know, blonde *is* much more special than brown. *Everybody* knows that!"

"No, it is not!"

"Is, too. It *is* more special. I get my blonde hair from my mother!"

Madeleine shrugged. "So?"

"And my blue eyes, too. People say I look exactly like her, that I am her spitting image!"

Madeleine was getting exasperated without quite knowing why, while Cecily seemed to enjoy having the upper hand.

"And my brother's hair is dark and wavy, just like my father's!"

"So?" Madeleine said again. "Who wants to be any-body's spitting image, whatever that is? Not me. And anyway, I don't have a brother!"

"I already know that - why don't you? You know, children always look like their parents. *They have to.* And you know what else?" Cecily frowned and looked

Madeleine over. "You don't look like your mother *or* your father, not one little bit! Why don't you? And another thing, why don't you have a sister or a brother either?"

"Because I don't!"

"That is not a real reason!" Cecily shouted.

"Is, too! It's true, that makes it a real reason." Madeleine shouted back at her.

"No, it doesn't! You don't look like your parents, not at all, and I still think that is strange, strange, strange. So there!" Cecily screamed back.

Before Cecily could say anything else, Madeleine shouted as loudly as she could, "I don't want to talk about this anymore and I'm not playing tea party again, not ever again and - and I'm going home!" She jumped to her feet. "I'm leaving, right now, this minute and - and I'm not coming to your birthday!" She was sorry as soon as the last words had slipped out.

"Fine!" Cecily yelled back, "Don't come! I have other friends, lots and lots and lots of them. I don't care!"

"I don't care either!"

At that moment the door opened.

"Girls! Girls, for heavens' sake, what is all this shouting about?"

Crying, Cecily ran to her mother. "She called my tea parties silly, she did! And she's not c-coming to my b-birthday!"

Madeleine pushed her way out of the playroom, past Cicely's dumbfounded mother and a curious servant girl who ran after her, down the stairs and outside to make sure she arrived home safely.

She ran upstairs to her room where Nanny was sewing. She was always sewing. Setting her work aside, she said, "Back so soon, but what is this I see? Tears? For heaven's sake, darling, what is the matter?"

Why did grown-ups always say "for heaven's sake" before they asked if something was the matter? Angrily, Madeleine gave her bed a kick which hurt her toes and made her cry even more loudly before she threw herself onto her pillow.

"I want my m-mother!"

"I asked you what is the matter"

The question produced no answer but more and louder wailing. After a long silence Nanny repeated her question, then adding sternly, "It is not polite to ignore adults when they ask children a question."

That brought forth, not unexpectedly, the loud "I am not speaking!"

"That is also very impolite," Nanny admonished.

"How many times have I told you that? Did the two of you have an argument, darling?"

"I said I am not speaking!" Madeleine shouted again. She turned towards the wall and buried her face in her pillow. .

"Well brought-up girls learn not to pout, dear. And you are old enough to remember that it is very bad manners to shout at your elders."

The child was entirely too willful, too stubborn. At her age she ought to know better. But how could she, with a mother one of those undisciplined artist types. Now her Henri, he knew the rules and the boundaries before he was three years old!

When Anne came into the room, Madeleine was still crying.

"I cannot do anything with her, she only wants you," Nanny said, shrugging. Her lips settled into a thin line of disapproval.

Anne sighed and suggested she go down and get herself a cup of tea. Then she sat down on Madeleine's bed, put her arms around her daughter and waited. Stroking the damp curls from her forehead and letting her cry over whatever was hurting or bothering her was the only way to get her to calm down and, eventually, to talk. What could have made her so unhappy?

"Something happened at Cecily's today, is that it?"

she guessed when the sobs started to subside. Madeleine sniffled and nodded. Anne waited, handkerchief in hand.

"And?"

"And n-now I c-cannot go t-to her b-birthday."

"I see - is it really so bad?"

Madeleine nodded. Anne wiped her daughter's face, handed her the handkerchief, said "blow" and waited.

"You didn't get along today? Did you fight?" That was a distinct possibility, given Madeleine's quick temper. She sometimes said things out loud that other children would not even let themselves think. And she could be a merciless mimic.

"Not like boys do, but we yelled at each other. Loud, really loud."

"Madeleine, you didn't you use bad words, did you?"

"Not even one, but I wanted to."

"Well, I am glad you didn't. I think you girls will have to apologize to each other; friends can always make up again, and then you can go to Cecily's birthday. I know how much you want to go."

Madeleine started to wail again. "No, I c-can't go n-now, and I d-don't want to go, not n-now. I t-told her I wasn't going, and I'm n-not! Cecily said 'fine'. She doesn't care! That's what she said. And last night the b-boy didn't come b-back either!"

More sobs. That boy again. Why? Who was he?

There had to be more to the girls fight. Perhaps Cecily, being older, minded that Madeleine liked getting her way and often did. They'd had several talks about this - but what could have caused such a violent reaction?

It took another half hour of patient coaxing to get the rest of the story from Madeleine. At last she blurted out, between sobs, "Cecily says I d-don't l-look like you or Papa, and that I d-don't look like anyone in my family and *that I have to, I have to!*"

A chill went through Anne. She held her child close while thoughts raced around in her head. 'What do I say, dear God, how do I say it? I was afraid this would happen someday, I knew it would, but not so soon, not when she is still a little girl. How could she understand? She is too young, how can we get her understand? What do we tell her? How? What can I tell her *now*?'

She waited until the wailing stopped and went to get a glass of water for the hiccups that always followed Madeleine's crying. After she took the empty glass from Madeleine, she sat down on her bed again and said, "Sweetheart, not all children look like their parents."

"Yes, they do, they do! Cecily says they *have* to."

"Listen to me, Madeleine: Cecily may be almost twelve, but that does not mean that she knows everything. No one should ever think that they know everything, that they have all the right answer, no matter how old they are. Listen to me: children *do not have to look like their parents!* Some do, some don't. Some look like an aunt or an uncle, or even a grandparent. People always said I looked like my grandmother."

"You did? Children don't *have* to look like their parents, really not?"

"Really not." Even if there had not been such hope in Madeleine's voice Anne would have repeated, as she did, firmly, "No, they don't have to!"

Sniffling, Madeleine thought this over, slowly and carefully, but then she seemed to accept the answer.

'I did tell her the truth', Anne thought, 'a partial truth only, but that's all I can give her now. This is far from over. She is much too inquisitive to let it rest. What will Henri say? Oh dear God, what are we going to do?"

Chapter VIII

When Henri came home after a meeting that had lasted longer than usual and found Anne in the salon, sitting in the dark, an unopened book in her lap, he knew something was wrong. She always waited upstairs for him, reading in bed.

He was at her side in two steps. "Anne, what is it? Is Madeleine ill? You are not feeling well?"

"No, no, we are both fine."

"Thank God for that - then what is wrong?"

Anne told him what had happened between the girls.

"Damn!" Henri said, several times. He had never said that in her presence before. He asked what had provoked the argument.

"I didn't get a chance to ask for details; she was crying so hard that all I wanted to do was calm her, but somehow it must have occurred to Cecily that

Madeleine does not look like either one of us. She said that to her."

"Damn! Damn! Damn! What did *you* tell her?"

"Only that some children do look like their parents and some children don't, which is true, and that I looked like my grandmother, which is also true, but Henri, she is too young to understand. What are we going to do? What, Henri?"

"Well, that was a good enough answer for the time being, what else could you have said? All I know is there's nothing we can decide tonight. It is late. I've had a long, horrible day and am too tired to think, too exhausted to go over this. Damn, damn - but you know, I did just think of something. Perhaps I ought to get in touch with Jean. You remember the Gautiers, don't you? Who had a similar situation on their hands, two or three years ago? Of course, their son was older at the time than Madeleine. Still, I might learn something useful from how they handled it. Damn that this had to happen so soon - come, love, let's go on up."

Neither one slept much that night.

When Anne walked into Madeleine's room the following morning, she was just stirring. She sat up quickly and rubbed the sleep from her eyes the way she always did and announced, "I want to see photos of my grandparents."

"Didn't you forget something?" Anne asked.

"Good morning, Maman. Please?"

"That's better. You want to see photos; well, we don't have any from when they were young. Photography was still very new then and very expensive, so all we have are photos of my parents when they were older and none at all of my grandparents."

Oh!" Madeleine was disappointed. "And Papa's parents are not alive either and they only took pictures of palaces and churches."

"That's right. After your father and I were married they traveled a great deal, all over the world, and they both took sick in a place far away from good doctors or good hospitals - "

"I know, in a place that sounds like India but isn't. It's a longer name. I don't member what they look like."

"Well, you remember that they went to Indonesia, and that's remarkable. Of course you can't *re*member seeing them: you were not even one year old when they left. And by the way, it's *re*member, not member!"

"All right, *re*member. Can I see the old photos now?"

"After you get dressed. I'll send Nanny in."

Immediately Madeleine fell back onto her bed with a moan. "No, I cannot get dressed, my tummy hurts."

"It does? Perhaps you're hungry. Nanny said you hardly ate any dinner last night."

"It hurt last night, too," Madeleine moaned again, very convincingly, she thought.

Anne knew that there was nothing wrong with her stomach. She couldn't face going to Cecily's house for this morning's English lesson, that's what it had to be. She was not about to insist she go until she had found out more about yesterday's trouble.

"All right, no English today. I'll let Cecily's mother know. But it's still time to get dressed."

"I cannot - my tummy - "

"Will get better soon, sweetheart."

That is what her own mother had always said to her. Anne hadn't thought about this in years, but it all came back to her now. She remembered using 'the hurting tummy excuse' at that age, especially when she needed an excuse to get out of visiting Great-Aunt Amélie. Being hard of hearing, the old lady would shout strange things at her visitors that only she thought were amusing, then cackle-laugh delightedly to herself. Her person, actually her entire house, gave off the most peculiar musty odor. Anne always tried to make her breaths as shallow as possible which invariably ended in a coughing spell. Immediately, Great-Aunt Amélie would start on her litany about the new generation's 'sickly children'.

Anne never touched anything, especially not the strange-looking cookies which emitted the same odor, only stronger, from their ancient tin box. It had dawned on her that she was offered the same seven cookies at every visit.

Madeleine seemed fine when she played in the play-room and later, when she accompanied Anne on an afternoon walk in the park, except when she asked, "Why don't you talk?"

With difficulty Anne tore her thoughts away from wondering what Henri would have to tell her after speaking with his friend. What if he hadn't reached Jean, or hadn't learned anything helpful?

When he did come home that evening she immediately knew that he did not bring good news.

After dinner, during which they barely spoke, she took him into the small salon where a chilled bottle of wine and two glasses were ready on the table next to the small sofa. Henri poured the wine, raised his glass to her, sighed and asked, "How was she today?" They never discussed family in front of the servants.

"Relieved that I didn't make her go to the English lesson. And she wanted to see the photographs of my parents. How did you do?"

Henri leaned back in his chair and sighed again.

"Not very well, I'm afraid. I wish I had something

better to report. Jean was surprisingly open about the whole unhappy episode. Their Olivier was nearly fifteen when he overheard a conversation at his uncle's house, put two and two together and rushed home to confront his mother. Yvette, taken by surprise, denied everything and insisted that he must have misunderstood. Olivier shouted at her that he wanted to know the truth; she repeated her denials. He called her a liar and swore he would never believe her again before he stormed out of the house. That evening he waylaid his father before he came into the house and apparently asked, "So, what are *you* going to do? Lie to me like Mother?" Of course Jean knew this was about the adoption; he grabbed Olivier, marched him into his study and tried to explain that his mother never wanted him to know while *he* felt Olivier ought to know as soon as he was mature enough to understand."

"And then?"

"Then Olivier accused him of keeping up the lie ('How long did you think I had to be? Twenty? Thirty? A hundred? I bet you had no intention of *ever* telling me!'). He ran screaming out of the house. Later, they heard the door to his room slam and when he didn't come down to dinner they had a plate brought up. It was left outside his door because the room was locked. Yvette checked later. The plate was gone; naturally they assumed that Olivier had taken it inside before locking the door again.

There was no answer when Jean knocked at his door and called his name several times before he went to bed. They thought that the boy was still too angry to speak to them, or that he had fallen asleep. But later that night Olivier apparently climbed out of his second-floor window. How the damn idiot didn't break every limb of his body getting down ...

Anyway, he was found several days later by the police and brought back, unhurt, hungry and dirty and unrepentent. He is still at the Rennes Military Academy because he threatened to run away again if he was made to live with 'those two liars.'

Henri drained his second glass. "The only advice Jean gave me was to try to be united as parents. I think he may be right about that. If we are not, the same could happen with Madeleine. *He also said not to wait too long.*"

"But we can't do it now. Olivier was fifteen; she is only ten!"

"I know that. Do you honestly think she is not going to talk about this again, ask more questions? We must tell her."

"But she is - "

"Please don't tell me her age again," Henri interrupted her. "I am well aware of how old she is!" he added in a sharp tone that hit Anne like a blow. "I know you want to protect her, but the truth has a way of coming out, sooner or later, and just how are you going to teach her to be truthful while we keep telling her a lie, such a big one? Madeline is intelligent and, if not right away, she will understand in time. She'll have a harder time the longer we continue lying to her."

Henri didn't notice her uncomprehending look, wasn't looking at her at all. He had never spoken to her so sharply. He was always so even-tempered; this had to be a sign of how distressed he was.

"Henri, please listen to me. Now is not a good time. She still talks about this boy she 'sees'. She says that it is not a dream, that he is real, not someone she knows, but she does see him and he looks like her. He has the same color hair and the same blue-green eyes. She doesn't know what to make of this, of course, and I don't either. She is confused, but it is obvious that he is very important to her. She has seen him several times." Anne noticed that Henri was getting impatient and finished in a hurry. "I don't know what is happening with her, I realize that she has a vivid imagination, but I also know she is really troubled by this because she doesn't understand it. To burden her now with something else that is much harder to understand - it is too much. It is. We cannot do this *now*, Henri, we can't."

A tear rolled down her cheek; she brushed it away before he could notice.

"Anne, will you please forget about that boy, whoever

he is, wherever he comes from? Can't you ever concentrate on the issue at hand, on what is important? How did she take your explanation? Was she at all satisfied?"

"She seemed to be, yes, but what if someone else brings up that she doesn't resemble us? Henri, I'm so afraid of that."

"Then you tell her again what you have already told her! When you spoke to Pamela, you didn't tell her anything else, did you?

"Of course I didn't! No one around here knows about the adoption, most of our neighbors moved in after us, but that doesn't help, not really. What if others start talking about her not taking after you or me - oh, Henri, nothing can help that, nothing."

"Especially not such defeatist thinking!" Again he had spoken very sharply.

He pulled out his pocket watch. "I have to get some paper-work done for tomorrow, why don't you go on up? I'll try to get home early tomorrow, and we'll talk again. Sorry I nearly lost my temper there for a moment, but we have no choice. *We must do it now.*"

He was gone from the room before she could say anything.

Anne sat, feeling ill. This was the first time they were disagreeing so strongly about something important, the first time she did not know him, could not reach him; she didn't even believe he had meant the 'sorry' he had thrown her way so casually.

But that was not what mattered, not when she knew with a certainty she could not explain that Madeleine would not understand her parents being united about something that would turn her world upside down. She would feel alone, deserted, betrayed - I cannot lose my girl, I cannot lose her. The thought banished everything else from her mind.

I cannot lose my girl, I cannot … She wiped the tears from her eyes and ran upstairs. Lying in bed, she thought about all that had been said, all that had not been said and feigned sleep when Henri came into the room.

Anne didn't want to read something into Henri's earlier-than-usual departure the following morning and decided to go see Pamela. Over several cups of tea, the two mothers agreed that *both* girls should apologize - they missed spending time together and needed to be reminded that there are better ways of settling differences than shouting at each other. Pamela readily accepted Anne's remark that she looked like her maternal grandmother. She offered that Cecily had always had her coloring but that only recently had she started to truly resemble her.

"Children can change so suddenly, can't they?"

Anne nodded.

In the afternoon, she lost several turns at Madeleine's

favorite game because her attention kept straying towards the past evening's discussion.

Henri was not happy that she had talked to Pamela without first consulting him.

"I had to," she protested. "Both girls were miserable, and how can we arrange for a tutor if the girls don't speak to each other?"

"That's true," he conceded. "I imagine we both have thought of little else; any chance you have changed your mind?"

Anne shook her head. "No. I cannot. You keep saying Madeleine is intelligent, but this is not a question of intelligence. She is too young to understand. I am afraid of what telling her will do to her. And she had that dream again, about the boy. She always says he looks 'not 'xactly like her' but 'very much like her."

"Didn't I tell you to quit bringing him up? I don't want to hear about this boy again, not ever! Could you please try to remember that? For God's sake, now is not the time to go off on wild tangents! Why can't you concentrate on our real problem? We must tell her *now*. Surely you can see that."

"No, I don't see that at all. She is too young."

"How much difference can it make whether we tell her now or a few years from now? At least she'll know we're not lying to her!"

"And you think that is more important to a ten-year-old girl than finding out that we are not her true parents? That is *not* how she will look at it." Anne clenched her fists, unable to control the angry tremor in her voice.

"And just how do you know that? Are you willing to take the chance she'll find out by accident? I'm surprised at you. What do you think *that* would do to her?"

"What chance is there of that? No one knows!"

"No one that we know of. We can never be completely sure, and that is precisely why we must act now. We must tell her now!"

"No, you cannot do that!"

"Don't tell me what I can and cannot do! Someone has to make the decisions in this house: kindly remember that final decisions are up to me. You always let your feelings govern your decisions, without looking at problems logically, calmly, and - "

At this, Anne's control slipped.

"While you, Henri, talk about this as if it were one of your business deals! It is not! Madeleine is not a business. We're talking about a child, our child, about how what we do will affect her, whether she is mature enough to understand."

"I take exception to your tone and your words, Anne,

the strongest exception. I've let you have a free hand in how you manage the house; that does not mean I allow you to go against my decisions!"

"Allow me? A decision about our child that *you've* made *on your own*?"

"After looking at it from every angle, yes. It is the right decision."

Anne bit back saying 'You are wrong'. There was no use talking to him now. A wall of angry silence was growing up between them. When she realized that he wasn't going to say anything else she stood. Fighting the inclination to flee upstairs, she held on to the arms of her chair and fought to breathe normally.

"I cannot and I will not be part of this. I know Madeleine better than you do. You'll give me the courtesy of informing me when you intend to do this." Her voice broke on her daughter's name, and broke again. She rushed from the room.

Henri remained seated, exasperated and frowning. This hard, bitter anger, it was so not like Anne. There had been disdain in her voice, dislike even. What was happening to her? She had always deferred to him on important decisions. It was what a wife did, was supposed to do - of course until now, no crucial decision had revolved around Madeleine, but there were bound to be others as the girl grew older - and as for knowing the child better, that must be the overwrought mother in her talking! Nanny was right; Anne was too doting, too easily swayed. She lacked firmness, informed purpose. He had every right to stand by his decision.

Still, he couldn't get the image of Anne out of his head, the way she had stood stiffly erect, finger-tips turning white as she pressed them into the arms of her chair - but even so, compromise was out of the question!

Chapter IX

Fortunately, the tutor question was solved quickly.

Colin Webb was a young teacher who had only one reference which was of concern to both fathers in spite of its glowing terms. The mothers, however, liked his personality and background and the decision was made to give him a try. Surprised that the girls were also supposed to gain 'a little knowledge' in mathematics and science, he had presented himself with lesson plans and reading lists, all of which met with the parents' approval.

Meanwhile, Anne tried to keep up a semblance of harmony and to behave 'normally' around Madeleine.

After some days of watching silently, Madeleine stood in front of her and said, "Maman, I *know* you let me win sometimes when we play the Goose Game, other games, too, but not all the time! Yesterday, I won three games in a row, and just now I won again - you are not even trying! Is it because of a new headache, or do you still have the old one?"

"It's only a small one and almost gone."

Madeleine looked her over, unconvinced. "How can it be small if it lasts so long?"

Anne shrugged. "Perhaps you played very well - did you think of that?" She despised lying to her daughter, and here she was doing it over a silly board game.

Madeleine slid off her chair and went to stand in front of her. She reached up and touched Anne's forehead. "Temperature normal," she announced in perfect imitation of the doctor's tone. Anne reached down and enveloped her in such a tight embrace that Madeleine protested, "Ow, you're choking me!" Squirming out from under her arms she saw that her mother was weeping. This frightened her and she started to cry, too. It took Anne a long time to reassure her. Madeleine stubbornly shook her head, unconvinced also of the explanation that Papa was busy with a heavier-than-normal workload.

She set about watching both parents more closely. They were always serious now, hardly looked or teased each other anymore. They didn't laugh; they only smiled polite smiles, not real ones. Papa said that he had so much work that he couldn't make dinner - which didn't mean that he couldn't prepare it as she, silly goose, had at first hoped: it only meant that he would be home late. He was late most evenings. Sometimes she ate with Maman; it was nice but did not feel right enough.

The only good thing that happened was that she and Cicely were friends again. Apologizing isn't so difficult once you make up your mind to do it. The birthday party was good, and she liked most of the other girls.

Some evenings later, Anne waited downstairs for Henri to come home. Again, he was very late. Like that other night, he sat down opposite her and said nothing.

Anne finally broke the silence. "We cannot go on like this, Henri."

"I agree. However, I believe I made my position very clear."

"You did, but please don't talk to me as if this were business. How would you have reacted being told that you are adopted at Madeleine's age? What I am asking is this: could you reconsider and wait until she is at least twelve years old?"

"And what would that achieve? Why take such a chance?"

"Because we could use these years to talk about many things that might help her when the time comes. Two or three years could make a considerable difference in her understanding."

"I suppose - I suppose that is possible," he conceded reluctantly, pacing back and forth, "but it only postpones what should be taken care of now. To let it drag on for years, take that chance - I just don't know - I don't like it - well, I'll have to see."

Anne consoled herself that 'I'll have to see' is not 'no'. She told herself to hold on to that thought, careful not let too much hope into her voice. "It would give us and Madeleine time, that's the way I look at it. Time she needs. There is a difference between ten and twelve or thirteen. I know, I remember." What she did not say but hoped he would hear was that she didn't expect him to understand girls the way she did.

"I said I'll think about it."

"Thank you." There was more she would have liked to tell him but could not, not after the dismissive formality of his last words.

Tutor Webb started the following Monday and the girls immediately liked him ("He is young and good-looking; this is so much better than being taught by *our mothers!*"). He found the girls challenging, especially Madeleine who kept him on his toes with questions. She devoured books on almost any subject, and he was surprised that she was also interested in travel books and wanted to learn some Latin. He explained to her that he was not qualified to teach Latin but would be happy to compile a list of Latin sayings for her.

Cecily was easy to please and a willing reader as long as he assigned her stories that dealt with the trials and tribulations of royalty. He was thankful for all the princesses of French history and the Perrault fairy tales.

After a few weeks, feeling that the girls' command of the English language was more than up to it, he submitted an additional reading list to the parents: Charles Lamb's 'The Adventures of Ulysses' for the young; the abbreviated 'Travels of Marco Polo'; 'Robinson Crusoe'; Charles Darwin's 'The Voyage of the Beagle'; 'Oliver Twist' (in the newly available book form since serialization in Bentley's Miscellany had come to an end), and Hans Christian Anderson's 'Fairy Tales'. He also requested permission to use the Desrosiers globe.

The list was accepted with two exceptions: Darwin's name had been vigorously crossed out, and next to 'Oliver Twist' one of the parents had written, 'Not appropriate for young girls!!!'

Of course. Tutor Webb understood perfectly, even before he substituted 'sheltered' for young.

Anne wanted to give Henri as much time as he needed to change his mind, but seeing how intently a worried Madeleine kept watching them, decided that enough time had gone by after three weeks. They could not continue in this manner; it was up to her to take that first step.

Again, she waited for him downstairs, and before he could take the chair opposite her, she asked him to sit next to her.

"Please tell me what you have decided. We are both unhappy, and so is Madeleine. You haven't seen much of her, coming home so late, but she is confused and worried. You once told me you wanted me back - well, now *I* want you back. I need you back. Just tell me what to do."

Henri looked at her. It remained his decision, was his decision. Absolutely. No doubt about it - but perhaps there was something to what Anne had said earlier: what if a few years would make a difference to Madeleine? What did he know about what went on in ten-year-old-girls' heads? He often didn't understand Anne at all either, but damn it, she was right about one thing - he was unhappy. Work was bad enough, always had been, and coming home to all this tension - still, he hated the idea of giving in, in spite of all the thinking and soul-searching of the past weeks.

"All right, all right," he said after a silent struggle with himself. "We could wait until she is twelve, I suppose - but don't ask me about that book again. I won't have Darwin in my home!"

Anne was relieved beyond words and glad to let him have a small victory.

Everybody was happier. Madeleine ignored Nanny's scolding that she was too old to run up and down the stairs again the way she always had. She had decided not to mention the boy dream to her mother again because it seemed to upset her; she just wouldn't understand that it was not an ordinary dream. Seeing the boy always left her with an unsettled, sad feeling. That never happened with other dreams which also never repeated themselves. But whatever had bothered her parents was gone and that meant that life was good again, even though nothing very exciting or interesting was happening. She wished she could grow up quickly and get to fifteen or sixteen in a jump overnight!

Tutor Webb's suggestion of using British newspapers to expand their knowledge of the written language and to learn about what was happening in the world was accepted. An atlas and the globe were transferred into the school room. Cecily was still mostly interested in fashion, theatre and ballet while Madeleine followed the news with growing interest. She also asked for more Latin sayings and Tutor Webb wrote down another half dozen.

The annual visit to Louise was planned around Madeleine's birthday. Madeleine had started to correspond with her aunt as soon as she could write and had recently written to her, asking whether she could bring some of her old baby toys for Louise to give to the children. They were stored in boxes in the attic, doing nothing and were good as new. And hadn't Louise mentioned more than once that there were almost no toys at her hospital? Madeleine was quite sure she would not have a new sister or a brother. What sense was there in keeping these toys? They now brought a box of toys and children's books every time they visited. And every day, Anne had thought that Henri would tell Madeleine when she was twelve, and here she was nearly *thirteen* and he hadn't said one word. She couldn't imagine what was holding him back and was afraid to ask.

The time spent with Louise, this time without Henri, was joyous as it always was. Louise tried to hide that she wasn't quite well, but Madeleine, always keenly observant, insisted on finding out what was wrong.

"I expected you to notice that I am pale and that my habit looks big on me," Louise answered with a smile. "Well, we don't get out very often. That accounts for being pale, and as for my habit, it is new and not my size. We all get the same large size, but I assure you that it will shrink and become a better fit. Our laundry manages to shrink everything."

Anne and Madeleine looked at each other and were not convinced.

"Listen, both of you: there is nothing to worry about. The doctors are taking excellent care of everybody, me included, and for the time being, I am not even on night duty. I'll be fine."

"Aunt Lou, would you tell us? I mean if something were really, really wrong?"

"Of course I would."

That satisfied Madeleine who thought of her aunt as the most truthful person in the world. Anne accepted her explanation because she wanted to believe it. Again she thought how Henri had not said one word about talking to Madeleine. She had let so much time go by because he had never wanted to talk to her about business, but she finally decided to ask him if more or new difficulties at work were responsible for his longer hours.

"No, it's nothing new," was his quick response, "only the usual ups and downs. Fluctuations one has to expect," but then he sat up abruptly, rose and started to pace.

"No. No, I've been thinking about telling you, I just don't know how to go about it, how to begin. This is something I should have told you years ago. I wish I had. Don't look so worried, my dear, it's nothing terrible.

Well, you know that Father started Desrosiers with only one partner, but I never told you the rest. It was a foregone conclusion that I would work for him. I was never asked, I was commanded. And I knew that Father always wanted to travel the world with Mother - except travel to him meant 'accumulating as many countries' as possible, the way others acquire rare books or ancient coins or paintings. He even kept a 'countries visited' list so he could top their friends and acquaintances! That's what they started to do as soon as *he* decided I could manage without him. Not only that, he expected me to explore opening branches in other cities during his absence and was angry and disappointed when I showed no interest in doing this. He used to leave me notes - 'other sons would give anything to have the opportunities that have fallen into your lap' is one example and 'where is your sense of gratitude and responsibility?' another. Over and over again I was told that this is what sons do - grateful, appreciative sons, that is. But what was much worse to live with: Father was always right, or rather, he was *convinced* that he was right. Right about everything. He saw no point in discussions, no benefit that could be gained from the exchange of different opinions - because he knew all the answers. Anne, working under him was difficult, unpleasant; what am I saying? It was a nightmare, at least for me! When I tried to talk to him, he didn't listen. Anne, I never told you this, but over the years I've come to *hate* the idea of spending my entire life managing his fine goods emporium, yes, it is still his. I hate it, but I had no choice. There was nobody else. Father's partner never married. As you know I have no brothers."

Anne listened and didn't know what to say. Why had Henri kept this to himself for so long?

"Mother was kind, but very quiet and went along with whatever he wanted and decided. Never questioned his decisions. I suppose that's what wives did then, or had to do. When his partner died suddenly some years later, I stupidly hoped Father might come back - of course I was wrong. I was tied to the prison of

Maison Desrosiers more tightly than ever. For the rest of my life."

Anne was aghast. "Henri, why did you never tell me? And please don't say you didn't want to burden me with this!"

"Well, that was pretty much my thinking at first, but now that I am nearing fifty and have already spent more than half of that time working at something that provides us with a very good life - which I do appreciate, of course I do! - but that I cannot regard as my life's work, I am beginning to think …

"Henri," Anne interrupted him, "I think I have an idea where you are going with this. You want to do photography more seriously, spend more time at it. Am I right?"

"How on earth can you know that? I have never talked about this!"

Anne smiled. "You didn't have to. How do I know? I know because I know you, and well, you must know that you are a different person when you talk about photography and what your photographer friends are up to."

Henri was almost but not quite speechless. "That almost sounds as if you wouldn't mind, at least not very much - are you saying you wouldn't?"

"Well, I do have a practical side, even if you don't always give me credit for one. I'd have to know what it will mean to our lives before I can answer that. Can we afford to do this? Would we have to move? Live differently?"

"No, not at all! Maison Desrosiers continues to do well, profits have been invested throughout the years; safely, I might add. And I would still keep an eye on things while leaving the daily management to two young men who are honest and capable."

"You *have* thought about this then - why two and not one?"

"Because there is enough work for two and I think it is the safer way to go."

"I see," Anne said, although she didn't. "Then - then you should do it."

"You mean it?" Henri wrapped his arms around her. "Really?"

"Of course I mean it! But explain to me what photography means to you."

He laughed. "Gladly. As an art form you might say it is still in its infancy, but innovations are happening all the time, and just think what photography can do to make people aware of events or conditions not only here at home, but the world over!"

"Events and conditions like - ?"

"Like reporting what is happening everywhere, not

only in words but with pictures. Photos of leaders in their various fields, their achievements, documenting living conditions here and abroad, on all continents, studying nature just for the beauty of it but also for its darker side, erupting volcanoes, earthquakes, tsunamis, floods. In time, perhaps being permitted to photograph new developments in surgery for medical books - isn't there a saying that a picture is worth more than a thousand words? There are so many possibilities - in the future taking pictures of people in action; sporting events ..."

"Yes, I am beginning to see that, and your enthusiasm is catching, but I don't ever want you near volcanoes, not even the non-erupting ones! And I don't like the sound of tsunamis! What are they? And won't you have to travel to some of these events and places?"

"Sometimes, but there is enough happening right here, in Europe. By the way, a tsunami is a tidal wave. It usually occurs in an ocean after an earthquake. I still have much to learn - and - and not only about photography," he added slowly.

Anne looked up at him. "Are you ... you are now talking about ..."

"Yes, I am talking about our Madeleine. I've tried and tried to find the best words to tell her, but I am coming to the conclusion that there aren't any best words. And no matter how I look at the situation, it is, or seems to be, unlikely that anyone knows. What I am trying to say is that that yes, I have come around to thinking we could wait, even longer than I thought."

After the first few seconds of relief, a seed of suspicion suddenly took root in Anne's mind. How could he have changed his mind so completely? Without any indication that he was considering moving away from his decision, when he had been so adamant about telling Madeleine. What if - was it possible that he was giving in, in exchange for pursuing his photography? No, and it was unworthy of her to think that of him! Yes, it was, but the thought was there and wouldn't go away.

"Well, what do you think, Anne? Why aren't you glad?"

"I am glad, of course I'm glad, more than glad. I just don't know what to think. I've never known you to change your mind so suddenly, so completely, about something that is so very important to you. I am confused. I can't help wondering: Why so suddenly? Why now?"

"Of course you're wondering, Anne, and talking about this is long overdue. I've thought about this for a long time. It is difficult; I have never talked about this. Not to anybody." He reached for her hand.

After a long silence, still holding her hand, he said slowly, "I had to change my mind. It took me months to know what I had to do. I went over and over our conversations - until one night I realized that I sounded exactly like Father. Always right, ordering everyone to do his bidding. Not listening, never hearing the other side. Pushing, always pushing. Pushing to get what *he* was after. It was hard for me to see him for who he was, harder to see myself in him, becoming like him. I know he was like that with Mother; I don't know how she put up with it all her life. I am not going to repeat this with my own family. I don't want to do this to you, Anne. You do understand that, don't you? So we agree on waiting?"

"Of course we do! Yes, now I understand, but I wish you had told me a long time ago; I should have asked you sooner what was wrong, and yes, of course I agree with waiting. I hope we never have to tell her."

"Anne, that is not possible. The one thing I know is that we must do it before she marries. It would be wrong, irresponsible, not to."

"Yes, I know, I know, but that is so far off in the future."

She was almost giddy with happiness.

Chapter X

In the following years, Henri pursued his photographic studies whenever possible in Paris and London. He met Roger Fenton and the two quickly became friends. Anne was doing charitable work in Rennes and was looking forward to be the first woman exhibiting some of her work at the Municipal Gallery.

Nanny had become very strange as she got older and had to retire. She mumbled incessantly about invisible devil-fisted persons and grabbed everyone by their sleeve so she could bend their ears about her 'darling boy Henri'. She was living out her life in a comfortable home for retired governesses and didn't recognize any of her visitors.

Best friends Cecily and Madeleine took riding and dancing lessons (with Madeleine excelling at riding, Cecily preferred dancing), continued with Tutor Webb and, as in the past, spent summers at the Desrosiers country home near Beg-Meil on the Brittany coast.

By the time she was seventeen, Madeleine was completely at home in English and more interested than ever in what was happening in the world. She read every article about Florence Nightingale she could find. Aunt Louise had met her and had been impressed by her dedication to her profession, her organizational talent, and her incredible stamina. They had shared the strong belief that a change in attitude towards nursing was long overdue.

She still 'dreamed' about the boy but hadn't talked about him for years, until one day when they were both working in the studio, Anne on a still life and Madeleine sketching something - not very successfully, judging by her grunts of displeasure.

"Need help?"

"No, I don't think you could help. You don't see him."

Anne put down her brush. "See *him?* What, I mean whom are you drawing? Oh, it's the boy again, isn't it? You still dream about him?" She had hoped that he belonged to the past. Madeleine hadn't mentioned him in years.

"I don't dream about him. I *see* him."

"All right, you see him. Can you make *me* see him? I could do a drawing, make changes as you tell me?"

"Would you?" Madeleine brought Anne's sketch pad and pencils over to the big table.

"He looks like me, or I look like him. Not 'xactly, as I used to say, but he has the same cowlick going to the left like mine does, but his hair is much shorter than mine, of course. And only wavy, not as curly."

"Face - square, round, oval?"

"Squarish, but not too much."

"All right, I can always fix that later. Eyes, nose?"

"We have the same eyes."

"Don't tell me he has your dark lashes!"

"He does, but perhaps I have *his* lashes!"

Anne suppressed a sigh. "Eyebrows? What about his nose?"

"Like mine, a little bigger. And his eyebrows are bushier, and he has a scar on his chin, right about here."

As Anne tried to follow directions her unease grew. Why was Madeleine still dreaming about this look-alike boy? Where did all of this come from? What, if anything, did it mean?

"What do you do when you 'see' him? Do you talk to each other?"

"No, we can't. He reaches for me as if he wanted to, but then he always disappears."

"He never says anything?"

"No. I want to call to him, to tell him to wait, but I cannot make a sound, and then, suddenly, he is gone. Oh yes, that is really good, your drawing looks almost like him. Can you put in color, too? Please, please, please?"

"I can," Anne said, "but you know, I thought you were going to ask me to draw a portrait of Jean-Luc, that nice young man from your dancing class. You still see each other at dances and other parties, don't you? Isn't a real young man more interesting than a make-believe one?"

"Mother, the boy is not make-believe! I cannot explain it, but he is real. He must be. And as far as Jean-Luc is concerned, he is very nice, just not to dance with. I was taller and I could always see the top of his head with all that dandruff. And his hands were always so sweaty! He never wore gloves. He still does'nt."

Anne, still working on the sketch, laughed. "Yes, I remember, that can be quite a problem! Come here, take a look."

"Oh, that is almost perfect! Just make his ears stick out a bit more, and the white scar on his chin is more angled, like this."

Madeleine watched while her mother made the corrections, added color and put the sketch on a shelf to dry. Then they hugged and talked about the festivities planned for her eighteenth birthday and going to see Louise the way they did every year.

Several weeks later, Tutor Webb announced to the girls' parents that, much to his regret, he could not continue teaching them. The news coming out of Turkey and Russia was bound to have an impact on France and England; war seemed inevitable, and he felt it was his duty to join the British army. He intended to leave as soon as possible.

Cecily's parents were relieved; it solved the problem of their daughter who kept complaining that she'd had as much schooling as she could stomach. Henri answered that, of course, he understood loyalty to one's country. He did not say that he, too, was convinced that war was inevitable, and that he had heard that, for the first time ever, it was to be to be documented by a photographer. He merely asked the tutor to explain the situation to the girls, especially to Madeleine.

"And be prepared for her questions. You know how she is. Before you leave, come by my office for your letter of reference."

The tutor arrived the next day, armed with a large map which he tacked on the wall and a recent issue of the 'Illustrated London News' saying, "Time you young ladies learned what goes on in the rest of the world."

Before they could ask 'why?' he asked, "Anyone know how long Europe has been at peace?"

Madeleine and Cecily exchanged helpless looks, but

then Madeleine frowned. She had remembered something. "Was it since Napoleon?"

"Excellent, mademoiselle. Yes, since Waterloo. 1815," he confirmed. "Forty years ago, but now that peace is starting to fall apart. Remember, we also had a revolution here in 1848, a bloodless one, after which Louis Napoleon was elected President of France. But about the same time there were bloody uprisings in Austria, Hungary, and Germany."

He held up the 'Illustrated London News'.

"In here, the lead article speaks of 'thrones tottering and crumbling in the dust' which is a reference to the Ottoman Empire, and of France and Britain declaring war on Russia after it attacked the Turkish fleet. Read and please pass it on." He handed the paper to Madeleine and continued lecturing.

"There is another problem: the Eastern Question. Anyone know what that is?"

"No. Does it have to do with China or Japan?" Madeleine asked as she handed Cecily the newspaper; Cecily slid it down onto her lap so she could search for the fashion pages.

"No, you have traveled east all right, but too far. The Eastern Question refers to the uncertain future of the Ottoman Empire - I should have mentioned earlier that Ottoman is merely a fancier name for Turkey, here" - he pointed to the map with a bamboo stick - "and the growing tension between Turkey and Russia, here. Russia seems intent on gaining access through the Bosporus and from there, into the Mediterranean, right here. Naturally, this has Turkey worried. Britain, too, sees this as a threat to their naval superiority. Are you following me so far?"

Absently, Cicely nodded, having discovered a double page of fetching veiled hats and matching gloves.

Madeleine raised her hand.

"Yes?"

"Why would France and Britain get involved in this?"

"Because they see no other way of stopping Russia. Control of the Black Sea and the Mediterranean would be essential for expanding Russian naval power, and Britain is not about to sit idly by and watch that happen. There are, of course, other reasons and other problems, among them the fact that Jerusalem is part of the Ottoman Empire."

"Jerusalem belongs to the Turks? How did that happen?"

"Well, that is a very long and very complicated story, too long to go into here. What it comes down to is this: the Greek Orthodox monks on one side and the Roman Catholic monks on the other have been squabbling for

centuries over who is the rightful owner of the key to
Bethlehem's Church of Nativity. That's it. Really, you
might say that a part of the larger problem revolves
around a key. The row between France and Russia over
guardianship of Palestine's Holy Places has been going
on forever, it seems. The fact that Tsar Nicolas recently
ordered the invasion of Moldavia, here, and Wallachia,
here, both Turkish provinces, is not helping the situation … and Miss Cecily, I believe you have accidentally
stumbled on the wrong newspaper section. Please rejoin
us and study the newest fashions after class. Where was
I? Oh, yes. England and France, with Turkey, have entered into an alliance against Russia. I assume that one
of their main objects will be taking Sebastopol, here,
and destroying Russia's Black Sea Fleet - you can see
how important this naval base would be if Russia were
to expand its naval power into the Mediterranean. Well,
all you have to know is that the war will be between
England, France and Turkey on one side, and Russia
on the other, all of which is a much simplified version
of events because time is running out. I'll be leaving for
England within the week."

"So soon?"

"No!"

"Why?"

"Do you have to?"

He silenced the girls' protests. "Yes, I have to. I am

more urgently needed fighting for my country than teaching here. They were years which I have enjoyed, most of the time. I have your parents' permission to write to you, and I shall, whenever I find time, paper and ink, *and* if I have your promise you will write, too."

"Of course I'll write!" Cecily thought it would not be nice to let her relief show, but thank God the lessons were over at last. "But you are not a soldier!" she protested.

"True, but I can be. I used to be a crack shot when our place was overrun by rabbits, which happened regularly every year. I'm sorry, I know you think of them as adorable fluffy creatures, but that is a view not shared by farmers! Don't worry, I intend to be back," he added. "God bless you. And keep reading, both of you!" Not that Madeleine needed reminding.

That evening there was a lively conversation at the Desrosiers dinner table which started when Madeleine asked, "Papa, is Tutor Webb right? Will there be war between Russia against France and Britain in the Crimea?"

"War? Who said so? What war?" was Anne's immediate reaction.

Henri had Madeleine repeat what she had learned, quietly proud how well she had understood the information and was able to put it into her own words. She ended by asking, "Isn't it strange? France and England were enemies for such a long time, and now they will be fighting on the same side."

"Not all that strange," her father answered. "It all depends on whether nations find they have more common interests, more common goals than differences. I can see why fear of the 'Russian Bear' or 'Russian Eagle' would make allies of old enemies."

"Well, I for one am glad that you are too old to fight on any side," Anne said and resumed eating. "I don't mean that you are old, my dear, just too old to go to war," she amended.

"Thank you for that," he answered drily. "You are right, my fighting days are definitely over, but - I wasn't going to mention this yet, but I might as well do it now: There is a good chance that my friend Fenton will let me tag along when he goes to the Crimea."

"W-what are you saying?" Anne's spoon clattered into her soup bowl. "The Crimea? Didn't you just say that is where the war will be? Henri, you cannot go!"

"I hope you don't mean that, Anne. Roger is being sent there by a private firm to document officers' and soldiers' lives, the conditions under which armies live, how they fare before and after a battle, etc. etc. He has no intention of getting too close to the fighting."

"He is going to stay away from where everything is happening? How likely is that? And please don't tell me you have already decided to go. It is dangerous, far too dangerous. It isn't safe. I cannot let you go . . . "

"As I said before, I hope you didn't mean that, Anne. It is the opportunity of a lifetime to understand what I have learned, to watch one of the foremost photographers of our time at work, and when it is offered, I shall go. Actually, it will mean going to England first where Roger puts together everything for his expedition. After that, we'll travel to the Crimea by ship. I promise not to take chances. I assure you, I shall be careful. But meanwhile I am going to take some pictures of my two ladies, to take with me. How about right after we finish dessert?" He had no intention of giving Anne more time to raise more objections.

Madeleine's photos were the best he had ever taken of her; they captured her lively sweetness and the dreamy openness of her smile. Anne managed to force a smile but looked apprehensive.

"Couldn't I go, too?" Madeleine asked her father a few days later, knowing full well what his answer would be.

Unfortunately, she asked just as her mother entered the room.

"What was that? No, no, and no again! What are you thinking? Why doesn't anyone in this house listen to reason? And what did you mutter under your breath?"

"Nothing. I only said I had thought perhaps I could help. Miss Nightingale is going with her nurses."

"Yes, she is. *And* she is experienced and qualified. *And* she made very clear that from all her experienced nurses she is only taking the *older* ones, the ones in their *late* twenties, preferably even older! *Older*, Madeleine! *And* no matter where they have worked before, they can't have any idea about what awaits them over there. I know you'd like to help, Madeleine, but a first-aid course does not prepare anyone for war!"

After that, Anne turned towards her husband.

"And you, Henri, did you really think that hiding 'The Times' from me would keep me from finding out about 'the revolting conditions at the British Military Hospital at Scutari'? That is only one example and word for word *exactly* how your Mr. Russell put it. I've read many of his dispatches. Your friend Fenton is British, so you'll be wherever the British are, and that is where 'there is not even linen to make bandages for the wounded'! Yes, I know that fighting hasn't really started, but did *you* happen to read this, by any chance? It is hard enough for me to make peace with the fact that you are going, Henri, but now I expect, no, I *demand* your help in explaining to our daughter that there are things we can do right here at home!"

Anne stopped herself. Had she really said 'demand'?

Henri put an arm around her. "Anne, you never

cease to amaze me. And as for you, young lady, your mother is right. First aid courses do not prepare anyone for the Crimea. Not only because of war, danger and hardship, but because of exposure to typhus, cholera and dysentery. All that without assurance of adequate help. I know what you're going to say, that I'll be exposed to them, too. While this is true, I can take precautions for myself, but I could not look out for you at the same time - we wouldn't be in the same places. So I want your word that you're not going to give in to some wild and foolish impulse to try to follow me. That would be madness and I absolutely forbid it, Madeleine. Do you understand, do I have your word?"

Madeleine's 'yes' was almost inaudible. Henri made her repeat it more loudly and shake hands on it. She promised, thinking how her father knew her better than any other person in this world.

At least he had added, "I promise not to take chances." Mother and daughter needed to hear this again and again, but it did nothing to ease Madeleine's feeling of being excluded and useless because she was young and inexperienced and a girl.

Anne also worried about the weather. "I read that winters can be very harsh over there. When do you leave?"

"As soon as I get word from Roger. In a few weeks, I suppose. We'll meet at London's Blackwell Pier, so

I'll have plenty of time to familiarize myself with his van. What a capital idea, transforming a wine merchant's vehicle into a photographic van! You may not be that interested in the details, but there are two cisterns on the roof, one for regular and one for distilled water. He's had yellow glass windows fitted into the sides and shutters. There are dozens of cases of equipment, five or six cameras, racks to hold everything in place. What else? Trays to hold negatives. A folding bed that fits under a shelf. Boxes of meat preserves, wine, biscuits. A tent. His assistant will be along, of course, and a cook/handyman/driver. The most important thing, Anne, is that this van has become a mobile darkroom in which the exposed plates can be processed! But I see all these technical details are putting you to sleep."

"No, they are not. It's just that I am more interested in your ship."

"Of course you are. Our ship, the 'Hecla', is an armed paddlewheel steam sloop, a government vessel supplied to Roger by Secretary of War Sir Hubert Sidney himself. Roger will even carry a handwritten letter of introduction from Prince Albert to Lord Raglan, the British commander - my dear, could we travel under better auspices?"

"I suppose not." 'And just how much good are princely letters in a bad storm?' she thought angrily before she added, managing a near-smile, "I'll still count the days until you are back, safe and sound."

"Of course I'll be back safe and sound, and we'll write to each other, but better be prepared: letters may take some time going back and forth."

"Some time? I'm not sure I like the sound of that. What exactly do you mean by 'some time'?"

"Several weeks; it could be even more."

"But that is awful, simply awful!"

"Yes, it is, Anne, especially if you think of the officers and soldiers over there and their families at home. For us, my dear, it is merely an inconvenience. Remember that it can take sailing ships five weeks or longer to reach Turkey. I might be able to send a letter back with someone returning to France; I promise to do that as often as I can. Or I'll send a telegram - but should you get one, for heaven's sake don't jump to the conclusion that it is bad news!"

Anne nodded. What else could she do? After more than twenty-five years of marriage, Henri's calm reasonableness still managed to achieve the opposite of what it was meant to accomplish.

Henri left for England, and Anne and Madeleine, accompanied by a servant, traveled to Paris - Louise had asked to see them. "Do you think that means she is not getting better?"

"I don't know what to think," Anne answered. "She has been the same for the last few years, hasn't she? Her letter only said that she was looking forward to having some time with us, especially with you, and that it would be good for us, both Henri and the tutor having left." Madeleine thought she was too old to be taken in by such a thin fabrication, but thought it wiser not to say so.

Louise had lost more weight and looked gaunt, but she greeted them with her old happy smile. Anne was so taken aback by the change in her that she couldn't speak. After hugging Louise carefully, Madeleine sat down on her footstool, looked up at her and said, "I can see something is wrong. Please tell us what it is, Auntie LouLou. We have to know."

"Well, the last time you were here, the doctors weren't sure yet," Louise said, smiling about Madeleine reverting to what she had called her when she was a little girl. "I had nothing to tell you then. Now they know, after tests and some treatments, and there is no sense talking around it, so here is what I wish I didn't have to tell you: it is something that will not go away, something that cannot be cured."

"Aunt LouLou, you lied to us!" Madeleine shouted into the silence.

Anne, aghast, managed a tearful, "Madeleine, apologize to your aunt this instant!" Louise waved that away. "No, Anne, let's not ruin our afternoon with unnecessary apologies. I wish it hadn't come to this so soon, but … "

"But now that it has, please come home with us and

let us take care of you," Anne pleaded through her tears. "Please. We'll take good care of you, and it would mean so much to us."

"Yes, come home with us," Madeleine begged. "We have so much room and there are very good doctors in Rennes, too, and I want to help and ..."

"I wish I could do that," Louise interrupted her with a gentle smile. "I love both of you dearly, you know that, but this has been my home for most of my life. *My life is here*, with the Sisters. This is where I want to be, where I need to be, especially now. I know it is hard for you to understand, but you can help me most by accepting my decision."

There was a long silence.

Anne knew her sister well enough to realize she would not be budged. Helplessly, she looked at her daughter who seemed to be struggling with something she had trouble putting into words.

"Auntie LouLou," Madeleine said at last, slowly, "I hope I am wrong - dear God, I so hope I'm wrong - but I have this feeling that you're saying more than wanting to remain here. Am I right? What you are saying, but not in words - I am so afraid you're telling us that ... that this may be the last time we are together." She wept quietly.

"Madeleine!" Anne exclaimed.

Louise reached out to both of them.

"It's all right, Anne, Madeleine. It's all right. Just keep writing to me, won't you? I treasure your letters, and I thank you both for understanding and letting me do this the only way I can. No more tears, please. Instead, let's talk about the many happy memories we have together."

This is what they did, even sharing a laugh or two, until Louise grew tired and there was a knock at the door. "Five more minutes, Sister Louise." Those minutes flew by much too fast.

When they hugged good-bye, Anne whispered to her, "Thank you, Lou, thank you, thank you, thank you. I owe you everything. Everything!" Madeleine was still weeping.

On the way home, Anne tried to comfort her daughter, telling her that Louise had always shied away from what she used to call 'those big emotional scenes'. That this was the life she had chosen, and that they had to understand and respect her decision. Madeleine said nothing. She was trying to understand why serenity and acceptance could not include them.

Louise died in her sleep two weeks later, and Anne and Madeleine traveled back to Paris for the funeral. Anne, all in black, wore her black jet mourning jewelry - necklace, ear-rings and a large pin. She offered Madeleine the loan of a jet bracelet, but Madeleine declined. She wanted nothing to do with what she thought of as 'the awful death etiquette of mourning jewelry'.

"Why not, sweetheart?"

"I am wearing these black clothes and that black veiled bonnet with all that black crepe dangling down the back *only* because I have to. At least I don't have a beady-eyed black bird perched on top of my head like some ladies do. Why does the whole world have to know? I cannot help it, all that black makes me feel that we're putting on a show so people can say, 'Oh look, there must have been a death in that family. I wonder who died.' Why can't we just *not* wear any jewelry at all? The idea that jewelers are making money on mourning jewelry strikes me as ghoulish!"

"Madeleine, what an terrible thing to say!"

"I'm sorry, Mother, that is how I feel."

There was more Madeleine could have added. After one look at her mother's face, she did not. It would only upset her more. Her mother was sad. She was sad, too, but she was also angry. There was always anger in her when she felt sad and helpless. Her aunt LouLou was gone, and theirs was such a very small family - there were no other aunts or uncles. No cousins, not even one. Nobody.

For her, it was the first death in the family. She missed her father's reassuring presence and knew her mother did, too.

Chapter XI

A lain and Nicolas had completed their Lycée studies and for Alain the path was clear: law studies at the University of Paris. Naturally, his mother wanted him closer to home, in Rennes, but Alain had insisted that it was Paris or nothing. She tried to draw some comfort from knowing that her son would live with an aunt and uncle, at least for the first semester.

"And if you absolutely insist, Nicolas can go along with me to Paris," he told both parents, at the end of his patience after another heated discussion. "No one else!"

Nicolas heard him mumble angrily under his breath, "Why do they think I cannot get on a train and find my way to Uncle's house by myself? When are they going to stop treating me as if I were still a little boy?"

Docteur C. secretly sided with his son but was glad that Nicolas would be traveling with him. He thanked him and told him to take some days to see the sights before his return. "After all, this will be your first time in Paris."

When they got off the train and had commandeered a coach, Alain announced that he was not going to arrive at anybody's doorstep with a nursemaid holding his hand. "You can't be serious! I am a nursemaid now?" Nicolas laughed, but when he saw how serious Alain was, he added, "Just so you know, I have no intention of holding your hand, now or any other time. How about I get off earlier and wait on the corner of their street, out of sight, until you are inside. Then I'll join you. Fair enough?"

"No, not fair enough at all! You've done your job, you got me to Paris - now go! Go home! Disappear! Leave, and I mean now! You know how much I look forward to my classes and being on my own - when are they going to let me do things by myself?"

Nicolas was tempted to say 'when you stop behaving like a spoiled child' but didn't. "Well, all I know is that you are relieved that your father has given up on making Docteur Caradec the Third out of you. What happened to our seeing Paris together?"

"We can do that during my vacation. By then I'll really know my way around. I'd rather prepare myself, go over some notes. For God's sake, will you stop arguing? Why can't you leave me alone? You're beginning to sound like her!"

That stung, that and the way Alain was dismissing him. Sometimes it was difficult to believe that this was the same Alain who had loaned him his dictionary and had so patiently helped him to learn French. And Alain studying his notes? When he never spent one minute longer over his studies than absolutely necessary? That was hard to believe, too.

"All right, have it your way!" he finally said, but insisted that they go together to the telegraph office to confirm their arrival in Paris.

He was surprised when Alain hugged him goodbye, hard. Quickly he hid behind a tree and watched until he saw the carriage stop. Alain and his luggage disappeared into his uncle's home.

At loose ends now, he decided he had enough money for two nights at a student pension; it included morning coffee and two slices of bread. Not that two days were nearly enough for what he wanted to see. How could he leave without seeing the Cathedral and the Chapel and the Louvre, without walking along the Seine? Seeing Sacré Coeur? The Sorbonne? He enjoyed the very full days but wished he and Alain had parted on better terms.

On his way back to Fougères Nicolas replayed their last conversation In his mind and briefly wondered whether he should have stayed after all, at least for another day. No, absolutely not, he decided. If Alain ever found out, he would probably accuse him of being a spy in his parents' employ.

Besides, he had his own future to think about. Docteur C. had offered to pay for him to go to veterinary school, a generous offer - if that was what he wanted to do with his life. It wasn't. The possibility that Alain might look on this as usurping his rightful place had briefly crossed his mind but had nothing to do with his decision.

He still was not sure in what direction he wanted to go. Politics? Teaching?

Docteur C. expected an answer by the end of the month.

After the train ride, Nicolas decided to walk home. He liked to think over things while walking. The Caradecs were not at home; the servants were probably resting in their attic rooms, this being early Sunday afternoon. Nicolas saddled Duc and decided to visit Berthe whom he had not seen in over a month. Leisurely he rode towards Vezin-le-Coquet where she now lived with her daughter.

Marie was outside, taking wash from the line and waved to him. He reined in his horse, tied it loosely to a tree and grabbed the basket from her, then asked after Berthe.

"She is feisty as always; yer not to worry," Marie

answered with her ready laugh. "Likes to go back to her childhood more often, starts on somethin' but forgets what it was. The boys love her stories, 'specially the one about 'the boy with the thousand questions'. Ye ought to hear her tell it: Ye saved a boy from a bunch of armed thugs 'n' carried 'im home, then carried 'im back and forth to school for weeks until his poor broken leg healed. When I say, "Broken, was it?" she laughs 'n' answers, "What's so wrong with havin' a little fun embroiderin' stories? Well, yer always welcome here, come in, come in, the boys'll will be that sorry they missed ye; they're helping out at a neighbor's farm this week."

Berthe sat in her rocking chair in a sunny corner of the small kitchen. Marie picked up the knitting that had slid from her lap and gently touched her shoulder.

"Wake up, Mother - there's someone here to see ye!"

"I weren't asleep!" Berthe answered testily, "I never sleep in daytimes."

"Yes, Mother, I know." Marie made a face at Nicolas. "Look who's here. It's Nicolas."

"I got eyes, I see it be 'im. Come here," She stretched out her thin arms and enveloped him in her Berthe scent, the wild flowers of her home-made soap and her old woman aura.

"So, what are ye up to these days?"

Nicolas told her about Paris and traveling by train.

"On a train? Grand, was it? So how d'ye like the big city?"

"Some of it is very beautiful, there is so much to see, but other parts are poor and crowded, and very noisy; I really enjoyed riding through the quiet woods on my way here."

"And now?"

"Now I have to decide what to do. I could become animal doctor like docteur Caradec, but I'm not sure. Remember how I always wanted to see something of this world? I still do. I hope I will, some day, but I am also thinking I'd like to teach …"

"No matter what ye decide, ye'll make good," Berthe said as if this were a foregone conclusion. She had always had this unshakeable faith in him. He remembered how it had calmed his apprehension before he entered the Lycée.

They drank tea and sat in companionable silence and memory came surging back to Nicolas how he had always thought of Berthe as his mother.

"There is something I've been wanting to say to you for a long time." He said, twisting the empty mug in his hand. "I always - I always thought of you as my mother. Always. And I thank my lucky star that Rozenn left me with you."

Berthe set her mug aside and reached up to his face

with both hands. "But I already knows that, me boy, I knows that all these years - not that stars had anythin' much to do with it. Can ye stay awhile?"

'Of course I can, as long as I am back before dark." I have to tell the Caradecs that their son is settled in with his aunt and uncle in Paris. You know I'll be back as often as I can."

Chapter XII

When Nicolas reached home, the Caradec house was in an uproar.

Wordlessly, a servant pointed him toward the salon where Doctor C. was trying to talk his sobbing wife into taking a pill. As soon as she saw Nicolas she shoved her husband aside, stood up and shouted, "Why didn't you stay with Alain? Why? Now he is gone. Gone. I'll never see him again!" Wailing, she collapsed into a chair.

"I - I don't understand, Madame C. What happened?"

"What happened?" she screamed. Struggling to her feet again, she pushed past her husband and advanced towards Nicolas, hands balled into fists, ready to pummel him. "You have the nerve to ask what happened? Don't you dare act the innocent with us!" Her hands curled into claws as she lurched forward. "After all we've done for you, this is the gratitude you show us? This is how you repay us?"

Docteur C. managed to grab her arms. "Enough, Sylvie, enough! I'll take care of this. Now swallow this pill so I can take you upstairs. Yes, *now*, you need to lie down. Now, I said. I insist! Good, that's it. You" - he turned to Nicolas - "You stay here, understand? You have much explaining to do!"

Nicolas could only nod. Explaining? Explain what?

Something must have happened to Alain, but what? His mind was trying to untangle the possibilities - a sudden illness, perhaps some sort of accident for which he was being blamed? Why? He had watched Alain walk into the house, luggage and all, eager to begin his law studies - at least that's what he had tried to make him believe. Ripples of unease ran through him as he paced back and forth, staring at the loudly ticking wall clock. What could have happened? And what could Madame C. have meant when she sobbed that she'd never see her son again?

After endless minutes during which the ticking of the clock seemed to become louder and more menacing, Docteur C. came back into the room. He sank into the nearest chair. His face was rigid with anger when he spoke.

"Talk!" he ordered. "From the beginning and the truth this time!"

Nicolas thought he would choke on anger of his own. He had done nothing to deserve this. Nothing.

He decided to leave as soon as he had answered Docteur C.'s questions.

"We arrived in Paris. Alain didn't want me to come along to his uncle's house or even to watch him go in. He made that very clear. When he insisted I get off the coach early, rather than fight with him, I did. I waited where he couldn't see me until I saw the coach stop in front of his uncle's house. I *watched* him get down and walk inside. I *watched* a servant take his luggage in. I *watched* the door close after him. He was all right then, everything was all right. That is all I know."

"This is exactly what happened?"

"Yes, Sir, it is."

"A likely story. I've given you another chance to tell the truth. What really happened?"

A likely story? Another chance? *What* did he imply?

With difficulty Nicolas swallowed down his anger and asked, "Didn't you receive our telegram?"

"Oh yes, we did, we did! Both of them!"

"Both? We sent only one."

"Well, Alain sent another one. Two days later. Would you like to know where from? Marseilles! You heard right, Marseilles. The fool has enlisted. By now he may already be on a ship bound for the Crimea. Of course the telegram does not mention which unit or which ship! It is clear he doesn't want to be found. You are responsible for this, Nicolas! You! This is your fault, this is your doing!"

This was what Docteur C. thought of him?

"I know *nothing* about this! Nothing at all, Sir."

"Really? I find that impossible to believe. More than a year ago both of you talked about joining up - I'm sure you remember that rather unpleasant conversation and how I made my position very clear. I knew then that the whole thing had to be your idea, and I know it now: without you Alain wouldn't have a clue about what is happening in Turkey. Or anywhere else in the world, for that matter. Who else could be behind this but you? I expected better from you."

Well, Nicolas had expected better from him. He was too furious to answer. How could Docteur C. believe this of him? Was that what he really thought of him? Well, he had heard enough, more than enough. He was going to leave and slam the door shut on his way out, but not before he'd had his say.

Looking straight at Docteur C. he said as calmly as he could, "Sir, I am not lying. I did not know that Alain planned this because he did not say one word about this to me. Not one word. *I did not know* . That is all I have to say, Sir!"

He turned and was already at the door when Docteur

C. called out, "Wait, please!" He fixed Nicolas with a penetrating stare and sighed.

"I don't know what to do. Alain is so not cut out to be a soldier - his mother has convinced herself that he will be killed over there, it's not that I don't believe you, Nicolas, it was just such a terrible shock, it still is - and my wife, as you've seen, is making herself ill over this. I keep thinking, what if he enlisted under an assumed name? How could we ever find him? He is under-age although that may not matter much these days. What are we going to do? What can anyone do?"

Nicolas had never seen him look so defeated, so without hope.

What could they do? What cold anyone do? Nothing! Alain was gone. He had left. In his typically arrogant way, thinking only of himself. Nothing anyone could do about it now. Alain wanted to do something on his own and he did. Well, let him. As far as he, Nicolas, was concerned, all *he* wanted to do was get out of the Caradec house..

But suddenly there was another thought. It was gone before he could catch it. What was it? Something to do with - Here it was again!

Oh, no! No, no, a thousand times no!

Sure he could do this, but only if he had completely

lost his mind. He told himself to get rid of this idea immediately!

But the idea, as insane as it was, kept intruding into his chaotic thinking and refused to be ignored. Not out of a sense of guilt - he was *not* responsible for Alain's rash action. They had promised never to talk again about joining up again, and they hadn't. Not once. There was no way he could have guessed at what Alain must have been planning for quite a while. Without any thought of how this would affect his parents, without any thought that *he* would be blamed! Alain, the selfish, thoughtless idiot probably thought he was on his way to becoming a war hero ....

But there was something he could do. There was. He could go after him. He could go, try to find him.

Yes, he could - if he was mad.

The thought grew even as he tried to push it down and out of his mind. Who was the idiot now? This was crazy, insane, doomed from the start! What was he thinking - that he could go from regiment to regiment asking do you know this soldier? His name is Alain Caradec, his mother wants him to come home? Did he really believe no one would stop him? That anyone would bother answering? That he could even get himself there? What about when the fighting started? Then trying to find Alain would still be insane, only a thousand times more so! They could both be killed - for what? For nothing!

And yet - what an adventure it would be! The Mediterranean, Constantinople, the Black Sea, French and British and Russians soldiers. The government had predicted a short war just a few days ago, one that could be over in a matter of weeks.

And what was he thinking, looking at this as if it were an adventure? This was not about having an adventure! It was about … he knew what it was about.

Stupid, insane, doomed from the start, that's what this idea was, and yet he could not rid himself of it. He thought it through again and again and again, and what it might mean, and always ended up in the same place: there was no way of measuring what Docteur C. had made possible for him. It had changed his life forever. That was what should matter, and it did. More than anything. Even if Docteur C. still blamed him.

"Docteur C. ," Nicolas drew some deep breaths and waited until anger stopped strangling his words. Standing very straight and speaking very quickly, he said, "Docteur C., I had nothing to do with what Alain did, but I am going after him. With or without your consent. I want to leave as soon as possible and I won't need my birth certificate because enlisting is out of the question for me, I need the freedom to move around. Perhaps I can get to him before he embarks, or reach the Crimea shortly after he does. Frankly, I have no idea how to go about anything. I'll decide when I get there.

But just in case I ought to have a letter of authorization from you. Oh, and I'll need a compass and some money in case I have to grease a palm or two. And could you let me have two of the photographs that were taken of Alain last summer? I must be out of my mind, but I am going, Sir."

He had run out of breath - what had he just committed himself to do?

"I don't know what I can accomplish, but I intend to try, Docteur C.," he added while the only thought left bouncing around in his head was, Alain, you damn fool!

There was a long silence, broken only by Docteur C. blowing his nose and saying something in such a low voice that Nicolas could not understand it. After a while he rose.

"I apologize, Nicolas. I never really believed that you would - you have my apologies and my gratitude, Nicolas. My wife's, too. Take Duc, even though he is not trained for any of this, having your own horse will make it easier to get around, but look after him on the ship. Horses don't like sea travel. I thank the Lord that you came into our lives and think of you as Alain's brother. We shall pray every day for your safe return, Alain's and yours - I cannot say more, we'd better start gathering what you'll need."

He lifted a helpless hand, let it fall heavily on Nicolas' shoulder and walked from the room like a man suddenly grown old.

Just for a moment Nicolas asked himself whether Docteur C. would have let him go if he really were Alain's brother - but why wonder about something to which he already knew the answer?

Better think about what he was getting into.

From what he had read in the newspapers, one year earlier, Russia had moved into two Turkish principalities north of the Danube, Moldavia and Wallachia; three months later, the Turks had declared war. He wasn't sure of the sequence of events, but there was a Russian attack on Turkish ships during which only 400 of 4,000 Turkish seamen survived and a city was totally destroyed - Sinope, the name came to him - and after that, Britain and France signed a military alliance and in early 1854 declared war. So much for some of facts; at least his memory had not been affected by his crazy decision.

By now, thousands of French soldiers in their blue uniforms and the British (red coats) and Russians (long grey coats?) were supposed to be on the move towards the Crimea. Steamships and sail ships waited in Marseilles; some steamships apparently towed sail ships attached to them by cables, just how efficient could that be, and how was it managed in rough seas? He could not imagine it, but then, what did he know about moving troops? He didn't even know how many days it would take to get to Turkey. No, not days, surely it would be weeks.

He tried to picture the map in his mind: sailing east across the Mediterranean, through the Dardanelles into the Marmara Sea, then past Constantinople and into the Black Sea and Turkey. Where in Turkey? He had no idea but had dreamed of seeing some of these places, but not under these circumstances.

He had also read that all ships were infested with every kind of vermin known to man and shuddered - rats, bugs, flies, fleas and God knows what else. And wasn't finding Alain more impossible than finding that proverbial needle in the haystack? Of course it was.

'Well, at least I know what I'll do when I find him! I'll wring his neck!' he said to himself.

He made time to see Berthe before he left. Not wanting to worry her, he told her that Docteur C. was sending him to Lyon to do some work for him; he had business interests there. He might be away several months, he said, so she shouldn't worry. She looked at him long and hard. He sensed that she didn't believe he was telling her true, but all she said was, "May the Lord keep you safe."

He bent down so she could kiss his forehead.

During the days before his departure he made sure to commit all of Docteur C.'s instructions to memory: opium for sedation, castor oil for constipation, Epsom salt for purging, chalk and opium for diarrhea, quinine and antimony for lowering fevers, port and beef to fortify the sick, vegetable and fruit to guard against scurvy, watching out for frostbite.

"Frostbite?" he had repeated, incredulous, when Docteur C. mentioned it the first time. "Doesn't Lord Raglan expect to take Sebastopol in two weeks? That's what the newspapers say. It'll be almost summer!"

"Yes, I read the same nonsense," Docteur C. answered angrily. "The powers that be who are predicting a short and easy campaign have no idea what they are up against. I've spent some time over there. It is impossible to take Sebastopol with its many stone forts and gun emplacements from the sea which means a land campaign. The Russian army is huge, making Russia a formidable adversary, and just because there are some palm trees around Sochi does not mean that it doesn't get extremely cold in the Black Sea region. Doesn't anyone here realize that people can die of frostbite? As a matter of fact, Nicolas, remember this: if you ever have to sleep in a tent when it is very cold, or God forbid out in the open, *don't ever think of sleeping without your socks and boots on.* You might want to for one reason or another, like giving your feet some air, some freedom: but don't do it. Remember that. Also remember that cholera is a tremendous problem over there, and so is typhus. There is no treatment or cure for either. There was a cholera outbreak in London a few years back. I wonder if the authorities are aware of the fact that death can occur as quickly as three to four hours after onset!"

Nicolas thought, 'Thank you for this comforting bit of information which I didn't need just now.'

He promised to write or telegraph as often as possible.

Chapter XIII

He left two days later, still trying to get used to brand-new sturdy boots worn over two pairs of socks. Spare items of clothing and hastily assembled necessities were stowed in a knapsack, together with paper, pens, ink, and a rudimentary map. Two photos, identity papers, money and the compass were secreted in a water-proof pocket sewn into his shirt, as was a letter in an official-looking envelope. "Only in case of an emergency," Docteur C. had stressed.

The train taking him south was rapidly filling up with new recruits, most of whom had trouble sobering up; many looked neither close to eighteen nor near the posted minimum height, whatever that was: the number had been blackened out on all posters. No wonder they had taken Alain; he was only two months shy of his eighteenth birthday and fairly tall. Many years ago, he had embarked on a rigorous exercise program, hoping to gain some height, but he had remained a full head shorter. That still rankled.

It seemed to Nicolas that the army filled their quota with whoever understood 'at attention' and could follow that order! He was not wearing a uniform, but nobody bothered him about that. Not even when he got himself on a horse transport in order to remain with Duc.

In Marseilles he tried to follow the recruits, but the crowds made access to the harbor impossible. In the shoving confusion, he was yelled at to "get that damn horse out of the way" and was finally pointed in the right direction. Cursing the ear-splittingly loud marching music coming at them from two opposing bands, he searched for and found his ship, "The Himalayan". There he found out that he had to let Thomas Fellowes, an officer in Cardigan's 11th Hussars, put his horse into Duc's separate hold. Fellowes had apparently missed his British ship and word had come down from the captain that Lord Cardigan's Hussars were to be accorded every consideration.

Trying to keep the two horses calm was impossible from the start. They fought against their restraints until sweat glistened on their necks and flanks; they whinnied and snorted and roared in distress.

Docteur C. was right: horses hate sea travel. At least theirs were in side-by-side roomy stalls in a private hold - the conditions in the large lower hold which was near the engines were terrible. There it was not only steamy-hot, airless and dark. The horses, tethered in very narrow stalls, could not lie down at all. Nicolas knew that eventually their legs would cramp and continue to cramp. The steady pain would drive them frantic, and after this long ordeal they were supposed to be fit for duty? What genius had planned this horse transport? Why not go over land? No wonder the sounds coming from the large hold were so terrible. He found out later that several horses, struggling to break free, had suffered broken legs and had to be put down.

Thomas and he spent large parts of every day and night with their mounts during a sea voyage which was expected to last between five and seven weeks and became friends. Thomas didn't mind when Nicolas, seeing him for the first time in his Hussar dress uniform for the Captain's dinner, could not contain his laughter about the skin-tight dark-pink trousers and the tall fur hat he carried under his arm.

"How can you sit in the saddle for hours without - well, what shall I say, without being *extremely* uncomfortable? And that short jacket loaded down with all that gold braid in the front, that's more for show than protection, isn't it?" He was overcome by more laughter. "I do apologize, but how in the world do you get that strange furry thing to stay on your head, not to mention that it makes such an inviting target?"

"All right, all right, I fully expected you to come up with some disparaging remarks. We get them all the time," Thomas grinned, "but could you show a little respect? The hat is not a strange, furry thing. It is called a busby. As I said, we get questions all the time, and I might as well tell you this: because of the lovely color of our trousers we are known as 'the cherry bums' of the Peacock Regiment. No, I am no*t* joking. Naturally, in polite society 'cherubims' is substituted for cherry bums."

"Naturally. " Nicolas was still laughing.

"Enough, Nick, enough. Most of us have black leather patches sewn into the seat, not that they prolong the life of our trousers by much," Thomas continued his explanation. "And either way, the pants are, as you guessed correctly, pure torture. I might as well also ask you, do you know "Punch"?

Laughing, Nicolas mimicked a drinking motion. "Of course I do."

"Not the beverage, numbskull, the satirical weekly. It recently published a ditty in our honor. Under the dir-est penalties imaginable you will not, I repeat, *you will not* commit these lines to memory:

"Oh, pantaloons of cherry,
Oh, redder than raspberry!
For men to fight in things so tight
It must be trying - very!
Gainst wear, though fine the weather
They would not hold together.
On saddle-back they fly and crack
Though seated with black leather."

Nicolas didn't have the heart to tell Thomas that, effortlessly, the eight lines had embedded themselves in his memory.

"You've never considered another regiment, one with more 'normal' if less eye-catching trousers?"

"Well, the 11th Hussars are a family tradition, so that never came up."

"Oh."

They had other, more serious concerns. There had been a great many cholera deaths on board and rumors had it that both cholera and typhus were raging in the Crimea. Raging? In other words, if you didn't sicken and die from one, the other was bound to get you. Compared to that, their other traveling companions, scurrying rats and mice, bugs, other crawly beasties and the ever-present flies and fleas were mere nuisances.

If he had known all this? He still would have gone.

They were becalmed in Malta and the captain decided to use the time for some minor overhauls.

Nicolas knew nothing about the island. Thomas informed him that Malta, only eight miles wide and eighteen miles long, had a history going very far back, was given to the Knights of St. John of Jerusalem in 1530 in perpetual fief but had become a British Crown Colony in 1815.

"Forty years ago. How do you remember all that?"

"It was drummed into our heads in school. I have no idea why I retained this particular lesson. Forgot most of the others. Due to lack of employment opportunities, Malta is now one of the world's poorest countries; all well-paying jobs are held by the British."

"Why?"

"Well, it is what happens when the British Governor wears three hats: governor, legislator and chief judge. He controls all hiring. Might as well show you what is happening to the Maltese."

Thomas stowed away as much bread as his jacket pockets would hold. Nicolas decided do the same, also grabbed a bread bag from the galley on his way out and followed him. Walking up from Valetta Grand Harbor towards the Victoria Gate they suddenly found themselves on stone steps teeming with beggars; dozens, no, *hundreds* of men, women, sick children, all skin and bones and covered in rags, pleading weakly for something to eat. Most were lying listlessly about the stones; others sat leaning against the wall; none looked as if they had the strength to stand. Some seemed to be living there.

"These are the 'Nix Mangiare Steps', Nicolas - I'm sure I don't have to translate the name for you."

Both reached into their pockets, broke the bread

in smaller pieces and dropped them into out-stretched hands. Then they moved up a few steps and did the same until all the bread was gone. A fight erupted about the empty bag; they looked at each other and fled.

They arrived at the port of Varna on an oppressively hot day (why 300 miles west across the Black Sea from the Crimea? Nicolas wondered), with soldiers hanging sea-sick over the railings and others so weakened by fever and dysentery that they had to be carried ashore. Nicolas was well and remembered how, a lifetime, Marrec had thought of making a sailor of him.

The quay was crowded with Greeks, Turks, French and British soldiers, vendors out-shouting each other, beggars and mangy dogs. The air rang with the babble of several languages and the sound of fly-plagued horses screaming, kicking, biting and fighting against being off-loaded in harnesses and set down into wildly bouncing boats. Some fought loose and went for the water rather than be put into the slings. Not all made it ashore. All were mad with confusion and fear.

Waiting to leave ship, Thomas showed Nicolas a book.

"A cookbook?" Nicolas laughed out loud. "What does an exalted member of the Peacock Regiment need a cookbook for?"

Thomas gave him a friendly cuff on the arm. "Hey, this is no laughing matter. You French have cooks, pretty good ones, I hear. We have to cook our own meals. By 'we' I don't mean myself, I have someone do it for me. but still … really, that's the way it is. So in here are recipes against starvation. Russians, supplies and time permitting." He patted the book. "Don't know what I'd do without my Alexis."

In turn, Nicolas gave him one of Alain's photographs. Not that he held out much hope that it would do any good showing it to a British officer, but the only thing that made sense was to try everything. They shook hands and promised to meet "whenever this war is over. Meanwhile let's keep our heads down!"

Feeling suddenly very alone, Nicolas tagged along with a French cavalry unit of one hundred men who took over what looked to be the best campsite on a large plain, although, given the heat from hell, he could not understand why they had not gone a little further to where there were a few trees.

"You there - where in the bleedin' hell is your uniform?" A sweating sergeant suddenly stood before him.

Nicolas answered the first thing that came into his head. "They ran out of the larger sizes in Rennes, had only small ones left. I couldn't get the jacket over my shoulders and the pants." He mimed trying to get into clothes much too tight.

"Welcome to efficient army organization!" the

sergeant grunted. "Not to worry, I'll have a uniform for ye sooner or later."

Nicolas didn't wonder how; he was too relieved, having passed this first hurdle.

The heat never lessened, not even in the evening. By then Nicolas' feet were on fire and his mouth was dry from the whirling dust and grit clouds.

They watched another unit leaving on what was supposed to be an eight-hour march up-country, towards Lake Devna. Later he heard that men, horses and mules collapsed from heatstroke and lack of water. Some died.

Duc was still skittish but seemed otherwise all right.

Then British units settled on the other side of the valley and began full dress uniform drills. In this heat? What insanity! More British units were expected to disembark as soon as the harbor was cleared, but to everyone's consternation their first units had arrived without baggage ponies or mules. The French sent down theirs so supplies could be moved out of the way. The next ship also arrived without means of transport.

In the evening, two cooks from the 13th Light Dragoons walked over to Nicolas' unit and sheepishly told the sad tale of the bottom of their large pot suddenly falling into the fire, stew meat and all! After everyone had a good laugh about the mishap the British soldiers went back carrying a solid pot and another piece of meat and Nicolas developed his first doubts about British preparedness.

Not a single bullet had been fired yet, but already incredible stories were buzzing around regarding the Varna hospital, an old barracks nearly a mile long whose capacity was said to be 10,000 men. It was filling up rapidly with cholera and typhus victims. How could this happen so quickly? What if Alain was there?

Nicolas talked himself into riding over to the hospital. Still quite a distance from it he needed to press a handkerchief over his nose and mouth, but even so the stench was overpowering. He walked inside - this was a hospital? How could anybody recover in here? The soldiers were lying on their blankets on filthy floors, in uniforms which were stiff with dried mud, and there was barely enough room to walk between them. There were no cots, no pallets, no linens, no bandages, no water. Not even buckets to vomit into - only plenty of rats.

Nicolas had to leave after having looked at about one quarter of the place.

Outside he talked with the two orderlies, both in dirty uniforms and mud-encrusted boots. A doctor in a dirty apron walked over to them, absently twirling an unlit cigar in reddened hands. He listened for a while, then announced to no one in particular that his colleague would not last the hour. He shrugged tiredly, lit his cigar and walked away.

"So we'll be down to one. Started with three. "Yeah, - that's all we are, a damn burial squad," one man complained. "French, Brits, Turks, makes no difference. They can't nail coffins together fast enough but get the bodies to us anyways, wrapped in their own blankets. That's how we bury 'em, but every night the locals come and dig 'em up again. Why, yer askin'? Ye must be new. For the blankets, of course. People here have nothin'. How many buried so far? Fifty to sixty a day, I'd say; had to switch to mass graves. One loses count."

"But you keep records of names, causes, dates of death, etc., don't you?"

"Course we do, but it's hard with no proper place to keep them. No drawers, no boxes. Papers fly away," the other orderly explained. "Ye wouldn't catch me spendin' another minute in here if I had a choice, 'n' neither should you!"

Good advice. Perhaps he ought to be more careful, even wash his hands like Docteur C., but how could that make a difference?

It seemed to him that the gulf between thinking about something and doing it was becoming deeper every day. It had taken him every bit of willpower to keep his mouth clamped shut against his churning insides as he forced himself to go down the rows, careful not to step on a hand or a foot. If he didn't have the stomach for this now, how was he going to manage when the fighting started? When he'd be looking for Alain among the wounded and the dying?

Meanwhile nothing happened, except the girl in the dream had followed him. Again he had felt strangely lost when she was gone. They still looked like each other, but he was aware of some slight differences - well, after all, she was a girl.

Boredom set in during the long days and nights when there was nothing to do but keep weapons in good condition and wait. No one knew for what, but everyone had an opinion anyway - Varna is important, it is our base for invading the Crimea - no, what are you on about, it's too far away, it's only a landing site - Our target is Sebastopol, of course, don't ye know nothing … what is Sebastopol anyways - only a huge fortress with millions of Russkies inside waitin' to shoot ye dead - so why are we holed up *here* twiddlin' our thumbs - waitin' for more Brits to get here, they're always late - you really think them generals know what they're doin' - who the hell knows - salt pork and hard biscuits, I'm sick of 'em already - bet officers eat better - hey, that reminds me, d'you see them 'Traveling Gents' yesterday - what yer talkin' about? I'm talkin' 'bout fancy gents comin' in their yachts to 'watch the war' from that big hill over there, through telescopy glasses; on regular tours they bring 'em; I hear they have themselves fancy picnics under umbrellas, served up by their la-di-dah servants - yeah, 'n' we'll be runnin' out of food and water soon, for men *and* horses - course I mean it, have ye ever known me not to be serious about food?"

At long last the French and British set off along the coastal plain towards Sebastopol, with Ottoman forces bringing up the rear. No one knew how many miles; not so bad if it wouldn't be so hot early in the day, and if you weren't carrying a load of equipment and rations. Like marching inside a hot oven it was, and it got harder when the plain changed to rough terrain with boulders and rocks, ridges and hollows.

What was that? A shot? Where'd it come from?

Cossack riders. They're the only ones with those small horses. There could be hundreds hiding behind the ridges. Could pick us off, one by one. How big is that Russian army anyway? - Big, everybody knows that - no, I want to know *how* big. The biggest in the world, that good enough for ye?

Evening came, hot and swarming with flies which annoyed Duc. For the first time, they could see enemy fires flickering in the distance. They made Duc nervous; he didn't like where he was. Neither did Nicolas.

And again nothing happened - nothing - just waiting, waiting, waiting. Idleness hung over them like a curse. Nicolas started to feel like going in search of a fight.

Anything but this senseless waiting.

Chapter XIV

Tutor Webb's letter arrived after Henri's departure for the Crimea and Anne asked to read it.

"Mother!" Madeleine was surprised. "It is *my* letter."

"I know, of course it is. I only want to make sure there is nothing inappropriate in it."

"Father would never feel the need to censure it!"

Anne gave in; they were both worried about him, wondering whether he and Roger Fenton were still on the 'Hecla' or already in the Crimea, and what was awaiting them there. Anne could not face having words with her daughter and withdrew into her studio; Madeleine went up to her room to read her letter.

Dear Mademoiselle Desrosiers,

I embrace the opportunity of writing these lines, hoping they find you in good health as this leaves me at present. I bless God for it, and may I offer my belated good wishes on your recent birthday!

"The sails were fill'd and light the fair wind blew." Well, a fair wind may have blown for Lord Byron but not for us during a stormy voyage! Let me only say that it was full of surprises and took more than a month to get to Varna (look for it on our map). We finally went ashore on rotten planks laid down on rotting timbers, a scant two feet above refuse-choked water.

I confess I quickly looked away from two dead dogs bobbing up and down between cabbages. And the smell ...

We were immediately surrounded by beggars of all ages and vendors, dogs and cats, however the most alarming sight were dozens and dozens of our sick soldiers lying on the bare planks under a broiling sun! Awaiting transport to a hospital I was told, in some instances for days, apparently without water or food,

We arrived without mules and ponies but were able to borrow some from the French. Not a very auspicious beginning. I wonder why this landing site was selected: there is no real road leading from the harbor to camp, only a path of dried mud which turns into muck after every rain. Did I mention that it rains every day?

Everything here is very colorful, especially the Turkish caïques, the traditional fishing boats which are painted in vivid colors and furnished with equally colorful pillows. These boats are only about five meters long, and it seems every Turkish sailor wears a fez and smokes a long pipe.

I read over what I have written so far and find it extremely boring (I fear you and Mademoiselle Cecily would have 'nodded off in class!) so let me tell you about some Turkish customs and beliefs I have come across.

I was walking one of our horses along an area of dry grass; he had injured his leg on board ship and I needed to assess his condition. He was mostly chestnut brown with a great many white spots all over. Two Turkish soldiers watched me and shook their heads. The horse was fine, he did not limp, what were they worried about that I did not see? They walked over to me, and we bowed to each other. "No, no!" they said emphatically, "bad horse, ver' bad horse. Too much color: soldier die in battle. We know, is true, is true." I made them repeat this several times to make sure I understood their broken French. "Are you saying that many-colored horses are bad luck?" "Oui, oui!" they agreed, delighted that I had understood. "Peut-être we fight together, but only on one-color horse, yes?" They must really believe this: I have yet to see Turkish soldiers on two-colored horses (there must be a name for them).

They also shoe their horses in a most intriguing way. It takes four men: Nr. 1 ties a rope around the horse's leg and keeps the leg pulled up. Nr. 2 holds the horse's tail and swats away the flies (there are always flies). Nr. 3 holds the horse's head and talks soothingly to him, and Nr. 4 squats down and quickly hammers in eight nails.

We are supposed to leave on an eight-hour march soon, so this has to be all for now or I miss my chance of sending this with an officer who is going home sick.

I apologize for the dogs. Please let me know if I ought to exercise more restraint in my next letter which may have to be cross-written.

I remain very sincerely yours,

Colin Webb

Madeleine read the letter several times and decided to show it to her mother. Anne read it slowly, frowning every now and then, then gave it back.

"So - what do you think?"

"Well, I think Mr. Webb might have spared you the dogs. And those poor, poor soldiers just lying there - why did he have to write about them?"

"Because they were there and because this is where he is now. In his lessons he always tried to lay the facts before us. Just because the war has not started for him yet - what would you like him to write about? Pretty flowers with butterflies flitting over a sunny meadow? Bluebirds chirping in the trees? I want to know what is happening over there!"

"Madeleine! I am surprised at you. You ought to take my concerns seriously, not ridicule them!"

Madeleine gave her mother a quick hug. "I'm sorry. I intended no disrespect. Truly, I didn't. I simply want to find out and to understand."

Anne sighed. "Why don't I know this by now? I discovered this when you were three years old. You are so your father's daughter."

"And that is good, isn't it?"

"Of course it is good, very good. But one more thing: when you answer the letter, I hope you keep in mind that no matter how nice and interesting Mr. Webb is, that is all he is and can be to you, a tutor."

"Oh, Mother!" Madeleine rolled her eyes.

She decided to answer right away. On plain paper, not the pretty flowered one which, she had been warned, would suggest that she was welcoming a suitor's attentions. Such idiocy.

She sat down at her desk, unsure of herself. What was the proper way to address him? Never mind proper, she wanted to strike the right note. How should she begin? Suddenly it came to her. She smiled, grabbed a sheet of plain ecru paper, and began writing.

Dear Tutor Webb,

I was glad to receive your letter and astonished at the

exquisite formality of its first paragraph. It is so impressively correct that I keep wondering: did you by any chance lift it word for word from a letter-writing manual? Before I answer your letter I must tell you how much I appreciate that you are writing to me as an adult. Mother, of course, still thinks of me as a child; sometimes I fear this may never change. You are seeing and experiencing things I shall never see, but that doesn't mean I don't want to hear about them.

You didn't say what their illness was - is it cholera? I hear that is very contagious. Is there no hospital where you are? I am asking because my father is going to the Crimea with the photographer Roger Fenton. I cannot ask Mother because she started worrying before he had left. Things here are as they always are. Nothing changes. Can you think what we people at home could do? How to go about it? I cannot only read the newspapers or magazines and books, arrange flowers, sip tea and carry on inane conversations. Don't suggest knitting; we already do that. Did you write to Cecily, too? She is spending a few months with family in England. I miss her but I miss my father more.

I nearly forgot to ask: Why were ill soldiers so neglected? Is there or isn't there a hospital in the area? Who is in charge? What is going to happen when the fighting starts and soldiers have to be taken care of, too. Please write again and tell me everything!

Sincerely, Madeleine Desrosiers

Certain that there was nothing objectionable in what she had written, she asked her mother whether she wanted to read her response, expecting and hoping that the answer would be 'no', that making the offer was enough.

It was. Anne handed Madeleine enough stamps to cover several letters, adding pointedly, "These are also for letters to your father."

Madeleine decided to use the rest of the morning going through the newspapers. She was immediately sidetracked when the word 'Varna' jumped out at her. More than half of the town was destroyed in a fire that burned for three nights. British and French supplies waiting to be distributed could not be saved, among them a large shipment of boots. Mention was made that a previous shipment had been of *left* boots only (why weren't boots shipped *in pairs?*). Food was lost, too. Afterwards, the town was sacked. "Biscuits burn beautifully," according to one eyewitness. "What else was there to do later but get drunk like a skunk?"

Cholera was also claiming so many lives that formal burials were not held any longer, another report said. Earlier on, trumpeters had always led the processions by playing the 'March for the Dead', but hearing that lugubrious tune from early morning into deep night, day after day after day, was considered to be too demoralizing for the sick soldiers.

By now, she read, 27,000 British, 60,000 French and

7,000 Turks had disembarked. No one had a clear idea of Russia's strength: official estimates ranged from 20,000 to 100,000. That huge a difference - that couldn't be right; something had to be wrong with these numbers.

She read on. The Allied had no current Russian maps, only ancient ones - this was becoming too depressing, too grim. She wished she could talk with her father about the dispatches, there was no one else. Her belief that he would be safe in the Crimea was shrinking to the hope that he would be, but she had to keep that to herself.

Perhaps it was good that she had to get ready for a dance. It was certainly better than sitting home and knitting - all that knitting done by her mother and friends and thousands of women - by the time those scarves and mittens made it to the Crimea, it might be spring. They wouldn't be needed any longer because surely the war would be over by then.

There had been no other letter from her tutor; she hoped that was due to erratic mail service. For the first time she gave some thought to the hardship lived through by the those left behind, the mothers, wives, sweethearts …

She wished she had a sweetheart. Being two years older, Cecily had two and couldn't make up her mind which one she liked better which meant she talked about both of them all the time. Cecily also had an English cousin who was 'two years engaged' and had been told by her fiancé to read only books suggested by him.

"Only a question or two, if you don't mind, Cecily," Madeleine had said. "What gives him the right to sit in judgment over what she can and cannot read? And why on earth did she promise?"

That nearly led to a quarrel, but Madeleine had learned to hold back before it was too late. So she did not add that this young man struck her as insufferably conceited: did he have doubts that his fiancée was worthy of him - or didn't it matter any longer because she had three hundred pounds a year, or whatever the amount settled on her was?

It wasn't that young men were not interested in Madeleine. Jean-Luc of dancing school days had remained a faithful admirer and was now a head taller. No dandruff to look down on, but his hands were still sweaty. He was as nice as ever, but nice was not enough. He agreed with everything she suggested or said. It was the same with other pleasant young men, except that most of them didn't quite know how to deal with her interest in what was happening in Turkey and America and tended to think of her as too outspoken because she didn't agree sweetly with everything they said.

But enough of doing nothing. She had just enough time to go through some of the articles on Florence Nightingale she had set aside. She started with the one about her arrival with thirty-eight nurses (who *were* all in their thirties, Mother was right!) in Constantinople from where they were taken across to Scutari where an old Turkish barracks large enough to hold thousands of men was supposed to have been transformed into a hospital.

There, according to reporter William Russell, the sick, wounded and dying were lying on dirty floors, in their own dirty clothes, with rolled-up uniforms serving as pillows. The doctors accepted no help from the nurses; they looked down on them as interfering females, low-class, most likely of easy morals and given to drink.

Madeleine had already read that Florence Nightingale had come up against this attitude before. She was from a wealthy family and had no intention of waiting for governmental approval. She therefore bought the basic necessities with her own funds: hundreds of brushes and soap for general cleaning, boilers to start a laundry service, tin baths, towels and sheets, operating tables, folding screens, bed pans, small-toothed combs to get rid of lice, stump sleeves. Then she began the herculean task of trying to establish some sort of hygiene and sanitation, separating the ill from the wounded, providing good food and proper lighting.

Five days after her arrival large numbers of injured arrived after the first battle, the battle of Alma, and totally overwhelmed the hospital.

It took many weeks until the promised funding from the War Department came through and she was officially appointed superintendent of nurses. At least now the doctors could no longer ignore her.

She continued with her purchases of small stoves, chloride of lime and whatever was needed, and supervised her nurses. Often she could be seen at night, carrying a lamp. Not only to check on patients, but also to make very sure that none of her nurses slipped into the wards after the 8:30 p.m. curfew!

Madeleine was very much affected by these accounts. They had good news from her father, but none from Tutor Webb. Every day she looked for a letter, and naturally her mother misinterpreted her impatience and concern. They had words, Madeleine explained and apologized and Anne was relieved. Thank God this was one less thing she had to worry about.

'Stump sleeves' hadn't made an impact on Madeleine at first reading, but now she thought they might be even more important than those endless mittens and scarves. She went upstairs and knocked at her mother's door. Anne was sitting by the window, Stendhal's 'Le Rouge et le Noir' upside down on her lap.

"Do you ever tire of knitting those mittens and scarves?" she asked her.

"Of course, but it is for a good cause. You're not thinking of quitting, sweetheart, are you?"

"No, not at all, but when we go to the knitting circle tomorrow afternoon, I'd like to suggest that we also knit stump sleeves. Or better still, *you* should suggest it. Most of the ladies won't take a suggestion seriously if it comes from a girl."

"A stump sleeve? Is that - is that what I think it is?"

Madeleine nodded.

"I never knew such things existed." Anne sat up. "We'd have to make different sizes, I suppose. It is an excellent idea. *Your* idea. You propose it!"

That night Madeleine had trouble falling asleep.

When she did, her uneasy sleep was peopled by wounded soldiers in torn and dirty uniforms, getting soaked in a steady downpour, crowding around her to receive their stump sleeves.

When she had handed out the last one and showed them that her basket was empty, they angrily limped and lurched and pushed toward her, coming very close and threatening her with their crutches. She knew she would fall and be trampled, but suddenly, someone said, very clearly, "Leave her alone!"

Just for an instant he was there, the boy - a tall, young man now - and then he was gone. She woke up in a panic until she realized that she was at home, in her room, in her bed.

She pulled the covers tightly around herself, closed her eyes, and hoped he would come again but fell asleep.

Chapter XV

Nicolas felt that he had left Rennes and France an eternity ago. Days and nights ran into each other, weeks into months. He was stuck in a place which made it impossible to do what he had set out to do, but what he was witnessing often left him in despair and thinking that he was losing his mind.

For weeks he had been with another French cavalry unit and was still amazed at how easily that had come about.

When he had pointed to his tattered civilian clothing (the sergeant who had promised to provide him with a uniform had died of cholera) and protested that he was not a cavalry soldier, the new sergeant had walked around Duc a couple of times, nodded his satisfaction and said, "Fine horse ye got here. Welcome to the cavalry, son!" and tossed him a rifle. "I'll get yer particulars later."

Nicolas looked the weapon over. It was different from any he had ever seen. Impatiently, the sergeant grabbed it back and demonstrated it. "This here is called a Minié, named after the inventor of the long bullets it fires: that's right, long bullets. They're much more dangerous than round ones, and this here rifle is accurate over almost nearly 600 yards! Best thing about it? The Russkies have nothin' to go against it! Just follow the others: aim 'n' shoot!"

Before Nicolas knew it he was in his first skirmish. His only thought was to stay alive. He did as ordered: He aimed and shot. He knew he had killed.

"You're a cool one," the sergeant commented a day later, "and not a scratch on ye! Glad to have ye, whoever you are. Here, found ye a uniform."

From a dead soldier, obviously. Well, nothing to be squeamish about. It was a decent fit but he had to see about a patch for the jacket front. The previous owner, poor devil, must have been shot through the heart. He didn't need that bloody hole as a constant reminder.

First chance he had he took himself over to see the vivandière of his camp. Each French unit had one: she was usually a soldier' wife, marched with the regiment and saw to food, drink and laundry for the men; in some cases she even tended the wounded. She covered and stitched up the hole with extra fabric and sewed a sturdy pocket over it. When Nicolas asked what he owed her she refused payment, saying only that she had a sailor-son about his age aboard one of the French ships.

"It is a nice change to meet a well-mannered young man like you," she said when he thanked her. "Here," she handed him two apples, "Bet you don't get enough fruit." Nicolas hadn't seen an apple in a long time. Neither had Duc. Of course he smelled the apples on him and looked for them. They enjoyed them together, Duc's disappearing in a couple of great gulps. When he kept nudging Nicolas to come up with more, Nicolas gave him his other half.

He was stuck in a bad mood. He had survived several skirmishes, but now his feet hurt constantly; there was no way to dry his wet boots and wet socks. What was worse, he had been robbed of his money while he slept. He had intended to buy a thicker blanket for Duc at one of the auctions of deceased officers' effects. He'd had a glimpse into one of these tents - the list of what was available, provided you had the means, was unending: kits, clothes, boots, weapons, watches, telescopes, books, silver candlesticks (if 'your lordship' needed to go to war in style!), dishes, chairs, mattresses, pillows and blankets. That is *if* anything worthwhile was left after officers had gone through everything.

The thief had left him the photographs, not that they would be of much use now. Although army regulations demanded that officers and enlisted men be clean-shaven, by now almost all faces were hidden under beards. His own was long enough to do with what he had seen others do: wring rain water out of it. It rained every damn day. It was also getting colder and a beard provided at least an illusion of some warmth. Illusion was better than nothing.

He wondered if he'd recognize a bearded Thomas and realized how much he missed his friend.

His whole body ached with fatigue. He slept only fitfully, trying to fool himself into thinking that he was lying snug and warm under a pile of thick blankets, even though he couldn't stop shivering under the thin single one.

Damn Alain and his selfish escapade which had brought him into this hell. Already he had seen too many men die, too many wounded left lying where they had fallen, waiting for help which never arrived in time. Too many rider-less horses galloping aimlessly around, mad with fear.

Before he knew it he was caught in the eight-hour insanity of a real battle. Inkerman they called it. The fog was so dense that he and everyone else felt blinded, cut off from everything. Trying to remain standing in rainwater-filled gullies and ravines, alert to bayonet-ting the invisible enemy before he got to him. Weighted down by the mud clinging to his boots. Advancing with the others, running bent over even though he had ceased to believe that offered more safety. Retreating, never seeing how far. From the start it had been im-possible to make out shouted and trumpeted commands which were lost in cannon noises, shell explosions, the hiss of rifle bullets whizzing by, comrades screaming and cursing or praying loudly to their saints. From the beginning it had been impossible to know friend from foe.

He thought he was going deaf from the constant gun noise; there was a steady ringing in his ears, his eyes were tearing from smoke and grit and his head hurt. He struggled through the thick fog, straight ahead or what he assumed was straight ahead. How could anyone tell in this damn fog?

He came through Inkerman in one piece but with a nasty gash to his bridle arm which he didn't even re-member getting. He tended to it himself with his oint-ment and a handkerchief. After what he had witnessed, he had not much faith in military doctors and never ventured out without these two items.

Little was said about their hard-earned victory ex-cept that losses had been very heavy on both sides.

Instead, all the talk was about the desperate heroism of the Light Brigade which had been ordered to attack straight into Russian fire on October 25. He hoped that Thomas was all right. He had to be; the 11th Hussars, someone had said, had been part of this insane seven-minute dash. Fighting with sabers and lances against cannons - what madman had come up with this crazy plan?

After Inkerman, he had retreated to the French camp with his unit, and another wait to push further towards Sebastopol began. It was getting colder. Water puddles froze. And still no winter gear. He needed a warm blanket for Duc who was not ill but getting thin. He always looked for more food. All horses did. The men, too.

On the evening of November 14 an odd quiet, the kind that sometimes comes before a storm, settled over their camp. The sky turned a strange leaden yellow. When he heard, 'Hurricane! Hurricane!' Nicolas, riding Duc, followed the sergeant who was racing for the shelter of some huge rocks. He must know what he was doing.

Hurricane - what was that? Pressed against the rock and holding on to Duc for dear life, he found out quickly enough: A screaming wind arose, accompanied by thunder and lightning. Tent poles snapped, tents were lifted up, torn to shreds and tossed about like toys; barrels bounded down the hills, men and horses and equipment and uprooted trees flew through the air - if he hadn't seen it with his own eyes he would never have believed it. Not only was not one tent left standing, a hospital tent collapsed onto the sick and wounded, he found out later. And a regimental drum was found, more than two miles behind the Russian lines. The drum story circulated for days with the drum-mileage jumping wildly between three and twelve miles - while twelve may have been exaggerated, Nicolas had no doubt about the two-mile version! He was lucky; he and Duc were unhurt, but he also knew that if Duc had been his old self, he would never have been able to restrain him.

"Worst damn hurricane ever!" everybody kept saying, working at clearing debris. Whatever it was called, he hoped it was his first and last one. It was followed by torrential rains. Nothing could be done about the twenty-one British ships out on the open sea waiting to come into harbor. They crashed into each other, ground each other to pieces and went down with their crews and cargo.

Losing the men was bad, of course. But they had all counted on urgently needed supplies: Winter clothing and food for the men; twenty days' worth of hay and barley for the horses and mules, badly needed new boots. Boots were supposed to last a year but fell apart much sooner, remaining wet all the time. The last shipment had been of *left* boots only - instead a shipment of left boots, now only small sizes? Who was the genius in charge? Someone mentioned clothing still stuck in knee-high harbor mud. "Couldn't we at least get those out?" Nicolas asked, trying to warm his hands by shoving them into his armpits. He shivered in spite of the sheepskin jerkin he had taken off a dead Cossack. Sleet and snow turned the camps into places of ankle-deep mud which weighed down the boots and the horses' hooves, sometimes freezing overnight. Dry tent floors were a distant memory.

"Why? On three miles of mud instead of a road?" the sergeant asked, "Bet everything's already moldy, rotting away."

And as had been predicted, the hurricane was followed by another outbreak of cholera, a particularly ferocious one. Nicolas wondered why; he knew he ought to check the hospital again but couldn't get himself to do it.

Duc had become his main concern. He still valiantly did what he was asked to do but slowly, lethargically. He hadn't been himself for some time. It was pitiful to see how his flanks started to cave in. The sparkle was gone from his eyes. The incessant noises had frightened him into trembling and shaking, but now he often also seemed unwilling or unable to get up and move. Nicolas had bartered away Docteur C.'s compass for barley weeks earlier, but that was almost gone. He had nothing left to sell. What in hell was he going to do when that bag was empty? At least Duc didn't seem to be running a fever. All he could do was hope that this was a good sign.

Snow was still on the ground in late March when a strange-looking van pulled by one horse struggled up to their camp. British, Nicolas thought when he heard the two men speak. 'Photographic Van' was stenciled on both sides of the contraption. Curious, he walked over to it.

"What are you photographing? Vous prenez des

photos de quoi?" he asked the two men who started to unload equipment.

"Oh, good, a Frenchman who speaks English! The war, of course! Been doing it for the past two months; just left a British camp. None of us speak French, by the way, except the boss's friend."

"Mind if I watch?"

"Well, wait . . . you aren't a photographer, are you?"

"No."

"That's good then, wait here." He went off to talk to someone and returned a few moments later.

"By the way, I am Marcus Sparling, assistant to Mr. Roger Fenton. He said all right."

"Thank you. My name is Nicolas Favreau, and I am not a soldier."

"You're not? You could have fooled me. You'll have to explain that some other time."

Marcus kept up a steady stream of explanations while he carefully positioned a tripod on which the camera was going to rest. He talked about glass plates which had to be coated with an emulsion of wet collodion in the van, then rushed from there to the camera to be exposed and rushed back into the van *in not more than five minutes* because only wet plates developed well.

"Collodion is a solution of nitrocellulose, alcohol and ether; it is used to coat photographic plates," he added before Nicolas could ask.

"So you see," he ended his explanations, "this van is our darkroom, most likely the only one of its kind in the world. The subject or subjects have to be planned and ready ahead of time. And this gentleman here, Monsieur Desrosiers, is Mr. Fenton's friend and colleague."

The man kept staring at Nicolas.

Nicolas thought it couldn't be because he was dirty and unkempt. Everybody was, but it felt strange. He shrugged and started to think: the photographer had been around for two months and might - well, chances were probably slimmer than slim - but what if he had come across Alain, had photographed him? Would Mr. Fenton let him look through the pictures? He was stuck here without other ideas, not knowing where to search next, doubting that he would ever find Alain - what could he lose by asking?

Since he was the only Frenchman around who spoke English and every courtesy and help was supposed to be extended to the British photographer, Nicolas was asked to accompany Fenton on some of his outings. As all he was doing was waiting for the next skirmish or battle and nothing was happening, he was glad to go and immediately noticed that no photographs were taken of wounded or dead lying on a battle field, not soldiers,

not even horses. They had all been removed along with
other reminders of war such as weapons, shells, bits of
clothing, caps, saddle bags. It even looked as if sand had
been poured over places where blood must have pooled
- everything was gone, except sometimes cannon balls.
Left there, or had they been put back again, later? He
was about to ask when he was told this was in order to
make the photographs creditable *but also* palatable to the
reading public. In other words: the sensibilities of the
people at home had to be protected. They were not supposed to see the war.

For the first time in his life, Nicolas felt like getting
drunk.

Every time they went out, Monsiur Desrosiers' eyes
were on him. Why? He had never seen the man before.
Once he asked him whether he had any family back in
Fougerès - parents, a brother, a sister?

"Non, Monsieur, I have no family."

Strangely enough the gentleman seemed relieved by
his answer. Well, whatever the reason, this was a good
moment to ask him whether he would take a letter for
Docteur C. back to Rennes and mail it from there. And
might it be possible to see the photographs of French
soldiers? He explained why.

"I don't know. You've set yourself an impossible
task, finding one among so many thousands," Monsieur
Desrosiers said, "but I can ask Mr. Fenton for you. And

of course I'll take your letter and see to it that it is sent on."

As Nicolas had expected, Alain was not among the photographed French soldiers, but he was given a two-day pass to check the nearest hospital ('nobody's goin' nowhere right now'). Alain was not there either. The place looked tidier, but again he wondered how anybody could recover in such stench, among such awful sounds - and why had he tempted fate by exposing himself to cholera again?

The photographers had left by the time he got back, but the French chef Alexis Soyer, a friend of Florence Nightingale, had just arrived. The story made the rounds that he had worked in a famous London club for some time, and that he had cooked a state dinner for Queen Victoria and Prince Albert! He came full of ideas of how to improve cooking for the British soldiers and with many copies of his 'The Modern Housewife'. Thomas' book!

He had also brought along several of his patented portable stoves and demonstrated their use; also another one of his inventions which he had named 'the Scutari Teapot', an eight-quart tea kettle. His first order of business, however, was to have all boilers lined with tin, maintaining that copper is poisonous.

For his tea he used an over-sized coffee filter, spread out the tea leaves on it, poured boiling water over them, shouted, "Et voilà!" and bowed to the admiring spectators. This was not only a more economical way of brewing tea but resulted in a vastly improved beverage.

Nicolas was fascinated by the man and his inventions and hoped that he'd have the chance to tell Thomas about having met the author of his 'favorite' book - if they both were still alive when this war was over.

He was bone-tired and discouraged. The unrealistic hope of finding Alain had dwindled down to no hope at all, leaving him with gloomy thoughts and a growing resentment. What was worse, he realized, he was afraid now. How long could his luck last? He thought of the many comrades whose luck had run out. Why for them and not for him?

When he had dreamed of seeing something of the world, this was not how he had imagined seeing it. How could he have been so naïve?

Chapter XVI

Only a semblance of calm had descended on the Caradec home since the arrival of Alain's telegram.

"Am well home soon Alain"

It was after lunch and his mother sat in her favorite armchair, surrounded by photographs of her son, clutching the telegram which was about to disintegrate from being handled by her tear-dampened hands. "Only eight words," she repeated over and over again in a dull voice. "Why didn't he tell us where he is? How he is? What does 'soon' mean? How soon? And how long did this telegram take to reach us?

Perhaps he was well then, but he could have been hurt again the very same day, or the next week, and ships are dangerous, they break up and go down in storms, and Alain doesn't know how to swim! Why didn't I let him learn how to swim, why? What if he is - no, I cannot let myself think that." Then she'd stare at the stack of laundry-fresh handkerchiefs and chose a new one to weep into.

Docteur C. had given up explaining that being in the military meant *not* divulging certain details such as locations, but he was worried, too. He sat at his desk, unable to concentrate. According to the news, the Allied armies were supposed to push towards Sebastopol at last. Soon, they said. Hopefully before the Russians secured their naval base by adding even more trenches. Soon? The papers had been talking about 'soon' for months.

He was worried how and why Alain had been sent home. How badly wounded was he? There was no reason other than having been wounded which sent a soldier home, something which he deliberately withheld from his wife. Had Alain received adequate care? He went back and forth between worrying about his son and being angry at him. He also hoped Nicolas was all right. He hadn't heard from him in a very long time, either.

He was trying to catch up on paperwork when a servant came to announce that two women were at the door.

"The older one said, "Tell Docteur Caradec that Berthe is here with her daughter Marie and that she has something important to tell him about Nicolas."

Docteur C. got up immediately and ordered the usual to be brought into the small salon.

Dear Lord, I hope Alain is all right, and Nicolas, too, of course. Perhaps she has news of Alain. No, how could she? She doesn't read, she doesn't get the papers. He took a moment to regain his composure before he went in to greet his visitors.

"Madame Berthe," he said, relieved to see that she was not in tears and quite calm. "It is a pleasure to meet you at last. I hope everybody is well?"

He shook hands with her. So this was the woman who was so dear to Nicolas. After he greeted her daughter he sat down and waited until apple juice had been poured and a plate of cookies placed within their reach.

As soon as the servant had left the room he asked, "You came to tell me something that concerns Nicolas?"

"It be a long, long, story, Docteur."

"Where Nicolas is concerned, I always have time."

"Good, I have to start at the true beginnin'. Now this woman Rozenn brung him to me when he wasn't two weeks old. At her wits'end she were, not knowin' nothin' 'bout new-borns. She said she were his mother, paid me to look after him 'n' promised to visit Sundays. Missed most o' them, to tell ye the truth. Now Nicolas, he never took to her. Never. He was five when she come for the last time 'n' what does she tell me?

That she were *not* his mother! That a friend o' hers was! Said she'd pay good money if I were of a mind to keep 'im. Very angry she makes me, talkin' 'bout the boy like he's a piece of goods. So I tell her of course he stays, but to stuff her money where the sun don't shine - beg yer pardon, Docteur, oughtn't to put it like that in polite company, but that's 'xactly what I said."

"Mother! You promised you wouldn't!"

Berthe took some sips of apple juice while her daughter, blushing furiously, hid her head in her hands.

"Never mind, Marie. What's said is said 'n' what's done is done." Serenely unembarrassed, Berthe continued.

"Anyways, haven't seen her these many years, didn't know if she be alive or not, but here she suddenly is, early afternoon yesterday, at me daughter's house where I lives now. Real bad she looks, legs all swelled up. Old. Not breathin' good, either.

'Why d'ye come when it be so hard on ye?' I ask.

'Can't ye see I'm real sick?' she says. 'Priest said to make me peace with God, get this thing what bothers me so much off me chest afore it's too late.'

She catches her breath 'n' this is what she says to me: 'I be with my friend Jannet when she had her babes. Yeah, ye heard right: *two, not one.* A boy first, then a girl, but already she, Jannet, is bad with the fever ... so I takes the boy 'n' tell her he be dead.

'Ye tell her what?' I shout. 'Ye heard me, I tell her he be dead!' she shouts back at me. Shoutin' makes her choke. I push a glass o' water closer so she can reach it. I yell, 'How could ye?' but not in such polite words.

'I look at her 'n' can tell guilt has gnawed at her somethin' awful. Terrible bad she looked. Anyways, she says she took her friend to the Hôtel-Dieu, made her leave the girl for the Sisters 'n' walked home with her. Found out she died the next day. Was a widow, too, the poor thing, such a young widow."

She sat back, spent. Marie gave her another glass of juice.

Docteur C. sat unmoving, stunned into silence.

"Now this be the important part: Nicolas *has* to know. Ye see, all them years he dreams 'bout a girl who looks like him, he tells me. I say it's only a dream, what else can it be? He keeps sayin' no, it's more, it's - he thinks real hard 'n' comes out with 'she's *another meself.*' I asks ye, how does a boy only five or six think of puttin' it like that? But me, *I'm* gettin' 'round now to thinkin' he is right. Bein' twins 'n' all, there could be more to this.

Marie here says that places like Hôtel-Dieu must keep records. What if he could find his sister?

And there is one more thing. Near a year ago, Nicolas, he come by to say good-bye afore he leaves with a story 'bout workin' for ye in Lyon. He says not to worry if he can't come see me for a long time. Now he never stayed away so long, so I worry, 'course I worry. Then I think 'bout what he said 'bout workin' for ye 'n' not believin' it then. Don't believe it now. That boy never learnt to lie good enough so ye'd believe 'im! But Docteur, *ye* must know where he is. *We have to tell 'im.* Please tell me where - oh my, now it's me gettin' out o' breath!"

She waved away another glass of juice.

"Where is Nicolas?"

Docteur C. quickly filled her in on how Alain had enlisted without telling anyone, and how Nicolas had left nearly a year ago to try to find him.

Berthe shook her head in exasperated disbelief.

"Who goes to war when he don't have to, who? Nicolas, he would! Thinks 'n' thinks 'n' does what he thinks is right. Now Docteur, tell me true: ye *order* 'im to go to this Tur - ye knows, I means the place he went?" Her dark eyes bored into his with an intensity that would have made him think of the Spanish Inquisition if it hadn't been for the gentle expression that remained on her face.

"Did ye? Order him?"

"Mother, take a rest," Marie interrupted. "This is too much for you."

"Don't need rest, just want an answer."

"No, no, Madame Berthe, no, of course I didn't order him. I would never do that, but I did accept his offer."

Berthe said quietly to herself. "That's me boy Nicolas. Thinks 'n' thinks till he finds what needs doin' 'n' does it, even if it look crazy to others. He write ye?"

"A few times; he was all right then, but the last time was more than two, no three months ago."

"Three months ? And yer own boy?"

"He was wounded, we don't know how; he is supposed to be on the way home, but we haven't heard anything from him for quite some time either."

Berthe nodded. "That be the hardest, the not knowin', the waitin' 'n' more waitin', always the waitin'," she said quietly. "I know, I remember. My Marrec …" She shook her head. "Thank ye, Docteur, that's all I come to say 'n' to find out. Time to go home, Marie."

They all stood.

"How did you come here?" Docteur C. asked, looking out through a window. A strong wind had come up, together with the first drops.

"In our cart," Marie answered.

"I'd like to send you back in a carriage. It looks like rain. We Bretons are known for understanding and predicting the weather, aren't we, Madame Berthe? Someone will follow with your cart as soon as it lets up."

"No, thank ye. I don't mind gettin' wet."

"Today I would like for you to arrive home without getting wet. It is a small way of thanking you, Madame Berthe - not only for coming here today and talking to me, but for all you have done for Nicolas. He learned much from you when he was a boy."

Berthe, speechless for a moment, nudged her daughter. "Ye hear that, Marie? How can we say no with Doc puttin' it like that?"

Docteur C. saw them into the carriage as the rain began to fall. "I will send word as soon as I hear from Nicolas. Meanwhile, if you ever need anything, and I mean anything at all, let me know."

He turned and went back into his house.

With a contented sigh, Berthe leaned back into the velvety comfort of the Caradec coach. "Marie," she said, "now this be a true gentleman, 'n' I'm not talkin' 'bout this here ride."

"I know, Mother, I know."

Before he went back to work, Docteur C. looked in on his wife who had fallen asleep. He wouldn't tell her that Nicolas had a sister. Not yet. Not without knowing whether the girl was alive - not a certainty by any means for any infant left in a hospital foundling wheel, and if she was, what had happened to her.

Not until his son and Nicolas were home.

Chapter XVII

After an absence of nearly three months, Henri arived back in Rennes to a tumultuously happy welcome from Anne and Madeleine.

"You're home, Henri, you're home! But you lost so much weight!"

"And feel the better for it, I do! I was acquiring too much of it right about here." He patted his waist. "So please don't think of 'fattening' me up again with tempting dishes and rich desserts, Anne. Please?"

"We'll see, we'll see. Why didn't you have enough to eat?"

"Getting supplies was difficult at times."

Dear Anne, he thought, so oblivious to what is happening outside of her world.

"Mother! I am sure Papa saw things that would have taken anybody's appetite away!"

"That was part of it, too - I cannot tell you how good it is to be back with my two favorite ladies."

"Henri, I still think you must need a good rest, a vacation."

"Perhaps later. I have been away from business for months; it's time I took a look at the books and at what has happened during my absence. As a matter of fact I also have to see someone in Fougères. I think I'll do that in a day or two, get it out of the way. Meanwhile, if you ladies will excuse me, I am going upstairs to take a very hot and very long bath. I've already told the servants."

"Again? Didn't you already have one this this morning? Before you let us welcome you properly?"

"Yes, I did," he grinned, "but it will take additional ablutions to make me feel that I got rid of all that Crimean mud. You cannot imagine how wonderful hot water is after doing without."

He was already out the door when Anne called after him, "Henri, who is in Fougères?"

She shrugged when there was no answer. He probably didn't hear her; besides, they didn't know anyone there.

Henri had been able to think of little else since he had first seen Nicolas. The resemblance to Madeleine was astounding - or chilling, depending on what it meant to you. Same birthday, same year. Madeleine's blue-green eyes and the dark lashes? Nicolas had them, too. There was a definite over-all facial resemblance. The small differences could easily be attributed to one being a young woman, the other a young man. His hair was a darker brown, but how much of that was due to the fact that he had seen it when it was dirty, unwashed for who knew how long? They were both left-handed: he had watched Nicolas write the Caradec address on the envelope. He held his head slightly to one side when giving someone his full attention. Exactly like Madeleine.

But only Madeleine had been brought to the Hôtel-Dieu. Why not her brother? Or could Nicolas be a cousin - no, what was he thinking? They were *twins!*

After much soul-searching, Henri had decided to deliver the letter Nicolas had given him in person. Nothing else made sense. Docteur Caradec had to know a great deal more about Madeleine's brother, this young man who had lived with them for years.

He also decided not to say anything to Anne until he had answers. Originally he had toyed with the idea of mailing Nicolas' letter and not pursing this further - what if the resemblance was merely a quirk of nature? But much as he would have liked to believe that, he could not. He had no right to keep this to himself.

He sent a messenger with a note to Docteur Caradec that he had recently returned from the Crimea where he had met Nicolas Favreau who had given him a letter, and that he would like to deliver it personally. A date and time was agreed on.

Henri left Rennes early and, as expected, arrived at the Caradec residence around eleven. The men shook hands and after brandy was poured into their glasses, Henri pulled out the letter and handed it to Docteur Caradec.

"Please, go ahead and read it; I can imagine how anxious you must be for news."

Docteur C. ripped the envelope open, read the letter and sat back with a sigh of relief.

"Nicolas writes that he knows no details about Alain except that he was invalided home with a leg injury according to hospital records. You have my thanks, and my wife's, for bringing this to us so quickly after what must have been a tiring voyage back from the Crimea. Naturally I am curious to learn how you met Nicolas, but first let me tell you how he came to live with us."

Docteur C. told him the story of how Nicolas had come to Alain's aid, how he moved into their home and how the boys had attended school together. How Alain, their only son and still under-age, had enlisted without telling anyone, and how Nicolas had offered to go and try to find him.

"Looking back," he admitted, "I should never have permitted that."

Privately Henri agreed. Talking about a highly dangerous, really wild goose chase with no chance of succeeding!

He, in turn, related how, traveling with the photographer Roger Fenton across the Crimea, he had come across this young French soldier who questioned every aspect of their photographic equipment.

"Yes, that sounds like him," Docteur C. said. "He was always curious, always asked questions, and he has a phenomenal memory.

'Like Madeleine', Henri thought.

"Well, when I told him I would deliver his letter personally, he was able to confirm that at the time it was written your son's name did not appear on any of the wounded lists, nor lists of the missing or dead. I apologize for putting it as bluntly as he did."

"No, no, I want to know. I need to know."

"By the way, he has a friend who is with the British army. He showed him Alain's photograph, too, just in case - and speaking of photographs, this is the main reason why I needed to meet you. This is what I haven't mentioned yet." He pulled a photograph from the inside pocket of his coat and laid it down on the desk.

"Our daughter Madeleine."

"Dear Lord," Docteur C. said bending over the

photograph. He sounded as if he were in shock. "Dear Lord. I don't know what to say. It is one face! Brother and sister. No, twins, they must be twins, and they don't know each other? How wonderful this will be for them!"

He looked back at Henri and immediately realized that his reaction was not shared by his visitor.

"What is wrong, Monsieur Desrosiers? You look ill. Better lean back in your chair. Perhaps another brandy - I could do with another one myself." He picked up their empty glasses and refilled them.

"Thank you. Do you have a recent picture of Nicolas, one without a beard?"

"Of course. You say he wears a beard now? I cannot imagine Nicolas with a beard. He was always clean-shaven."

"Well, almost all the soldiers I saw over there had beards. The officers, too. Lack of water, soap, razors. Also time, I suppose ... "

Docteur C. walked over to his desk, took a photograph from a drawer and placed it next to Madeleine's.

Both stared at the young people. They had to be twins. It was impossible not to see it, impossible to think otherwise. 'Twins, yes, they are twins', Henri thought in despair, getting up and pacing back and forth. Dear God, what is this going to do to us? How do I tell Anne, how do we tell Madeleine?"

"What a wonderful gift for them, finding each other after all these years!" Docteur C. exclaimed again, looking up from the photographs.

"But what is wrong, Monsieur Desrosiers? You look as if you had seen a ghost. You are not happy for your daughter?"

Henri sat back and shook his head. "I cannot be happy," he said tonelessly. "I - how could I be? Madeleine doesn't - she doesn't know - that she is - We never told her that she is adopted."

"I see."

There was a long silence before Docteur C. spoke again.

"I don't know what to say, except to assure you that I shall not tell anyone about this, except Nicolas. Of course we don't know when he will be back. It could be weeks, months even, but when he is back he has the right to know. Naturally I shall first ask for his word to keep all of this to himself until you are ready to meet with him. You can trust him. He will keep his word, he always does. I just cannot in good conscience keep this from him. I hope you understand ..."

Henri nodded. Of course he understood. Nicolas had every right to know. And so did Madeleine. He slid her photograph back into his pocket and stood up slowly.

"I do understand. And I am grateful for your

understanding. I shall pray for your son's and Nicolas' safe return."

At the door, as they shook hands, Docteur C. said, "If you don't mind one more question: is your daughter left-handed, too?" Henri could only nod.

On his way back he had hours to deliberate if and how he would tell Anne and Madeleine. Every way he thought of was bound to wreak havoc on the family.

What if he said nothing? No. Out of the question. But he needed time to think. Could he delay his decision? Surely it would take Nicolas more than 2 months to travel back to France and then -

After hours of going back and forth in his deliberations another thought struck him suddenly: What if they were to tell Madeleine about being adopted with Nicolas there? He wouldn't be there during the telling of it of course, but immediately afterwards. That might lessen the shock, would give her something to be glad about. It might. It was definitely something to keep in mind.

When he arrived at home, Madeleine was waiting to show him two letters from Tutor Webb, both cross-written. "It has taken me forever to try to read these. I think he used too many sheets of paper in his last letter. He could not have written any smaller! I think you are supposed to start with the horizontal lines. They were written first, please see if you can decipher this, right here? The second page is cross-written on both sides. I cannot read it at all. I wish he hadn't run out of paper! I keep switching sides and am not getting anywhere."

Henri reached for a magnifying glass; together they turned the pages this way and that, poured over the lines and managed to read perhaps one tenth of the writing. One letter was two, the other three months old. The tone was decidedly more somber, but Tutor Webb repeated that he was unhurt (miraculously so!) and that now, at last, the end was in sight *if* Sebastopol could be taken soon. Whenever 'soon' would be. He wrote that this 'conflict' had to answer for too many dead and injured. He mentioned some numbers, adding that, of course, he could not vouch for their accuracy.

"Those numbers, tens of thousands - that can't be right, Father, can it? Surely they are too high."

"At this time no numbers are exact, how could they be? But I wouldn't be surprised if they were to climb even higher before this is all over. There were so many deaths due to illness, and that predicted short campaign of two weeks turned out to be wishful thinking and lasted nearly a year and a half."

In a postscript,, Tutor Webb had added that no mail had reached his outfit in several weeks and that he didn't expect any improvement while being encamped near Sebastopol.

Madeleine dashed off a quick letter to him. She didn't tell him that one of the pages had remained unread.

Chapter XVIII

At about the same time Nicolas received a message from Thomas. He had shown Alain's photograph to a French officer whose unit was moving towards Sebastopol; Alain might be in that troop - or at least someone who looked very much like him if you added a bushy beard. But who didn't have a bushy beard these days? Of course one couldn't be certain, it had been a verbal message passed on through God knows how many soldiers, drunk and sober, but what was certain these days?

In a postscript he asked after Duc. Sir IV had been shot right out from under him, shot in the chest, and was suffering so terribly that he said, 'To hell with Lord Lucan's orders' and immediately did what had to be done.

Nicolas remembered how angry they had been about the senseless order that only horses with a broken leg or sick with Glanders were to be shot. No exceptions and severe punishment for non-compliance. It was a cruel and inhuman directive, one which could only come from someone totally in the dark about what was happening in the field. He thought of the dozens of horses he had seen, lying abandoned by the side of the road, dying slowly of starvation or the cold, too weak to fight off the wild dogs and the vultures circling low and lower overhead until they plunged. He would never let this happen to Duc. Never.

As expected Thomas' message ended with 'To good gunnery for us and to vanquished foes, and wherever we are, let's keep our heads down!'

From what Nicolas was hearing, many more thousands of French soldiers were already encamped. More were expected to arrive. Digging trenches continued while both armies poured lead into each other and the valley reverberated with booms.

When he had arrived in the area with his unit, during the usual afternoon deluge, water had already filled newly dug trenches, turning them into treacherous gullies. Thick, heavy mud clung to boots and shovels, but the digging went on, always under heavy Russian shelling that threw up stones and heavy mounds of dirt, injuring and killing men and horses. Some trenches and tunnels were so close that one could sometimes hear Russians laugh or complain. His comrades all agreed that 'mudák' had to be a very popular Russian curse, judging by the frequency of its use.

Nicolas decided to keep Duc back at the tents and to hell with the consequences. "He'll be a danger to everyone when he bolts, and even the shape he is in now he is still very strong." he said to the new harried sergeant who grunted his usual unintelligible reply.

He greased his boots, hoping that might somewhat water-proof them, but the next day the leather gave way and his toes peeked out. Like everyone else's. He hated how steady rain ran down his collar and knew he smelled as bad as everybody around him. What did anybody expect, unwashed and living in the same unwashed clothes for months?

Every muscle in his body was sore from digging. There were angry knots in his shoulders, his head pounded with the constant loud noise, his painful blisters developed blisters which hurt like hell and put him into a foul mood. Sometimes, he had decided, the only life you should try to save is your own. He worked on mindlessly every day until he went back to Duc at dusk. Cursing, he'd gingerly take off boots and socks; then he would lie down, exhausted, keeping one hand on Duc and stroking him. If this continued much longer, his feet would never recover.

More than once he was screamed at by his sergeant. "Bloody 'ell, ye want both yer feet to freeze *stuck together* so ye can lose 'em at the same time? I seen it happen! Keep 'em covered, you idiot!"

Wasn't that what Docteur C. had talked about? He wrung out his wet socks, put his wet boots on over them and wished he were elsewhere.

He didn't stay awake at night the way he used to. Trying to dodge what the Russians threw at them in the dark made no sense, but snatching at least some fitful sleep during the night cannonades did. He tried to empty his mind of everything; there was nothing he could do to avoid what was going to happen.

Coming here had been insane. What he had read in books about war had nothing to do with the reality of it. Nothing could prepare you for the savagery. And searching for someone? The right thing to do, maybe, but idiocy, utter idiocy.

Looking back he was surprised at how easily Docteur C. had let him go, but then, why wouldn't he? Alain was his only son. Who was he, Nicolas? No one's son, not even Berthe's, although she thought of him as one. And all of this was getting dangerously close to feeling sorry for himself, something Berthe despised. Didn't she always say, "If ye can change somethin' what troubles ye, do it. If ye can't, forget it, let it be. And don't worry ahead to the next day: all that does is double yer worries!" He could almost hear her voice.

He got up and caressed Duc. Poor Duc who had gone through so much with him. He deserved better. Ever since a shell had burst only a few feet away, throwing up stones and clumps of earth all over them, Duc had been badly spooked. Unhurt except for some superficial scratches, but really spooked. All he wanted to do was to lie down. His head always hung low now; his eyes were dull. He shook. With remembered fear, Nicolas understood that. He did, too, at times.

They were both always hungry and cold. The barley stash would last for one, maybe two more meals - damn the high and mighty brains who had miscalculated so badly about feeding men and animals. How could they not know that horses require twenty pounds of fodder a day? How else could they be expected to carry two hundred pounds? And where were the promised winter clothes and blankets? How could those damn high and mighty brains be so damn consistent in their damn miscalculations? Suddenly, something struck him as funny: Docteur C. would be speechless about how freely and loudly he cursed these days.

Meanwhile the wait was getting to everybody. *'We French are doing nothing and the British are helping us as fast as they can'* - the joke, hilarious when it first circulated among the men, had turned into a tired, bitter comment on what waiting for action was like. Nicolas realized he hadn't heard laughter in a very long time.

After the day's digging he'd go back to Duc who did not move from his spot by the bush. Nicolas gave him barley and some water, none of which he seemed to want or enjoy and rubbed him down before he covered him with their two blankets. That would keep at least some of the pesky flies off him. Wasn't it supposed to be too cold for flies?

"You take it nice 'n'easy now, boy," he stroked him. "You'll be all right. All of this craziness will be over soon and then I'll take you home. I'll figure out an easy overland route for us: no rush, and no more ships for you, I promise. And soon you'll be back home where it'll be nice and quiet. No more cannons but plenty to eat and you'll have an apple every day. Maybe two."

He wished he believed what he was saying.

The night was chilly, with the usual dew settling on and drenching everything. He woke early, shook out his coat and rubbed down his weapons; fighting rust had become a daily chore. He took the top blanket off Duc who was still asleep when he left.

Minutes later there was no doubt that the bombardment of Sebastopol had begun in earnest: word was that over seven hundred allied guns were bombarding the Russian positions; of course the Russians retaliated with everything they had.

Bombardment went on without let-up, creating columns of smoke and dust. A thick white fog crept above the ground and hid everything. Mortar rounds and ear-splitting booms continued. Shrieks and groans and curses and pleas for water traveled ghost-like through the reloading pauses.

There was a short lull around noon during which he helped clear debris and level the pits created by enemy shells, but then it started up again and lasted until nightfall. Strange how you never see the fighting when it starts, but you hear it as it comes closer.

Duc was worse when he got back to him. He didn't go for the last handful of grains or the water, didn't raise his head. Nicolas kept pleading with him, not sure any more that Duc heard him. There was a new wheezing in each labored breath. He knelt and put his arms around him, kept talking and stroking, telling him they'd be going home soon. Soon . . . until much later when someone tapped him on the shoulder and said, "I think he's gone."

Had he dozed off? "What? What d'ye say?"

"I said I think he's gone. What yer goin' to do now?"

Do now? Duc's head was low. Nicolas put his ear against his horse's flank. Nothing. He waited and listened again, and again, even though he knew. Nothing.

"And now?"

Nicolas tried to string words together for a sentence but managed only, "I have to bury him."

The soldier whom Nicolas knew only by sight nodded and said, "All right, I'll get more men."

He came back with five buddies and their shovels.

Together they dug for hours by the light of a couple of lanterns. One of the soldiers kept cursing under his breath, "What's so special about this horse? Horses die every day," but someone else always hissed at him to shut up. They kept digging until the hole was deep enough, thankful that the earth wasn't frozen. It took all of them except Nicolas to shove Duc downhill. Nicolas did not watch, but when it was over he helped shovel earth back over him. When that was done, he said "wait" and brought out two brandy bottles and his battered tin cup for the diggers, apologizing that he didn't have more and had no money. That didn't seem to matter. Many soldiers believed that enough brandy kept cholera away; brandy had become a more valuable commodity than money, not only a way to forget. His helpers left singing; he was down to his last bottle now.

When he was alone he wept as he had never wept before.

The next day Nicolas managed to drag a soldier out of a newly formed bomb crater. The soldier did not seem to be injured but just stood there, his mouth opening and closing without making a sound. It was obvious that he could not move on his own. When Nicolas got close enough to look down into the crater he realized that the soldier was standing amid body parts.

Does anyone ever recover from that?

He didn't think his own luck could last much longer. And now he didn't have Duc to get back to.

And then came the day when everyone knew that something big was about to happen: they were issued two days' rations. Orders came though: storm Sebastopol and take the Malakoff. How? By putting ladders on the outside of the fortifications, climb up, get yourself down on the other side and give the Russians what for - if the Russians who were no doubt just waiting to pick them off one by one didn't get you first. That was the best plan the lord generals could come up with? Nicolas was sure of one thing only: it was going to be a very bloody day.

He might die, and for what? Not for a glorious cause. Could there ever be a cause worth so many deaths, so many broken lives? And what the hell was the use of asking unanswerable questions?

He was not afraid, not the way he had been. There was a new kind of detachment in him. He was angry. Angry about losing Duc, angry at Alain, angry at himself for thinking he could do this. Angry for throwing his life away.

But - if these were to be his last days, he decided, anger was a damn sight better than fear!

He did what he expected of himself, enlisted or not. Once again hoarse-voiced and trumpeted commands were lost in the tremendous noises; once again it was every man for himself. He advanced so far and so fast with a handful of others that he was able to enter through a break in the wall, but immediately he was caught in hand-to-hand combat.

Knocked down twice, the Minié was wrenched from his hand and he narrowly escaped being bludgeoned by a rifle stock. Reaching out blindly he was able to grab a pick-axe off the ground before he struggled back on his feet. Screaming like a madman he swung it at anybody and anything that came near him, hating who he was becoming.

He deliberately did not see the bodies on the ground. He just wanted it to end, to be over. Where the hell were the others?

When the noises abated and the last Russian had fled, far into town he hoped, he heard a weak voice calling his name.

No, he was imagining this, or, more likely, he had at last lost his mind. Or he was hearing things with what little mind he had left. Keeping a wary eye and ear out, he listened - here it was again.

"Hey, Nicolas - over here! Give us a hand. *Today* if possible?"

"Thomas?" Exhaustion dropped away from him as he turned around.

"Could you hurry?"

Thomas was immobilized, caught under a giant dead Russian. Or was he? Nicolas couldn't be sure, but he kicked the Russian's pistol out of the way. Then he drag-kicked the Russian off his friend who sat up, groaning, and tried to support his right arm with his left. His right hand was bleeding. Nicolas pulled out his last almost-clean handkerchief, dabbed ointment on it and wrapped it around Thomas' hand; it looked like something had pierced it. Then he searched for something else to use, spotted a large two-headed eagle flag among the bodies. He picked it up, mumbled a few words, tore it from its wooden support and fashioned a sling from it.

He helped Thomas to his feet and carefully positioned his arm into the sling.

"There. You look terrible!"

"Thanks. Not as terrible as I feel!"

Nicolas noticed that Thomas was trying to stand on one leg.

"What happened?"

Grimacing through the pain Thomas said, "Who knows? I think that Russkie giant damaged my chest when he decided to sit on me. I definitely heard something crack. Made me twist my ankle, too. Why couldn't he have been one of the skinny Russkies? Most of them look like skeletons. Oh, and what were you muttering before - it wasn't a last prayer for me, I hope!"

Nicolas looked around while he answered. "Don't be an idiot! I apologized to my namesake for stealing his flag, that's all. What are you doing here? I thought you Brits were supposed to come in *after* us."

"Stealing the Imperial flag?" Thomas' laugh turned into a grimace. "Don't make me laugh again, it hurts. Well, according to the protocol of pillage . . ."

"There is a protocol of pillage?" Nicolas interrupted, keeping an eye out for returning Russians.

"There is a protocol for everything, don't you know? Anyway, you had every right. Naturally officers get first choice, before the men. And about what I'm doing here: I'm here because someone got their signals crossed as usual; isn't it what our generals do best? Nick, one more thing before we leave this lovely place: could you take a look at Billy over there? He is in a bad way."

Nicolas walked over and bent down to the boy. Thomas was right. Billy sat against a piece of wall, shivering; there was a blank stare in his eyes and his mouth was an awful, bloody mess. He looked like he had been crying; he sat, clutching a trumpet to him with both hands.

"You're coming with me, Billy; Lieutenant Fellowes needs your help," Nicolas said in his most commanding voice. Billy got up and followed him.

Nicolas realized that suddenly it was quiet, eerily

quiet. Must be noon, when bombardments ceased on both sides. To reposition guns, according to his sergeant. It was a miracle that none of the Russians had come back. Enough talk, they had better get away as quickly as possible.

They left through the same opening, trying not to see the bodies, with Thomas' left arm around Nicolas' shoulder. He was limping badly but insisted it was nothing. Billy followed wordlessly, doing his part as rear look-out.

The way back was a walk through unimaginable horror, worse than anything he had ever seen. So many dead, so many wounded, begging and screaming and no help in sight. No help anywhere. Stumbling through rocks and rubble and mud, wading through water running red. Suddenly shells hissed down again, to their right and to their left, missing, missing again - how much longer would they go on missing?

Thomas' face was ashen. Nicolas didn't know how he managed to keep walking. Every now and then his fingers dug painfully into Nicolas' shoulder. They trudged on until they were out of reach, finally arriving at the spot where Duc had been buried.

Thomas looked up. "Duc?" he asked quietly.

Nicolas nodded. He gave his friend the last of his brandy, keeping back a small amount for Billy who dribbled it carefully and slowly into his mouth. Then he went in search of help. He was able to get two or-derlies to follow him with a stretcher; they promised to rush Thomas who kept staring at his hand to the French field hospital.

"Hey Tom, it doesn't look that bad. They'll stitch you up and you'll be good as new and I'll see a lot of you."

"Nick, I'll never forget what you did today. You saved my life, back there, I know you did. I was sure I'd never make it out - and if you want that Russian flag back, you know where to come to try to get it. Make sure Billy goes with me."

"Consider it done. What is wrong with his mouth? He can barely talk."

"Or eat or drink, either. Poor boy, he's not even fif-teen, forgot to warm the mouthpiece in the usual mad rush on a freezing morning some days ago and his lips got stuck to it. Actually froze to the metal. Damn painful, I should think. Starts bleeding again with the slightest movement. I'll have the doctor look at him."

Suddenly Nicolas found it hard to speak. Alain had been his first friend, but Thomas - Thomas was his real friend. They could talk about everything together, be serious or laugh, and Thomas was, he didn't quite know how to put it, but he knew with absolute certainty that he was a thoroughly honest and good person. The way he had kept walking, uncomplaining, his face white and drawn with pain, nearly fainting but still looking out for Billy -

There followed the last days of bombardments which inflicted such heavy damage on Sebastopol that repairs could not be made overnight longer.

Very early on the morning of September 8, the Allied camps were startled by extraordinarily loud explosions, one following the other. Scouts discovered that the city was being evacuated over a pontoon bridge. When the troops were across, all the bastions, batteries and powder stores blew up, regardless of the fact that wounded soldiers of both sides had not been evacuated.

Sebastopol burned. The Allies had reached their objective.

For Nicolas the war was over.

A few days later he caught up with Thomas in the field hospital. He was practicing writing with his left hand but dismissed his efforts as not even comparable to the efforts of an uncoordinated three-year-old.

"Want me to write a letter for you?"

"No, thanks. I already sent a telegram home."

"Just like that?" Nicolas was under the impression that at present only governmental telegrams could be sent and received. Thomas shrugged innocently, and when he learned that Nicolas had not been able to make sailing arrangements yet, said 'perfect' and told him they would be traveling together since he was going home by way of Rennes. In about three weeks.

"So quickly, and why Rennes?"

"Because Mother's orders are to see this surgeon there. She wants him to look at my hand and my broken rib and my ankle. You know how mothers are" - he caught himself, said "sorry" and added quickly, "Billy is going home with me. He has no family. He was given a salve that seems to be helping and I'll find him some work on the place - and by the way, there are some new clothes for you to wear in those boxes over there. Time to retire your old ones. Your uniform stinks to high heaven!"

"And yours doesn't?"

"Please! Cherry-colored pantaloons? Never!"

A few days later a telegram arrived from Rennes: "Come home Alain here September 1."

"What? Damn it, no!" Nicolas shouted. He was too furious to wonder how the message had caught up with him.

Alain was home during the worst bombardments? All the time when he dug trenches until his hands were bleeding and his back permanently sore, when Duc died and when his blistered feet made walking and standing hell, while he was shot at, while he was getting too close to cholera and typhus - during all this time Prince Alain was safe at home, slept in his soft bed, had as many blankets as he wanted, had clean clothes and dry socks and dry boots, gorged on his favorite foods? No!

When he calmed down he was surprised to find in himself, but buried very far down, some gladness for Alain's parents' sake. But he was choking on a new anger which frightened him.

Chapter XIX

Weeks after Henri had returned from Fougères, Anne and he were sitting at the dinner table (Madeleine was at the theatre) when Anne suddenly put down knife and fork and said, "Henri, you are keeping something from me and I want to know what it is. I have to know. If it is an illness, we'll see it through together; if business problems are worrying you, at least tell me about them, and if it is something I have done, or should have done and didn't do - I need to know about that, too."

"Am I that transparent?" he asked, moving from his seat across the table to sit next to her. "First of all: no, I am not ill."

"Thank God for that. And you are not transparent, my dear; you are preoccupied. Ever since you have been back I've had the feeling that something about you is different. At first I thought it was the awful things you must have seen in the Crimea, but I think there is something else. I have seen how you look at Madeleine since you're back from Fougères. There is something strange about it. Why, I ask myself, and it frightens me. I was waiting for you to tell me, but I cannot wait any more. What is it?"

"Where did you say she is tonight?"

"At the theatre with Cecily and her parents. She may be spending the night at their home, or she may not. And please don't change the subject."

"I did not change the subject. I do have something to tell you - it concerns her and I wouldn't want to talk about it now if she were home. Please, Anne, don't look so scared. Yes, we are in a difficult situation and we shall deal with it, but there is also something very good and wonderful connected to it." He had thought long and hard about how to do this and still wasn't quite sure.

He took her hand.

"Anne, during my last weeks in the Crimea I met a young man who bears the most amazing resemblance to our daughter. Same face, same eyes, even same mannerisms. Now all we know is that Madeleine was brought to the Hôtel-Dieu by her mother, Jannet Favreau, who had contracted childbed fever and was very ill. She knew she would not survive. Remember?"

"How can you ask me that? Of course I remember."

"Until very recently what was *not* known to anybody

except the friend who went with her - who turned out to be anything but a friend - was that Jannet had given birth to twins."

"What did you say? Twins? Oh, no, Henri - no - but ..."

"Yes. First a boy whom this so-called friend secreted away for herself; apparently she had lost a son some years earlier. She kept telling Jannet that the high fever was making her imagine things, that she'd had one child only, a girl, not two. Then Jannet died and the 'friend' whose name was Rozenn, had to travel from Paris back to Brittany with a newborn and could not manage. She left him with a wet nurse named Berthe who lives near Fougères, paid monthly fees and promised to visit her son on Sundays. Any questions so far?"

"What is his name?"

"Nicolas."

"And this Berthe knew nothing about the twins?"

"No, no one knew about them for years. Berthe always believed Rozenn to be the boy's mother, but according to her, 'Rozenn didn't have a maternal bone in her body' and Nicolas never liked her. Rozenn visited less and less often, sometimes not for months, and when the boy turned five, she left him there for good. Berthe refused to accept further payments. Living with her meant that Nicolas had to go out every morning early and beg for food, like her own children, work hard the rest of the day - ”

“The poor boy.”

They both thought of Madeleine's early years and how easy and different her life had been compared to her brother's.

“A few years later he moved into the Caradec house, and why and how that came about is another story, as are his years with Berthe who must be a remarkable woman. For the first time in his life, thanks to this Docteur Caradec, he attended school with their son Alain; after a rocky start he apparently turned to be an excellent student.”

Here Henri had to stop for some sips of wine which gave Ann the chance to ask, “But why did he wind up in the Crimea?”

“That's another incredible story. The Caradec's only son, Alain, was supposed to begin law studies in Paris. He was under-age but enlisted in the French army any-way, without his parents' or anybody else's knowledge. Nicolas went to the Crimea to find him.”

“He did? Why on earth would he do that?”

“I don't know. Gratitude to the family, a sense of responsibility? I doubt it was looking for adventure.”

“And you saw him and immediately thought of Madeleine?”

"Immediately."

Anne gave up on holding back her tears and asked, "And that means that we have to tell her? I know, but how? When? Are you certain it couldn't be a coincidence? People can resemble each other and not be related."

"Not those two. They are brother and sister, we know that now. Twins. We must tell her. Together, of course."

"I wonder … now I wonder if Nicolas could be the boy."

"What are you talking about?"

"The boy she used to see in her sleep, or in a dream and still does, although she doesn't mention him anymore. Do you think that's possible, that there could be such a strong bond between twins? Even if they don't know each other?"

"Anne, please, not that boy again! I don't understand any of this, I never have. I've never known what to make of this dream thing. It is completely beyond me and there is not a shred of logic to it. At this point we don't even know if he had the same experience. What we do know is that Nicolas is her twin brother. And that we don't have the right to keep them apart. Isn't that enough?"

"I know, I know, but that means … " She buried her face in her hands.

"Yes, I know. She will have to be told about the adoption. I've gone over this and over this, and no matter how we approach it, it will be a shock. I know, dear, but please stop crying and hear me out: What if we waited until Nicolas is back from the Crimea? I dislike putting it so bluntly: Naturally I hope that he will be back, but there are no guarantees. The war will be over within days, true, but these are very unsettled days and who knows how much time will go by before he is back or what might happen in the interim. It's a miracle that he survived this war and illness - I don't even know where and how he is now. I hope you agree: We do nothing until he is back in France."

When Anne didn't say anything, Henri continued. "We will have to tell her about the adoption, but I hope you agree with me about waiting."

"I do, Henri, of course I do. I agree, having Nicolas here might help."

"So we wait?"

"We wait."

They remained in the small salon, talking but staying away from the subject that was uppermost in their minds until Madeleine came home.

"How was the theater?"

"Eminently forgettable." She threw herself into a

chair. "I wish they'd do something other than those silly seventeenth-century farces."

"But you thanked Cecily's parents?"

"Several heartfelt times. You trained me well, Mother."

"Sweetheart, must you put it quite like that?"

"You mean 'trained' evokes a picture of a ball-balancing seal?" She laughed. "You *taught* me well - is that better? Why are you *up* so late?"

"We were talking and were just going up when we heard the door."

They all went upstairs, but Henri had caught that quick questioning look on Madeleine's face.

He hoped Nicolas would be back soon.

Chapter XX

Nicolas arrived in Fougères several weeks later, wearing one of his new suits and new boots.

Thomas had prevailed. "As I told you, you cannot continue to wear your old things. And your footwear - the less said about it the better! Pay me back when you are a wealthy lawyer or an influential politician if you absolutely must, but I wish you could let others do something for you once in a while! Why is that so damn difficult for you? You saved my life, for God's sake!"

Nicolas had managed a mumbled 'thank you'. He had no idea how Thomas had been able to purchase the clothes so quickly.

The closer he came to Fougères, the more uncomfortable he was. He was not looking forward to confronting Alain but felt the loss of Duc more keenly than ever and blamed himself.

He waited a few minutes before using the door knocker.

Before he could say anything Docteur C. who opened the door with his wife at his side took full responsibility.

"Welcome home, Nicolas, welcome. I can tell you must be thinking about Duc, but please remember that taking him along was *my* idea, *my* suggestion. Duc was always high-strung and not meant to be a cavalry horse, I knew that, but I also knew that he liked you better than any other 'human'. There was such a strong bond between you two. I should never have let you go, not you, not him. I have no doubt that you took the best care of him and did everything you could. Could we speak about this again, perhaps later tonight?"

"Certainly, Docteur C."

All this time Madame C. hadn't said a word, just stood there with barely the hint of a smile on her face. She stood stiffly erect, as usual, and was tightly buttoned from her waist on up to below her chin. She had immediately noticed his new clothes.

"He's here!" He heard Alain's excited shout before another door swung open. Alain made straight for Nicolas, limping slightly.

"Nicolas, welcome home! I had no idea that you came looking for me, that we were in the same hell, not until Father told me. No hard feelings, I hope?"

That was it - no hard feelings? That was all?

"Well, I'm not quite ready to say that! As a matter of fact, I used to dream of strangling you."

"Nicolas, no!" Frightened, Madame Caradec recoiled.

"Mother, he is joking." Alain managed an unconvincing laugh. "Aren't you joking?"

Nicolas's quiet "No, I'm not," wiped the smile off Alain's face.

"Dear God, no!" Madame Caradec put her hand to her mouth.

"When were you injured?"

"Well, my leg got in the way of a Russian bullet, but I was damn lucky at that. Fellow next to me took one that ripped his chest open; he bled to death in less than a minute. Sorry, Mother, I know you don't like hearing such details. Let's go in and eat. I'm starving."

"Before we do that, Madame and Docteur C., may Alain and I have some minutes alone?"

Madame C.'s urgent whisper, "No, tell him no!" could scarcely be heard under her husband's hearty, "Certainly, we'll leave you to it," as he prodded her towards the dining room.

"What's this all about?" Looking uncomfortable, Alain toyed with the top button of his shirt.

"You don't know? This isn't going to take very long, Alain, but I need to know what you were thinking, leaving the way you did."

"I had to get away, that's what I was thinking." Alain didn't quite manage to sound unconcerned.

"I understand that, but not the way in which you went about it. Your parents were convinced that I had helped you plan everything. They blamed me and accused me of lying when I said that I knew nothing."

"Isn't that typical! They still can't believe I'm capable of doing anything on my own! But Nick, how could I know they would react like that?"

"That is not the question, Alain. The question is, 'Did you think of *them*? Did you think of *me*, leaving the way you did?"

"Well, no one forced you to come after me!" Alain flung at him.

"True."

"So why did you?"

Nicolas stared at him. He had no intention of explaining something which should need no explanation. An unsettling silence grew up between them. Nicolas let it stretch out.

Alain finally broke it by saying, "Nicolas, we both came back in pretty good shape. Isn't that what matters?

Of course it is - and by the way, I guess you do realize that Duc was an expensive horse. Father is being damn decent about losing him over there, isn't he?"

"Yes, he is." There was no point in telling Alain what he thought of him for needing to make this last comment.

"Just one more question. Do you know what happened to Chien?"

"Your mutt? He disappeared on the day you left and supposedly hasn't been seen since. Well, that's what you have to expect from his kind. Now Purebreds, they are different. They know how to be loyal. Now let's go in - if there's one thing I dislike it is a lukewarm meal."

They walked into the dining room together. Madame C. looked up, relieved, and Nicolas wondered if she had expected them to come to blows. Of course the meal was excellent. He ate sparingly; he was not yet re-accustomed to such rich fare and large portions.

During dessert, Madame C. put on the thinnest of smiles and asked, "How long can you stay, Nicolas dear?"

"Just tonight, Madame. I want to see my friend again before he leaves for England."

"What a shame." Her smile did not quite cover her relief. To everyone's surprise except Nicolas', Alain went out immediately after dinner.

Later in the evening, Docteur C. took Nicolas aside and asked him to come to his office. "I'd like to know - tell me about Duc, if you can. It wasn't Glanders, was it?"

"No, sir. There was never any of that greenish discharge and he didn't have a fever as far as I could tell. Actually the trouble started in Marseilles before we embarked. The noise from two military bands with drums, trumpets and horns blaring against each other was deafening; many horses shied and tried to get away from the noise and were difficult to restrain. That and the general disorder frightened Duc."

Docteur C. sighed. "Of course it would. I suppose patriotic fervor insists on these send-offs. Too bad the people in charge know so little about horses. I ought to have remembered that without an adaptation period Duc would have a difficult time - how did he do in the hold? He was there by himself, wasn't he?"

"He was with one other horse, and at first everything was fine. Once we started sailing it was another story. The British officer and I spent hours every day and many nights with our horses; both fought constantly against their restraints and wanted to run from the sounds of distress that came from the overcrowded large hold. I cannot tell you how many horses stood in there: they could not lie down, not even once - that's how awful the situation was. We looked in a few times; it was horrible, and there was nothing we could do."

"And once you were on land?"

"Of course both fought against being off-loaded into barges - why wouldn't they, being buckled into those harnesses and lowered into small boats that kept bumping against the ship's hull. They calmed down once they felt solid ground under their hooves again. Duc was doing better, even though it was beastly hot marching and we ran out of water on the way to our camp site and ..."

"On your first day there?" Docteur C. interrupted.

"Yes, sir, and it happened again, much too often. We ran out of food, too, but that was later. Which reminds me: I owe you for the compass. I was robbed, and the compass was all I had left to barter with."

"You owe me nothing, Nicolas. I am the one who owes you."

"Thank you, sir. At first I'd had no choice but to ride Duc into some of the skirmishes and one battle. He did incredibly well for months, but the infernal cannon noise that never stopped, the exploding landmines, hearing men scream and seeing horses fall, seeing dying or dead horses lying everywhere - I know all that did something to him. Months later, when I became part of another unit, I was able to leave him back by our tents where he was safe, but by then he was not himself. I'm sure those awful sounds and sights haunted him. Then suddenly his breathing changed. Not into wheezing exactly, but it did sound more labored. I don't know what his illness was; he didn't seem to be in pain, just tired, but he was getting very thin and like I said, he was not himself. I was with him at the end. Other soldiers I barely knew helped me bury him. I am sorry, that's all I can tell you."

"No, I am sorry - because of what you had to live through over there. I know that you did everything you could for Duc and you have given me much to think about. How could an army run out of food and water?"

"We were wondering about that, too, believe me! Many times. And it was even worse in the British camps. Of course it was supposed to be a short war, but that is a poor excuse. So is the fact that shipments were lost during a hurricane and that a fire at one of our landing sites destroyed stored food and clothing. That couldn't be helped, but sometimes shipments arrived without mules which meant that the goods could not be moved out of the harbor and went bad, and once we received an entire shipment of *left* boots."

"What idiots!" Docteur C. shook his head. "Well, I thank you, Nicolas, for everything - come back to my office after breakfast tomorrow. I have a very happy surprise for you."

Nicolas went up to his old room. A very happy surprise - what a nice change that would be! Perhaps Docteur C.'s promise to send him to veterinary school was still good? Lately, however, another idea had drifted

in and out of his mind, unformed as yet, but very com-
pelling. In the morning he was curious but not unduly
so when he Dr. Caradec asked him to sit down in his
office. As always he came right to the point.

"First, if you want to go to a university, and I hope
you do, I am going to send you. It's the least we can do.
Law, medicine, the classics, whatever, wherever, and I
want to repeat that this was *always* my intention. It has
nothing to do with your going to the Crimea. I hope
you know that."

He waved away Nicolas' thanks.

"And now I have some truly amazing news to tell
you. You'd better sit down. And if you wonder why I
didn't tell you last night? I knew you wouldn't sleep a
wink if I did!"

That really piqued Nicolas' curiosity.

First Docteur C. went over what Rozenn had confided to Berthe, then what Berthe had told him when
she came to see him, followed by the visit from Monsieur
Desrosiers, who had delivered Nicolas's letter.

"Now tell me something, Nicolas. Did Monsieur
Desrosiers keep looking at you when he first saw you?"

Nicolas could only nod, stunned by what he had just
been told, but he soon recovered his voice.

"As a matter of fact, yes, he did. Yes, of course! I

know I looked as bad as everybody else, unwashed, bearded, uniform in tatters, but I couldn't understand why he kept staring at me and then would look away quickly. Not confused so much as disturbed, almost like someone who has received unwelcome news. Now that you have told me I can understand his reaction on seeing me. I have a sister, I have a twin sister!"

He started to pace back and forth.

"That's all I can think of. I cannot believe it! No, of course I don't mean that. I believe it! I believe it! I have a sister. After all this time I have a sister! What a wonderful surprise!"

"It is that, but you have to keep in mind that your sister has never been told about her adoption. My understanding is that the Desrosiers had hoped they'd never have to tell her. Having to tell her now is what has Monsieur Desrosiers so deeply concerned ."

"Yes, finding out will be a great shock to her," Nicolas said quietly.

"Which means you may find yourself in the middle of quite some situation, but I trust you'll know what to say. I have told you everything I know; they are expecting you."

"Here." He handed Nicolas a piece of paper with the Desrosiers' address on it. "I know you are anxious to leave and they expect you as soon as possible. You know that I wish you all the luck in the world. Let us know what happens, and above all - remember that you always have a home here with us."

Docteur C. had spoken almost sadly, Nicolas thought, as he thanked him. There had been true affection and regret in his voice.

Chapter XXI

The return to Rennes seemed endless and yet it flew by as Nicolas imagined conversations, tried to anticipate questions and prepare possible answers, and most of all, wondered about Madeleine's reaction. He was surprised at how strongly he felt the need to make it easy for her, to protect her.

When he presented himself at the Desrosiers' home he was surprised again: the bell was answered not by a servant but by the lady of the house who stared at him and was so taken aback that she could not speak for a moment. Then she extended a hand towards him and said, "Welcome, welcome, Monsieur Favreau. I would have recognized you anywhere, just as my husband did!" She led him into a library. "Feel free to look at whatever interests you. Someone will come and get you when we are ready - I don't know how long we'll be; we could not think of a different or better way of doing what we have to do. I hope you don't mind waiting."

"I don't mind in the least, Madame, and please, the name is Nicolas."

He paced up and down as soon as she had left the room and kept pacing. The book which could have held his attention had yet to be written.

Madeleine and her parents were in the little salon.

"Anyone feel like a quick game?" she asked.

"Not tonight, sweetheart, let's just talk."

"Fine, what about?"

"Something so important," her father answered, "that your mother and I would like your promise to hear us out without running up to your room."

"Are you ever going to let me forget that I used to do that? I don't like the sound of this, it sounds so - so ominous somehow. I hope it isn't. I used to escape to my room when I was younger, I know, but I haven't done that in years. All right, I promise. What is so important?"

"I'll start," Anne said.

"Before I say anything else I want to say this: We could not love you more and will always love you as your mother and father. Nothing can ever change that. Nothing."

"Mother, what are you ..."

"But now ..." Anne continued quickly before Madeleine could say more.

"But now I come to the difficult part, so I'll say it quickly, in as few words as possible: Madeleine, I did not give birth to you. We adopted you. With Louise's help."

"You *what?*" Madeleine jumped up. "What did you say? You *adopted me?* You are not my real parents? You aren't?"

"Please listen to me, Madeleine. Of course we are your real parents, in every sense of the word, the only parents you have ever known, will ever have."

"But - but you are not! You made me think you were. You lied to me! All these years - you lied to me! How could you!"

She started to weep. "*Now* I know. When I was little, when I realized I didn't look like you or Father, remember? You made up that story, and such a sweet story it was, about looking like your grandmother. How could you? And I, so naïve, I believed every word of it. Why didn't you tell me then or sooner - and why - why didn't my real mother keep me? I know, because she didn't want to! Isn't that usually the reason why some mothers get rid of their children?"

"No, sweetheart, no! Your mother was very young, your father had died, and she was so ill after you were born that she was afraid she would not live. She had no family. A friend took her to the Hôtel-Dieu where infants can be left in the care of the Sisters. Your aunt Louise was on duty that night. She said one look at you and she knew this little girl was meant for us."

"Louise was in on this, too? This gets better and better! Aunt Louise - how touching, how convenient! Anyone else assist you in your deception? No? No wonder you didn't want me to run up to my room! And why should *I* honor a promise I made under false pretenses, a promise made to two people who lied to me all my life? Am I the only one who doesn't know about this?"

"No. You will get to know the only other people who do know, soon."

"Why should I believe that - or anything else you tell me?"

"Because we only kept his one thing from you. Nothing else. You were too young to understand."

"Oh, and now I am grown up enough that I can understand everything? What am I expected to say, 'Don't worry, it's all right?' Why now? Why not a year ago? Why not next year? Why tell me at all!"

Anne looked at Henri, unable to cope with Madeleine's accusations.

"I'll take over," he announced. "Why tell you now? Because recently we were made aware of something else, something very important that *we* did not know about until now: the young woman who gave birth to you had minutes earlier given birth to a son. She had twins, Madeleine. Twins."

"What? Did you say twins?" Madeleine fell back into her chair. "A boy? What happened to him? Why - why didn't you adopt him, too? You could have, you know. You should have. Oh, I know - maybe you could not, an adopted Desrosiers daughter was all right, but not an adopted son! Was that it? Where has he been all this time? Did another family adopt him?"

"Madeleine, could you just be quiet and listen? Let's leave details and accusations for later. *I saw him in the Crimea.* By chance. Saw him and thought I was looking at you. You have the same eyes and so much else in common. He is taller, of course, but even with that big beard of his the resemblance was striking, simply striking."

Madeleine had difficulty speaking. "My brother? Where is he now?"

She caught the signal passing between her parents. Her mother reached for the bell and rang it.

"You don't mean he is here? You can't! In our house?"

"Yes, he is."

Madeleine was too caught up in her anger to notice that the door was opening.

"Oh, no! I am not letting you do this. How can you spring another surprise on me? I cannot do this. Don't you think this is enough for one evening? It is certainly is for me. *You* go and entertain him, I'm going up to my room. I can't do this, I simply cannot, I …"

She turned around when she heard Nicolas walk in. He looked at the three people inside, nodded politely at the adults but made straight for her.

"Madeleine, I am your brother Nicolas. I know you. Until this morning I didn't know I had a sister, but I always felt you were somewhere in this world, and now I understand why: *You are the girl who looks like me.* I saw you when I was asleep and always believed it had to be more than a dream. I thought of you as 'my other my-self'; it started when I was quite young. Of course there is no scientific or logical explanation for it, but that is not important for us, is it?"

He looked at her. "You're almost smiling, and I can guess why. Because you had the same dream?"

Madeleine stood there, nodding and biting her lip for a long time. But all of a sudden both moved and her brother's arms were around her. "Nicolas, Nicolas," she said over and over again, laughing and weeping into his shoulder.

Anne, too, was in tears and wanted to give Madeleine her handkerchief, but Nicolas looked up and said, "Allow me." Henri wordlessly handed his wife his own handkerchief. His two ladies were in tears. Happy tears? He almost dared to hope when Madeleine suddenly pulled out of Nicolas's arms and faced her parents.

"I must hand it to you, this was masterfully orchestrated," she said coldly. "First, you tell me I am adopted, in just a few words, then you produce a twin brother I had no idea existed - tell me, what did you think? That I'd be so overjoyed I'd forget about having been *lied* to all my life? And ..."

"Madeleine!" Henri held up his hand to silence her. "Do you really doubt that we did what we thought was best? How much does a child of five understand, or one at seven, at ten? Of course we know that this is a shock for you, a great shock, and that you need time to get used to the idea ..."

"I'll never get used to the idea!"

Nicolas walked over to her parents and said, "It may not be my place to join in any conversation yet, but there is something I would like to say to my sister, if you'll allow me."

Not waiting for permission he went back to stand in front of Madeleine.

"You have parents who have been with you since you were a few days old; I can see how much they care for you. I never had parents. I was taken to a wet nurse before I was one month old, and I was lucky. Very lucky.

She took care of me as if I was one of her own children; I lived with her until I was twelve. You have parents who love you. *That* is what matters. You and I will talk again soon, but I think now you need time alone with them. Your father knows how to reach me."

He nodded politely to Madeleine's parents. She followed him to the door and whispered, "Don't go," but he said he had to.

Head down, she turned towards her parents. "I can't talk about this anymore, I just cannot - ". Her voice broke and she rushed upstairs without waiting for an answer.

"We have always kissed good-night. Always," Anne said unhappily.

"Give her time."

"I know, I know. What ... what did you think of her reaction?"

"It was pretty much what I expected. You know how she is, she always speaks her mind, often before she has thought everything through and did we get a sample of that tonight! I do think she took to Nicolas, and we are fortunate in him; when you meet the Caradec family you will understand even better what I mean. He is a remarkable young man. Look how he spoke to Madeleine: not one word about the poverty and hardship of his early years, no attempt to gain sympathy, only stressing what is important. And he knew when to leave."

"Yes, I noticed that, too. We were right in having him come here today, Henri - but goodness, what must he think of me? I ought to have offered him something to eat!"

"For heaven's sake, Anne! I'm sure nothing was further from his mind. Besides, do you realize what time it is? Of course we were right having him come here. I am also thinking of offering him the use of one of our guest rooms while he is in Rennes. What do you think?"

"Henri, do we know enough about him to do that? The servants will talk!"

"Yes, they will do that, don't they always? Let them. He is Madeleine's *brother*. And again, I have the advantage of having spoken about him with Docteur Caradec. Actually, I am more at ease about the future, knowing that he will be part of Madeleine's life. Which reminds me, she still shows no interest in any of her young men?"

"What makes you ask this now of all times? Not even a hint. They are either too young, even if they are in their late twenties or older, not interesting enough, or too tied to their mothers' apron strings (her words, not mine). Or too full of themselves, or like poor Jean-Luc they have sweaty hands."

"Well, let's not worry about that yet. One problem at a time, Anne, please."

"Wasn't it *you* who asked?"

"I know, I know, the thought just popped into my head. Now I think we both could use some sleep."

Madeleine came down in the morning and offered her parents only a cool "Good morning".

Henri announced that Nicolas would be back around ten. "I hope you have no other plans."

Madeleine's "No, I don't" was curt, and Anne sighed audibly. Henri shot her a warning look and mouthed 'patience' at her.

Nicolas arrived on time and suggested they go for a walk. "I have your father's permission. You do have something a little sturdier than what is on your feet now, don't you?" he asked, frowning at her dainty morning slippers.

"I do." Madeleine returned within minutes, more properly shod. They walked to the park which was only minutes away, found a bench and sat down. Accordion music drifted toward them.

Nicolas could tell that Madeleine was still out of sorts.

"Well, we have much to catch up on. Ladies first?"

She shook her head. "No, you begin."

"Why not? After all I am your older brother."

That made her smile. "Can't be by too many minutes."

"Hmm … I don't remember."

"But you were there!"

"Yes, but I didn't know how to count yet."

She laughed.

"All right," Nicolas began, "First question: How do you like the idea of having a brother?"

"It's wonderful! Like a gift I never thought I'd have. But what is anything *but* wonderful is finding out how long my parents have lied to me. All my life. First I am too young, then suddenly I am mature enough because they *have* to tell me."

'Which is not the only way to look at it,' Nicolas thought. "Want to know what I think?"

"Yes, always. Tell me."

"All right. What if you looked at it this way: When your father first saw me, he could have said, 'Isn't it amazing how much he looks like our daughter? They must be related, closely related - but what if it is only a coincidence? It could be, couldn't it? Isn't there a saying that everybody in this world has a double? If I say nothing and do nothing, that young man will go back to wherever he came from. He'll never know, Madeleine will not know and we won't have to tell her about the adoption, not now anyway. Who knows, perhaps never.' Do you believe this would have been a fair decision?"

"No, of course not."

She had immediately seen that it wasn't. Finding out that Nicolas had grown up without family, her father would never keep his sister from him. And he would see that she had the right to know her brother. Yes. It was the only decision her father could have made. But it didn't change the fact that her parents had lied to her

"Are you always so smart and so annoyingly right?" she came back at him.

"Yes, always!" he answered seriously and laughed out loud at the expression on her face. "No, of course I'm not. I am just so happy having found you, I want you to be as happy as I am. Next question: do you remember the first time you dreamt of me? I'm saying 'dreamt' for want of a better word."

"Of course I do. I was five and it was very confusing to see someone with my face. Mother says I asked her, "Where did boy go?" when she came into my room. She felt my forehead, thinking I was running a fever. I could never explain you well enough to her, and she always insisted it was only a dream. I didn't know your name, so I always called you 'the boy'. And … I never told this to anybody, but there was a child's standing mirror in my room then, about as tall as I was. I used to stand in front of it and hope you would appear inside or on the other side of it. Of course you never did. How about you?"

"I was confused, too. In Brittany all girls wear white

caps but you didn't, and at first I couldn't figure out whether you were a boy or a girl. I didn't see your hair, but your face was like looking at myself. Then it dawned on me that you were wearing girls' clothes. I told Berthe who said not to worry, that it was only a dream. It was and it wasn't."

"I like that. It is a good way to describe it: it was and it wasn't. Now tell me about Berthe."

"She is the kindest, smartest, toughest, the most amazing - wait, I would really like for the two of you to meet soon; that would be a lot better than trying to explain her to you. I lived with her for the first twelve years of my life; I want to go and see her soon. I'd like to speak to your father about this; do you think you'd like to go?"

"Tell me, what makes Berthe so amazing?"

"Well, when you look at her - I guess most people only see a hard-working peasant woman who doesn't read or write but speaks her mind, often in a disconcertingly frank way and not always in the politest terms." He grinned, remembering.

"There is so much more to her. She has the biggest heart and knows so much one does not learn from books, including all the old Bretagne fairy tales and superstitions but she always, always loved and understood me. That's why she let me move to the Caradecs so I could go to school. She is the closest I ever came to having a mother."

"Then I want to know her, too."

They talked for over an hour, walking through the park like friends who have known each other all their lives.

At one point, Madeleine asked if he ever talked about his time in the Crimea.

He shook his head.

"Why not, if you don't mind my asking?"

"You can ask me anything you want. Always. But no, I don't talk about the Crimea. It is still so close. I can still see the terrible things I saw, and I hear the awful sounds. Sometimes I even think that I smell the smoke and the gunpowder. I used to wonder why I was so lucky, but now - knowing, that if I hadn't been there I would never have met your father, and then you - what I mean is I don't question fate anymore. I am only thankful. I still feel that there is something unfinished about my time there, though."

He looked at her. "I'm sorry, Madeleine, I didn't mean to make you sad."

"You didn't. You made me think of our tutor; we had him for years before he enlisted. Because of him I am interested in history; he also gave me Latin quotations. I had three letters from him, then nothing for such a long time - it reminded me that must be a bad sign."

"It may be, but it doesn't have to be, Madeleine. Everything was in such disarray when I left. If I couldn't have traveled home with my friend I would still be there waiting for transportation. I also think that it will take a long time for the governments to bring all their records up to date."

They were back for the noon meal during which Madeleine managed to say a few more words to her parents.

In the afternoon, Nicolas wanted to look in on Thomas. When he had finished explaining who Thomas was, Madeleine said she would like to go with him. She looked at her parents; they looked at each other.

Anne seemed doubtful. Madeleine could tell she was weighing the propriety of such a visit, but Henri said, "Why not? She is with her *brother*," and Anne agreed once she realized that Nicolas's friend was in that small, exclusive hospital on the other side of the park

Chapter XXII

Once a mansion belonging to a wealthy family, the private medical facility Thomas and Billy had moved into wasn't a hospital at all, although everybody in the neighborhood referred to it as 'the little hospital'. It was a place offering medical aftercare to patients recovering from surgeries amid all the amenities one could possibly wish for. At present, most rooms were occupied by recovering French and British officers.

Thomas sat in a comfortable armchair, his taped ankle propped up on an upholstered stool, writing material spread out on a small table next to him. He thought back to the first time Nicolas had visited him here and how amazed he had been at the surroundings and service. Nicolas had looked around and was obviously trying to make up his mind about something. Thomas knew him well enough not to rush him.

"You remember, Tom," Nicolas said at last, "how I worked as a paid assistant in a veterinary practice for a few years and saved my entire salary before I went to the

Crimea? All of this must cost a bundle, even for someone on officer's pay - what I am trying to say is: that money is yours if you need it."

Trying not to show how touched he was, Thomas had answered that he appreciated the offer very much, but that he had enough put away, especially since he would be leaving soon.

"Well, all right then, if you really don't need it, but now I have another question for you. Who will help you at home? Is there someone who knows how to tape your ankle and change the dressing on your hand? Write letters for you? Your mother?"

"Don't make me laugh," Thomas pleaded, "laughing hurts my ribs. The very idea of Lady Lydia changing dressings - oh, damn, damn, damn. That just slipped out."

"Did it now? So it is *Lady* Lydia? Interesting. What else haven't you told me?"

"Nothing. I swear, hand on my heart. Let me explain: Mother was 'Lady Lydia' before she married my father, and the name stuck. That's all. Now don't go imagining that Father is a Lord. He is not, thank God. My parents live simply and in the country."

"Why do I feel the need to ask for a definition of 'simply'?"

"No need to be sarcastic, Nick. Why don't you come

and see for yourself? They're comfortable, that's all, and anxious to shake the hand of the friend who saved my life."

"There you go, exaggerating again!" Embarrassed, Nicolas had thrown the newspaper at him.

Thomas expected Nicolas in the afternoon. He was checking the time when there was a knock at the door.

"Entrez! Enter, whoever you are!"

He looked up and saw Nicolas, but his eyes immediately fastened on Madeleine. He shook his head, as if to clear it.

"There - are - two - of - you?"

"Evidently, but I've only known that since yesterday," Nicolas explained. He made the introductions, then asked, "How's the chest, the hand, the ankle, the rest of you?"

Thomas was still looking at Madeleine. He had not heard a word.

"Hey, Tom, I asked how you are."

"W-what? Oh, sorry. I'm still on pain medication which accomplishes nothing - except a few seconds ago I was convinced those pills were making me see double! However, it goes without saying that you, Mademoiselle, are much prettier than your brother. Would you believe he never mentioned you to me?"

He glared at Nicolas. "Some friend you are!"

"Didn't I just mention that I met my sister yesterday? Are you really all right?"

"I am. Do I wish the giant Russkie who decided to sit on me had weighed less? Of course I do. With so many skin-and-bones, half-starved Russian soldiers around, did it have to be *him*? I distinctly heard a rib crack. But we shouldn't discuss such details in front of Mademoiselle your sister." He turned towards her with a smile. "My apologies, Mademoiselle, my abject apologies."

"None needed, abject or otherwise. On the contrary. I have read many of Mr. Russell's dispatches in 'The Times', especially the ones about the lack of preparation and proper care for the British wounded. I trust your experience was a better one?"

"It was, thanks to your brother: first he saved my life by dislodging the Russkie and bandaging my hand, then he made a sling of an Imperial Russian flag, then he drag-marched me to safety, then he filled me with brandy and made sure I was turned over to a French doctor. What followed is somewhat hazy."

"Just as long as there's no haziness about the fact that you are talking to my *sister*," Nicolas reminded him.

Thomas had not looked away from Madeleine since she had entered the room, and she kept sneaking glances at him whenever she thought herself unobserved.

Nicolas found it impossible to believe, but something was happening between those two, right before his eyes.

Time to change the subject. "When do you think you'll be leaving for England?"

"What? Oh, in two or three weeks. In her last letter my mother wondered why I seemed in no rush to come home. What about your plans?"

"I'd like to take my sister to the Bretagne, have her meet Berthe and the Caradec family."

"And also, I take it, give Caradec Junior a piece of your mind?"

"I may change my mind about that."

"Really? Only a few days ago I would have said that you were out for blood!"

"I know, but that was then. Now ... now I keep thinking that if I hadn't gone looking for him I would never have found my sister."

"True, true. *And* me, don't forget finding me. Well - after that, I mean, after the Bretagne, could you - would you consider - I mean at some later time, of course, whenever it is convenient for everyone - would both of you, I mean .... would you consider coming to see me in England?"

Thomas turning furiously red and stammering - that was so not like him! Nicolas looked at his sister who was sitting next to him, demure - and blushing most becomingly? What - she, too?

"Don't you think that is a question best put to her parents after you have been introduced to them?"

"Of course, of course. What could I have been thinking!"

Bet I know, Nicolas thought as an uncomfortable silence dragged on.

"Nick, I forget if I ever asked you; Alain doesn't have any older brothers, does he?"

"Only a dozen, and all handsome and over six feet tall … as if you didn't know."

Nicolas turned towards his sister, noticed the blush that still covered her face and said, "Time to take you home, little sister." "Already?" Madeleine and Thomas said at the same time.

"Already!"

"Please come back soon!" Thomas called after them. "Both of you! Please! Promise?"

Madeleine turned back at the door and, with her most radiant smile, nodded yes, several times.

Thomas leaned back in his chair, incredibly happy.

Nicolas wondered what he had started by bringing

Madeleine along. Going back to the Desrosiers house he kept stealing glances at his sister who walked right next to him but was definitely elsewhere. How could "it" happen so quickly, in mere minutes? There was no doubt in his mind about who occupied her thoughts.

At dinner that night, Anne and Henri extended an invitation to Nicolas to stay in their house while he was in Paris.

"You and Madeleine have much catching up to do, and you'll be close to your friend until he goes back to England. And besides, the coffee in this house must be greatly superior to the one served where you are living now! We will not take no for an answer."

Nicolas could not help noticing Madeleine's delighted smile when he accepted with thanks.

"I'd like your permission to take Madeleine to visit Berthe," he said a little later, "it's been too long since I've seen her, and I know she would enjoy meeting Madeleine."

"Capital idea," Henri said. "We could all go."

"If I might make a suggestion," said Nicolas after he had given this some thought, "Berthe has moved into her daughter's home, a very small house, two rooms and a kitchen. There are only four chairs, pretty rickety ones at that, and I don't know how Berthe is doing - four visitors at the same time might be - I don't know, perhaps too much? It would be easier for her if I go with Madeleine alone the first time, and that would give you time to get acquainted with Docteur and Madame Caradec. I imagine you have questions for them which could be asked and answered more freely without me there."

"Why not?" Henri said immediately with a grin. "And now I have a question for *you*. Did anyone ever suggest to you that you might make an excellent diplomat? That aside, do you know what you want to pursue now that you are back from the war?"

"I'm not sure. One idea is new, still too unformed to talk about, but I also go back and forth between becoming a teacher because school changed my life, or working for the government to help effect some long overdue changes."

"Meaning what?"

"At present, school is for boys from wealthy families only. I was permitted to attend solely because Docteur C. interceded on my behalf. There are still no schools for girls."

"I know!" Madeleine interrupted. "I cried my heart out when Father told me. I thought it was wrong then, and it is wrong now."

"Yes, it is, but as I told you many times, it is in the works. Even small changes take work and time, and this is a huge change. Meanwhile, let's find a date convenient for the Caradecs. Come, Anne, let's leave brother and sister alone for some more catching up."

"I know you have more questions, Madeleine. Your turn!"

"When did you become a mind reader?"

"I'm not, I just learned to figure out things on my own."

"Well, let's see how good you are. What am I going to ask you?"

"Why don't you ask me something difficult?"

"You don't know what I'm thinking about."

"How sure are you about that? How's this? I can think of two possibilities. One: You are looking for a way to ask me, *very* casually, about Thomas - ah, you're blushing again. Very becomingly so, I might add. Q.e.d. You did say you took some Latin, didn't you?"

"No. I only know the sayings and quotations our tutor wrote down for me. Q.e.d. was one of them; there was also 'pax vobiscum', 'cave canem', 'quo vadis?' and 'ora pro nobis.'

"An interesting assortment. Now for the second possibility: You'd like to know whether I wonder about our parents, whether I'd like to find out who they were. Of course I do, but we have almost nothing to go on. I wouldn't mind a difficult search, but for now I just want to be happy having found you. It is definitely something I would like to explore sometime in the future."

"Yes, I've thought about this, too. It would be different if they were alive. Then I would want to find out immediately, but, *my favorite mind reader*: for now I think I'll stay with your number one".

"Agreed. I shall tell you almost all I know."

"Why not everything?"

"Don't you want to find out some things on your own?"

Chapter XXIII

A few days later, Nicolas left early to see Thomas. There were some things he needed to get clear in his mind. Thomas was supposed to leave for home soon but seemed very uneasy.

"Come on, Thomas, out with it! You're as jumpy as spit on a skillet, as we say in Brittany, and that's not like you. You say it's not a delayed reaction to what you went through, that it has nothing to do with the rib and your hand and ankle. So - what does that leave? Your heart?"

One look at his friend's face told him that this was no joking matter.

"Oh," Nicolas said.

"Oh, indeed! How did you know?"

"Tom, I do have eyes. When two people keep smiling at each other as if they were the only people in the room the way you and Madeleine do, one tends to draw certain conclusions."

"But what am I going to do?"

"You're asking me? What I know about these things wouldn't fill a thimble if you even know what that is, but if you'd like me to hazard a guess - I'd say you write a polite letter to the parents of the young lady in question and ask for permission to call on her. Wouldn't that do it?"

Thomas sat up. "Yes, it would. Well, no, actually it wouldn't - wait, I just remembered something: first I need to get *permission* from the parents to *write* to her; then, and only then, may I write a letter to her. Except - except - I'm not sure whether Madeleine will welcome letters from me."

"For Pete's sake Thomas, you are not usually so dense. Madeleine likes nothing better than to talk about you. Doesn't that tell you something?"

"She does?"

"She does! How often do I have to tell you before you believe me?"

"You are certain?"

"Am I certain? Of course I am. I listen to her, don't I? She asks questions about you all the time, every day, whenever we are together! But as long as we are discussing this, how about answering a question for me: As Madeleine's brother I cannot continue this conversation without asking whether your intentions are honorable, if that is the proper word?"

"Nick, of course my intentions are honorable; try to be serious, will you? I have never been more serious about anything in my life! Never. I didn't believe it could happen like this, but it did. In one quick, glorious moment. My parents have been waiting and praying for a daughter-in-law for years, made sure I attended the parties and soirées I was invited to where I dutifully made polite conversation and danced with countless young ladies, all pretty, all nice, although some seemed only interested in gossip and fashion, but ... "

"But nothing happened?"

"Exactly! Nothing happened, not until now. I always imagined that love grows as you get to know a person really well, but I know Madeleine. Sometimes I even feel as if I had known her all my life, and yet, there is so much about her I still have to discover. I love her. I want to marry her if she'll have me and ... "

"Well, now I have a question for you," Nicolas interrupted him. "When that slipped out about your mother being 'Lady' Lydia - isn't your bride supposed to belong to those 'circles'? I will not have my sister's heart broken over this, especially not by my best friend."

"Nick, my parents will love Madeleine because I love her. Because she is lovely and sweet and kind and good and intelligent and knows her own mind and ... "

"I don't need more 'ands'. Have you forgotten that she is adopted? Can you honestly tell me that this not going to be a concern for your parents? All we know about our father is that he may have been a builder in Paris, some twenty years ago. And that he came from somewhere in the south, or the south-west, and died in an accident. We know nothing about our mother except her name."

"Nick, of course I've thought about this. I am not saying my parents would never wonder or talk about this, but once they get to know Madeleine - I just know they'll be happy and proud for her to become a member of our family. You, too. I know you. You are my best friend and whether you believe it or not, I know Madeleine. There is no doubt in my mind that your parents must have been fine people. Now what I would like is for both of you to come to England with me. I've already written to my mother - "

"Whoa! You're moving too fast for me! Given this quite a bit of thought already, have you?"

"Of course I have. Well, do think about it, but meanwhile, could you write that letter to her parents for me?"

"Don't you need to compose it first?"

"No. It *is* in my head, ready to go."

"Then start dictating."

Nicolas delivered the letter that night as promised.

Anne and Henri read it together.

"Well, if that isn't a sudden and unexpected development!" Henri exclaimed.

"Sudden, yes, but I don't know about unexpected," Anne said slowly. "I suspected something of the sort, but since I had no idea who it might be, I thought it was my over-active imagination that you always tease me about. I have seen Madeleine, sitting with a book but looking dreamy and smiling secret little smiles. Do you realize she makes sure to go along with Nicolas every time he visits his friend? Oh, Henri, why couldn't it be a nice young Frenchman instead of an Englishman?"

"Anne, you are not implying that Madeleine - she isn't - how could she be interested after seeing him only a few times?"

"True, she hasn't said anything … but how long did it take *us* to know? No longer than that. Remember?"

"Of course I remember," Henri smiled fondly at her, "but surely it is too soon to worry. Thomas is practically on his way home. I doubt anything will come of it. Of course we'll receive him; I shall send my answer over tomorrow. Tea on Friday afternoon suit you? I'll be home early, and you'll tell Madeleine and Nicolas. It will be only for a few weeks, you'll see. Then he'll be gone."

Unconvinced, Anne nodded to everything. Part of her wanted this for her daughter, but a much larger part wanted it to be simpler, happening with a Frenchman. This Englishman, however, might be a good way to start this new phase of Madeleine's life, and when he was gone she was going to see to it that Madeleine was kept very busy.

On Friday afternoon she tried hard but without success to find something, anything in this young man she did not like or approve of. She was always pulled back to how he looked at Madeleine, and how she looked up at him. How could she have been so blind? Henri took to him, too.

Permission to call on Madeleine was given and received by Thomas with an almost audible sigh of relief and a smile that remained on his face until he realized it was time to leave.

Travel to England was postponed. That, at least, was a good thing.

Chapter XXIV

Berthe sat in her rocking chair, in the same sunny spot in her daughter's kitchen where Nicolas had last seen her, her knitting in her lap, but this time she was wide awake. Her hearing was as acute as ever. She heard them approach and called out, "Yer here, yer here!"

"Don't get up!" Nicolas bent down for her arms. "Of course I came, and I brought someone to meet you."

He motioned to Madeleine who had waited by the door. She, too, bent down to Berthe whose eyes went from one to the other and back again after they embraced.

"It does me heart good to see the two of ye together," she said happily, "but Nicolas, yer not still angry at Rozenn, are ye?"

How did she know? Just because, for a fleeting moment, he had frowned, thinking of her?

Nicolas nodded. "Yes and no. I am grateful that she brought me to you, but I hated her visits; you know that."

"Sure do, but to be angry 'bout past things that can't be changed only makes for more hurt. She did a wrong to yer mother, to the both of ye, to ye most of all, Nicolas, but she never had any gladness of it. Ye found yer sister, that be all that matters now."

Marie brought out mugs of tea; they drank quietly, Berthe looking back and forth between them and smiling.

"Madeleine, tell me, did ye dream of him, too? Like Nicolas did?"

"Yes, many times. But it was never a dream like regular dreams. That last time - the last time I was somewhere in the Crimea with a basket of stump covers, and when I had none left, the soldiers were angry and began to push and shove towards me and go at me with their crutches. It was raining hard, I couldn't see very well, and I didn't know what to do, but then I thought I heard a voice say, "Let her be." The soldiers disappeared and there he was, only for a moment and then he was gone. You always disappeared so suddenly," she said accusingly to her brother.

"And so did you!"

"I wonder," Berthe said, "this could be the last time for ye both. The dreamin', I mean, there bein' no more need for it. Nicolas, I'm that sorry that I always thought it was only a dream. Ye know, after Rozenn left that last time, I think long and hard 'bout twins. Learned folks will say it is nonsense or that I be touched in the head, 'n' who knows, maybe I am - but now I feel in me heart there must be somethin' special between twins, even the ones that don't know the other. Who's to say no? Is nobody could *prove* different! That's why I made Marie take me to see Docteur Caradec right away, so I could tell him."

"Yeah, did she ever!" Marie chimed in. "There was no holdin' her. She said she'd walk there if I didn't drop what I was doin'. Had to leave wet laundry in the basket 'n' the bread dough I had started to knead covered up in a bowl. Strangest bread that turned out to be when I got 'round to baking it later!"

"Well, I'm truly grateful you went, both of you," Nicolas said. "There is so much only you could explain. But what I told you once, Berthe, that when I think of 'Mother' it is your face I see, that is still true. That will never change. I only wish I had told you much sooner, more often. I guess war changes how you look at things."

"War does that? What war? Oh, my, 'n' here I thought ye was toilin' away in an office down south a ways. For a few months, ye said. Seein' to Docteur Caradec's business interests. In … in Lyon, was it, Nicolas?" Nicolas hung his head and managed to look properly guilty. "Why didn't I guess that you knew all along? I should have known; you could always tell when I took liberties with the truth."

Berthe laughed out loud. "Liberties with the truth, is that what folks call tellin' a lie nowadays? Come here, ye two. Me arms 'round the both of ye, that is a gladness I never thought to have."

Suddenly there were tears in her eyes. Impatiently, she brushed them away.

"Nicolas, Marie could use some help with that old door lock. Hasn't worked right in years."

"In other words, you want to get rid of me, talk to Madeleine without me? I'm going, I'm going!"

Laughing, he followed Marie outside.

"Must have been bad, findin' out 'bout bein' adopted," Berthe said after a while, in the direct manner Madeleine was beginning to expect.

"Yes, all I could think of was that my parents had lied to me for so many years. All of my life really."

Berthe nodded. "Yes, that they did. To protect ye, child. It's what parents need to do sometimes, 'n' there be times when they can't. There are many kinds of lies: this one never meant to hurt. Now Rozenn, she paid no mind to hurtin' people, not till she were very sick. Cause of her Nicolas never had parents." She sighed and shook her head.

"I know, but he had you and he still does."

"He shared me with me own children, had to go out beggin' like they did, worked long hours each day; many's the time we all go to sleep hungry. His life could have been much different. More like yours, Madeleine."

"Yes, but he loves you as if you were his mother. That was the very first thing he told me about you, the most important to him."

"Did he now?" Berthe nodded. "I never said this out loud afore, only thought it, but I missed 'im somethin' fierce when he went to live with the Docteur family. Heart-sore I was, with missin' 'im. Had to remind me-self every day it be good that he was goin' to school. Smart boys like him belong in school, poor or not. But now tell me about how *ye* growed up."

Madeleine told her everything she could think of - about her aunt Louise taking her in from the found-ling wheel; about living in the same house all her life, fighting efforts to make her right-handed - "Exactly like your brother!" Berthe exclaimed - being schooled at home with Cecily, the shock of realizing that she did not resemble either parent and more - until she saw that Berthe was getting tired. Her eyes were closing, and her spectacles started a slow, down-ward slide. Madeleine grabbed them quickly and put them on the table.

"I used to do that all the time," Nicolas whispered to her, "I've been listening for a while." They walked away.

"Yes, the lock is fixed. Marie says she is fine, just tires more easily. I don't know how old she is; what I do know is that her life was hard, what with her husband at sea almost all of the time, raising children and then losing some when they were very young. She has three grown sons, seamen like their father who haven't been home yet this year, and her other daughter has moved away … I wish I could do more than visit her."

"You do. You love her and she knows that, and I don't think she would want to live anywhere else."

Chapter XXV

Thomas had become a frequent visitor at the Desrosiers.

If only there hadn't been a constant female presence hovering in the background who would cough or rustle the pages of the book she pretended to read or dust the same lamp over and over again when he tried to move closer to Madeleine. His ankle was much improved which meant she also followed them at a not-so-discreet distance when they walked in the park.

"When are we going to get rid of our shadow?" he complained to Nicolas. "What can I do about her?"

"Probably not a thing. And anyway, you're asking the wrong person. I've never been in your situation!"

"But if you were, what would you do?"

"Get down on one knee, propose to my girl and become engaged. For Pete's sake, you fought in a war and now you don't have the courage of a mouse! You love

Madeleine, she loves you: ask her to marry you, or ask her father first if that is how this is done, but … "

"But what?"

"Something has just occurred to me. What are you?"

"What do you mean, what am I?"

"Well, Madeleine was raised a Catholic; her aunt was one of the Sisters at the Hôtel-Dieu in Paris. So, what are you?"

"C. of E., of course."

"In plain English, please?"

"Church of England."

"Of course? Not on the friendliest of terms with Catholics, if I remember an old history lesson. Won't that be a problem?"

"No. I know my parents; we have written to each other about this and other subjects, it makes no difference to them. Madeleine and I have talked about it, too. We agree on so many things it feels like we have known each other for ages. According to Madeleine, the only objection her mother has to me is that I am not a Frenchman. I don't think that C. of E. will be a problem. "

"Let's hope so." They shook hands on that.

The more time Madeleine and Thomas spent together (always with the 'spy' lurking in the background) the happier they were. They discovered they liked the same books and music but differed about art; Madeleine liked newer painters and sculptors, Thomas preferred the old masters. Both read the newspapers and felt strongly about social problems, especially child labor and the limitations put on women.

"Wait until you meet my sisters," he told her. "I'm the youngest; they indoctrinated me at a very early age."

Thomas enjoyed the refreshingly independent way Madeleine had of looking at things. She loved his quirky sense of humor and his kindness, but more important than that, they both knew that they wanted to spend their lives together. Madeleine had had several heart-to-heart talks with her mother and finally convinced her that her happiness meant being with her Thomas.

On an evening two months later, Henri asked Thomas to join him in the library after dinner.

"Call me when it is over?" Madeleine asked her brother before she retired to her room. She wasn't worried but didn't want anybody to see how nervous she was.

Anne and Nicolas sat in the small salon.

"Tell me more about Thomas," Anne said. "All this is happening so quickly. The thought that our Madeleine will move away, it's just so difficult, so hard for me, for us - of course we want her to be happy, to marry the man she loves and who loves her, but why does he have to be English?"

Nicolas shrugged. "Well, all I can tell you is how much Thomas loves Madeleine and that she loves him. I haven't met his family. That's why he wants to take us to England soon."

"Yes, I meant to talk to you about that. It is completely out of the question for Madeleine to travel with you, Thomas, and Billy without a chaperone. It simply isn't done. I don't understand why Thomas didn't remember this. Henri is supposed to explain it to him tonight if it still needs explaining. And something else worries me a great deal. Madeleine is adopted - what are his parents going to think about that? I don't mean to sound as if I only see problems and obstacles ahead, I don't, but these are serious questions. They need to be discussed."

"I am sure they will be, if they haven't already been discussed. The adoption doesn't matter to Thomas. And I - I have met many people this past year, some good, some bad, some in between. Meeting Thomas and being his friend is the best thing that has ever happened to me, that and finding my sister, of course! I think the world of Thomas. I know Madeleine will be happy with him. And just between you and me: he has the strength of character which Madeleine's husband needs. I know how much Thomas loves her, but that doesn't mean that he will always answer, 'Yes, dear!'

Anne smiled. "Our girl can be rather headstrong; you've seen a few examples of that. I see that strength in you, too, except I think of you as very determined *after* you've thought everything through. She was always such an impetuous little girl, but at the same time so sweet and so funny. I wish you could have grown up together."

"We would have liked that, no doubt, but I wouldn't want to change anything. Some people think everything happens for a reason; I had stopped believing that when my two little brothers died. I kept asking why. There were no doctors where we lived, no help for people like us. And during the war, I saw so much misery, so much pain. Cruelty, too - how could anything be good and important enough to justify all of that? But now that I know that I would never have found first my best friend and my sister if I had not gone to the Crimea, I have to rethink this, change my mind. Perhaps some things do happen for a reason. I beg your pardon, I shouldn't get started on what Thomas likes to call my philosophical pet peeves."

"No need to apologize, Nicolas, I feel this helps me to get to know you. But how do you think Thomas' parents are going to react to the fact that Madeleine was adopted? And that we know nothing at all about your parents? That does worry me. And what if they insist on a wedding in England?"

Nicolas shook his head. "Not knowing them, I couldn't guess at their reaction or their wishes. The only thing I do know: if the parents are anything like their son ...

With that the door opened. A smiling Henri and a beaming Thomas entered the room. Nicolas shot up from his seat and dashed upstairs to get Madeleine. They were back down within seconds.

Ignoring his ribs, Thomas held out his arms. "Your father said yes, he said yes!" Madeleine flew into them.

Much later, when she disengaged herself in order to thank her father, Thomas sat down next to Anne and said, "And you have my thanks also, my heartfelt thanks. I love Madeleine; I will cherish her always. Always. Please visit us as often as you like and of course, we'll come here as well." He pulled an envelope out of his pocket.

"You may still be wondering about all of us traveling to England together. Mother never holds back, and did she let me have a piece of her mind!

"It is the paragraph which begins with 'Thomas, how ... '"

Dearest Thomas, how could a son of mine come up with such a hare-brained, ill-conceived and may I add, stupid plan? What were you thinking, or rather: were you thinking at all? What must Madeleine's parents think of you, of us? For the time being, please convey to Mr. and Mrs. Desrosiers that Father and I will be delighted to come to Rennes to meet them and their daughter at their convenience. I shall, of course, write to them very soon ....

And here, my father. This is what he writes:"

Don't make us wait too long, son. I am looking forward to meeting the young lady who has won your heart, and so are Charlotte and Catherine and the entire family, Father.

"But let me show you one more thing, something my mother added at the bottom of another, earlier letter and wanted me to show you. I know it will please you and also set your mind at ease:

I always wanted to attend a wedding in France. I am so happy it will be our Childrens' wedding,

Mother

Author's Notes

Foundling wheels where babies could be anonymously left had their start in twelfth-century Italy and were connected to a church or a hospital. Their use spread rapidly to other European countries (e.g. France, Germany, Eastern Europe), disappeared in the late nineteenth century but were reintro-duced in the 1900s. At present, Germany and Switzerland operate modern Baby-Klappen and so do China and other Asian countries..

I consulted "The Crimean War" by Paul Kerr, published in 1997, and as many soldiers' letters as I could find online for chapters of the novel which deal with the Crimean War. Readers interested in the Russian side of this conflict might like to take a look at twenty-five year old artillery officer Leo Tolstoy whose 'Sebastopol Sketches' were published in 1855.

William Howard Russell, 'Billy', an Irish reporter, was sent abroad by The London Times to cover the war. He remained in the Crimean for twenty-two months and is considered the first war correspondent. Public discontent and outrage about general mismanagement, especially the lack of planning, supplies and adequate treatment of the wounded as documented by him brought down the British government in 1855, and Lord Palmerston was installed as the new Prime Minister. Incidentally, he was Queen Victoria's *third* choice.

A few days after reading Russell's eyewitness account in The Times, Alfred Lord Tennyson, appointed Poet Laureate by Queen Victoria, wrote the poem "The Charge of the Light Brigade" which celebrates their exceptional valor and tragic heroism. The poem was published six weeks later and remains one of the most well-known English language poems. In Tennyson's own words: "My poem is founded on the phrase 'someone had blundered.'

The siege of Sebastopol which was expected to last only a couple of weeks took well over a year. Disease accounted for more than half of the 90,000 dead: more than 10,000 were killed in action, 20,000 died later of their wounds, and 60,000 were taken by disease.

The Victoria Cross, the highest British decoration for bravery in the face of the enemy, was created at the end of the Crimean War and was awarded by Queen Victoria not only to officers but, for the first time, also to enlisted men.

After the Crimean War the Tsarist regime was in

need of gold in order to pay off a huge war debt. Fearing that Great Britain, already a naval power to reckon with, might consider the acquisition of Alaska greatly influenced their decision to accept Secretary of State William Seward's offer. In 1867 he signed the $7.2 million deal, to be paid in gold bricks.

The U.S. paid about 2 cents per acre for "Seward's Folly".

CPSIA information can be obtained
at www.ICGtesting.com
Printed in the USA
FFOW03n0502251217
44176500-43588FF

9 781478 789482